Puzzle Pieces

by Chani Altein

The Judaica Press, Inc.

Puzzle Pieces
© 2007 by Chani Altein

ISBN: 978-1-932443-67-7

Also by Chani Altein:
The Gift of Friendship

Cover design and layout: Justine Elliott

THE JUDAICA PRESS, INC.
123 Ditmas Avenue / Brooklyn, NY 11218
718-972-6200 / 800-972-6201
info@judaicapress.com
www.judaicapress.com

Manufactured in the United States of America

Acknowledgements

I would like to thank my parents, Rabbi and Mrs. Yosef Yitzchak Kalmenson, and my in-laws, Rabbi and Mrs. Leibel Altein, for all of their love and support. I am blessed to have such wonderful role models to learn from and emulate.

I would also like to thank my husband, Rabbi Sruly Altein, for all of his encouragement and support. It is only with his help that I am able to work on my writing.

I am very grateful to the staff of Judaica Press for transforming my manuscripts into polished books.

And, of course, I owe infinite gratitude to Hashem for all He has done and continues to do for me. I am especially thankful for the opportunities that He gives me to get a personal glimpse of the *hashgacha pratis* with which He runs His world.

CHAPTER One

"Forget it, there is no way that I'm going on this ride," Hindy announced with a determined look in her brown eyes.

She and five other Pioneer campers were standing on line for the Ferris wheel, and after watching the ride for a couple of minutes, Hindy got cold feet.

"Come on, Hindy, it's really a lot of fun," petite, green-eyed Raizy said persuasively.

But Hindy was adamant. "It may be fun for you, but there's no way it'll be fun for me. Personally, I prefer to stay a little closer to the ground."

Blond, fair-skinned Leah tried arguing. "Just give it a try, Hindy. You'll see that it's not as bad as you think."

"No, thanks," Hindy replied firmly. "I'll just wait for you guys down here."

And that was that. Hindy's friends knew there was no point in saying another word. Once Hindy made up her mind, it was almost impossible to convince her otherwise.

"So who's going to be my partner?" Leah asked. She had been counting on Hindy to join her on the ride. "I don't want to go by myself."

For a minute, the others were quiet, trying to think of a solution to Leah's dilemma. They were surprised when the silence was broken by the girl standing right behind them.

"I'll be your partner if you'd like," she offered Leah.

Surprised, Leah looked at the tall, lean girl, dressed in a long-sleeved tee shirt and jean skirt. True, she was a stranger, but with her wide smile and friendly, blue eyes, she seemed sweet enough.

"Thanks," Leah responded, smiling back at her new companion. "My name is Leah Weiss, by the way."

"Mine's Nechama Greenberg. I'm here with my family, and no one wanted to go on the Ferris wheel with me, so I guess this arrangement is actually working out well for both of us."

As Leah and her friends waited on line, they chatted with Nechama. They had lots of questions for her.

"Where are you from?" Raizy asked curiously.

"Woodhaven," Nechama answered.

"Woodhaven? Isn't that in Pennsylvania?" Leora wanted to know.

"It is, but it's a two-hour drive from here. Where do you live?"

"In Lakeview City," Leiba replied. "We're just half an hour away from here. That's why our camp takes us to Thriller Park at least twice every summer."

"Oh, you guys are lucky," Nechama said enviously. "There are no amusement parks near Woodhaven, so my parents decided to make a big family trip and come here. When we leave, we're actually going to Lakeview City to have supper in the pizza shop there. There are no kosher restaurants where I come from, so for my family, this is really exciting."

At that moment, the lady working the Ferris wheel started letting people off the ride and helping new people get on. Before long, Leah found herself sitting beside Nechama, swinging back and forth as their booth made its gradual ascent.

Leah watched the scene below get smaller and smaller until she started to feel queasy. "I think I'm beginning to understand Hindy," she half-joked.

Nechama smiled reassuringly and advised, "Just remember, the key is not to look down."

Leah took Nechama's tip seriously and stared straight ahead. Nechama distracted her by engaging her in conversation.

"So what grade are you and your friends going into?" Nechama asked.

"Eighth grade. How about you?"

"I'm in eighth grade, too."

"Isn't it great?" Leah enthused. "I'm really looking forward to this year. Between yearbook, fundraisers and our graduation trip, we are going to have so much fun."

"Oh, it's nothing like that in our school," Nechama said ruefully. "In my class, there's just me and one other girl, so graduation isn't that big of a deal for us."

"Poor you," Leah remarked, her aqua-blue eyes sympathetic. "Don't you ever get lonely or bored?"

"Not really," Nechama shrugged. "I'm used to it, I guess. And I hang out a lot with my sister Rachelli who's a year and a half older than me."

This time it was Leah who sounded jealous. "I've always wished that I would have a sister. All I have is one younger brother."

Just then, the girls reached the top, and for a second, Leah let herself check out the view from above. Instantly, she regretted it. Nechama noticed the terrified expression on Leah's face and reached out to hold her hand.

"Don't worry. Being at the top only means that we'll be on our way down very soon," Nechama reassured Leah. "Meanwhile, tell me about your family."

"There's really not much to say. There are only my parents, my brother and I. My mother doesn't have a job, but she's really busy volunteering for different *chessed* projects all the time. She's very protective of my brother and I, and she is always making sure that we're safe and healthy and all that kind of stuff. My father's the opposite. He's easy-going and funny, and I love it when he's around. He's pretty busy with his work, though. He's a doctor. My brother Levi is a typical seven-year-old boy who loves to run around, play ball and have fun. That's pretty much it. What about your family?"

"There are four kids in my family. Rachelli's the oldest, and she's really sweet. She's responsible and organized and studious – basically as close to perfect as you can get."

"Oh, she sounds amazing," Leah interrupted dreamily.

"She is," Nechama agreed. "And let me tell you, it can be annoying sometimes since I follow right after her, and people compare us all the time. The truth is, though, it's almost impossible to get upset at Rachelli. She's just too nice. I'm second in the family, and then there's ten-year-old Yossi who is kind of quiet and shy. He spends a lot of time reading and thinking. Whenever he opens his mouth to talk, everyone listens because he usually has smart, interesting things to say."

"Nothing like Levi," laughed Leah.

"No, it doesn't sound like it. Sarala is the youngest in my family. She's four, though you'd never guess it by the way she talks. That girl knows exactly what she wants, and she has her precise way of doing everything. And then there are my parents. Both of them work in the Hebrew Day School that I go to. My father is the principal, and my mother is a teacher."

"So I guess you try to stay out of trouble," giggled Leah. "Is it hard having your father as the principal? I mean – " Leah stopped mid-sentence. "Nechama, have you noticed that it has been a while, and we still haven't moved from our place on the top?"

Nechama had to admit that Leah was right. Their booth had been suspended in the same position for several minutes already. "I wonder what's going on. Maybe someone on the bottom changed their mind about the ride or something."

Leah's heart skipped a beat. "I really hope nothing's wrong," she said, her voice trembling slightly.

"Don't worry, I'm sure there's a harmless explanation for this," Nechama comforted Leah, even though inside she didn't feel quite as confident as she sounded.

Leah tightly held onto the bar in front of her to stabilize her shaking hands. "You know, I've always heard people tell stories about these kinds of disasters, like rides stopping mid-air, but I never believed them. They seemed too crazy to be true. But now … I just can't believe this is really happening."

"Right now, we don't know anything for sure. I mean, any second, we can start moving again," reasoned Nechama, but her words sounded lame even to her own ears. With every moment that passed, the girls suspected more and more that there was a real problem.

Sure enough, a voice soon announced over the loudspeaker, "To those of you on the Ferris wheel, we are experiencing some technical difficulties right now. Please don't panic. We are doing our best to solve the problem as quickly as possible, and we apologize for the inconvenience."

At this announcement, Leah's face paled dramatically, and she looked as if she was ready to dissolve into tears. Nechama took Leah's hand again and said in a strong, even voice, "Why don't we say Tehillim together? That can only help the situation. Do you know any *perakim* by heart?"

Leah nodded yes.

"Okay, so let's start with the *perakim* you know, and then we'll say the ones I know. Come on, I'll repeat after you."

Leah obediently followed Nechama's instructions, and as she recited the holy words of Tehillim, she found herself feeling calmer.

"You know, this is really helping me," she remarked to Nechama after they finished the first *perek*.

"That's the point," smiled Nechama, adding, "Let's continue."

The girls had been saying Tehillim for nearly ten minutes when they felt their booth beginning to descend. A huge grin of relief broke out across Leah's face.

"*Baruch Hashem*," she breathed. "It looks like they fixed the problem." She gave Nechama a grateful look. "Thanks so much for keeping me calm. I don't know what I would have done without you."

"Well, I'm really glad I wasn't alone, either. Somehow, things seem less scary when you're with someone else."

"Yeah. I guess everything worked out for the best, after all. But next time we come here, I think I'm joining Hindy on the bench for this ride."

Nechama laughed. "I know what you mean. I'll probably think twice, too, before I go on another Ferris wheel again. But you've got to admit, this was quite an adventure. I'll have a good time telling my family about it when I meet up with them soon."

At that moment, Leah and Nechama's booth reached the bottom, and the ride attendant opened the bar to let them out. Leah's friends were all waiting for her outside the ride. They were talking together animatedly, sharing their comments on the scare that they'd just experienced.

"Bye, Leah," said Nechama. "It was nice meeting you."

"Same here," Leah answered sincerely. Looking at Nechama, it was strange to think that the two of them had only met half an hour ago. It seemed to Leah as if she had known Nechama a lot longer than that. "Wait one second, please," she told Nechama as she reached into her mini-backpack for a pen and scrap of paper. "Do you mind writing down your address?" she asked, explaining shyly, "Maybe we can become pen pals or something."

"Oh, that would be nice. I really like writing, and having

a pen pal would be fun." Nechama scrawled her name and address on the piece of notebook paper that was offered to her. When she was done, she said to Leah, "Okay, here you go. Don't forget to keep in touch!"

"I won't," Leah promised, and then she and Nechama waved one last good-bye as they parted.

On the bus ride home, Leah thought a lot about Nechama and the time they had spent together. Nechama had seemed really sweet, and Leah had enjoyed talking to her. Leah remembered the special piece of paper that was tucked securely in one of the pockets of her backpack, and she mused, "Wouldn't it be neat if a close friendship developed from today's accident?"

chapter Two

The phone rang four times before Yossi went to pick it up. "Hello?" he answered. A moment later, he turned to his older sister. "Nechama, it's for you."

Reluctantly, Nechama rose from the couch where she'd been lying comfortably, absorbed in the book she was reading. "Hello," she said when she got the phone.

"Hi, Nechama, what are you doing today?" asked Rivky Levin, Nechama's only classmate.

"Nothing much. Right now, I'm in the middle of a book my mother just bought for me."

"Oh, that's boring," Rivky said disapprovingly. Rivky was not a big fan of reading. In fact, Rivky was not a big fan of any activity that required sitting in one place. "Where do you want to go today?"

"Um, I don't know. Do you want to come over and hang out in my house?"

"Nah, that's no fun. I was thinking of taking a trip somewhere."

"Well, my father's in school, and my mother's out with the car, so there's no way they can drive us anywhere."

"Really?" Rivky asked in obvious disappointment. "That's a pity. My parents are home, but they're too busy making important phone calls to take me out. So what do you think we could do?"

"I'm not really sure, but it sounds like we can't go very far without parents to drive us."

"True," Rivky admitted. There was only a moment's pause before she exclaimed, "Hey, I've got an idea. Why don't we go to Regent's Park and go on the hiking trail there?"

"In this heat?" Nechama asked dubiously. "I don't know about that."

"Come on, Nechama, don't be such a spoilsport," Rivky urged her friend. "We'll take along food for lunch and have a little picnic by the waterfall on the way. You'll see, it'll be so much fun."

Nechama wasn't sure about that, but she didn't have the heart to argue. "Let me call my mother on her cell phone and see if she lets."

"Excellent. When you get permission, pack some drinks and fruit, and call me as soon as you're ready. Meanwhile, I'll go make sandwiches for both of us."

"Okay, I'll call you soon."

"Great, I'm waiting," Rivky replied brightly, oblivious to Nechama's lack of enthusiasm.

Rivky took a gulp of the bottled water that Nechama had brought for her and pushed a strand of curly brown hair away from her flushed face. It was really hot outside. "What a story," she told Nechama with an envious expression in her gray eyes. "I wish I would have been there."

"I did invite you to come along, but you wanted to go camping with your family instead."

"Oh, that's right," said Rivky. "But never mind, tell me more about Leah, the girl you met. It's pretty interesting that you landed up with another *frum* girl the same exact age."

"I know. Rivky, you should have heard her discussing her class's plans for eighth grade. I couldn't really relate. I guess things are different when your class is made up of only two girls."

"You can say that again," Rivky said emphatically. "Just think about making a yearbook for two graduates! As for a class trip, we go on class trips all the time."

Nechama laughed at Rivky's joke. "Are you implying that you don't like spending all your free time with only me?"

"Not at all," Rivky retorted, "but I wouldn't mind having a few more girls in our grade, too. Have you ever wondered why we had to be the ones to luck out with the smallest class in school?"

"Please, Rivky, it's not as bad as you're making it sound."

"Oh, really?" Rivky responded darkly. "I'm not so sure about that." But then, in a swift, characteristic change of spirit, she cried out, "Hey, look, there are the waterfalls. I'll race you there!"

And before Nechama could utter a word of protest, Rivky was off.

That evening Nechama was in the middle of playing a card game with Yossi on the living room floor when her father called to her that she had a phone call. Nechama reached for the nearest phone and answered.

"Nechama?" The voice on the other end sounded muffled and choked up. It took a moment for Nechama to realize that it was Rivky calling.

"Rivky?" Nechama questioned in alarm. "Are you okay? What's wrong?"

"Everything!" Rivky wailed, and she sniffled loudly. "Nechama, it's just terrible. I don't know what to do with myself."

"What's going on?" Nechama asked in concern. "Please tell me, Rivky."

Rivky gave a low moan and then said, "Listen, I'm coming over now, and I'll explain everything. Oh, Nechama, I just don't know what's going to be."

Nechama spent the next ten minutes waiting in trepidation. When Rivky did arrive, she looked awful. Her eyes were red and swollen from crying, and the color was drained from her face. She headed straight for Nechama's room, and Nechama followed after her.

When the two girls were sitting on Nechama's bed, Nechama pleaded, "Rivky, please talk to me. Tell me what's wrong."

"It's positively horrible," began Rivky. "This is the worst thing that's ever happened to me. I'm so heartbroken, I − " Rivky stopped and proceeded to burst into sobs.

Nechama soothingly put her arm around Rivky's shoulders and waited patiently until Rivky was calm enough to speak again.

"To think that all this time I was so unsuspecting! You know, just this morning, I was happily enjoying some fun outdoors, entirely unaware of the arrangements that my parents were making about the future of our lives. When I came home and they asked me to sit down on the couch because they had something important to tell me, I still didn't suspect a thing.

"So you can imagine how utterly shocked I was when they broke the news. It was a bombshell." Rivky paused and swallowed hard. "And it's all happening so fast. One week, and that's it. Do you understand? I have seven days – six and a half, to be exact – to pack up all of my belongings and say good-bye to the place I have lived in since I was born."

As Nechama registered the meaning of Rivky's lamentations, Rivky continued, "There are no words to describe my emotions right now. I don't know how I'll ever be able to deal with the pain of moving away."

"You're – you're moving away?" Nechama finally asked when she found her voice. "Where are you going?"

"To Los Angeles, on the other side of the country," Rivky replied, and with this she burst into a fresh torrent of tears. After a minute, she collected herself and explained, "My father's company offered him a job opportunity that he couldn't refuse. With this job, he will be able to work fewer hours and earn much more money. The only catch is that the position is available in their California branch, and they need it filled right away. So here I am, forced to leave my home, my neighborhood and my best friend and start all over in a completely strange city. I feel as if my world is turning upside down."

"This must be so hard for you," Nechama sympathized, her face full of pity. "Moving to another state is a big change."

"Yeah," Rivky nodded. "I don't know how I'll ever adjust. Everything will be so different in L.A."

"Well, the weather there is definitely something to look forward to," Nechama said optimistically. "It's supposed to be really nice all year round. Just think, no more bitter, freezing winters, and no more humid, sweaty summers."

"Big deal," scoffed Rivky. "I'll take Woodhaven's cold and heat over L.A.'s weather any day. At least in Woodhaven, everything's familiar to me. The school is like my home away from home. I know all the teachers and the kids. And now I have to go to this totally new school. It will be a building I won't recognize, with lots of girls whom I've never seen before."

"Don't worry, Rivky. It won't take long to learn your way around your new school. Besides, you'll probably be so happy to have so many new classmates. You've always wanted to have more friends, and that's what you'll be getting now."

"But, Nechama, I can't bear it. I can't bear the thought of leaving you. You've been my best friend since I can remember, and we've always done everything together. How am I going to survive without you?"

"Don't be ridiculous, Rivky," Nechama scolded her friend, cracking a smile despite the situation. "None of us is disappearing off the face of the earth, you know. We can always talk on the phone and write letters. And maybe you'll even come back and visit sometime."

"Even if I do, it won't be the same," Rivky insisted. "I don't know how I'm going to cope with all of this."

Nechama spent quite some time trying to reassure Rivky that everything would turn out all right. After an hour, Mrs. Greenberg knocked on Nechama's door and peeked her head inside.

"Rivky, your mother just called," she said kindly. "She said it's getting late, and she wants you home now. If you'd like, I can drive you."

"No, that's okay. I'll just walk," Rivky answered, rising from the bed with a sigh of resignation.

Nechama escorted Rivky to the front door. "Bye, Rivky, have a good night. And don't forget, I'm always here in case you need me."

"Thanks," said Rivky, a sad, half-smile on her face. "Good night."

Making her way back inside the house, Nechama started to despair as she thought about Rivky's news. When Rivky had been there, Nechama had been so busy comforting her that she hadn't had a chance to contemplate the full implications of Rivky's move on her own life. Now that Rivky had left, though, Nechama began to realize that without Rivky in town, things would be drastically different.

Besides losing her best friend, Nechama would also be losing her only classmate. What would it be like to go through school with no one else in her class? Was it even possible to go through school with no one else in one's class? Nechama went to her room to sort out her feelings. A short while later, Nechama, as if in a trance, walked into the kitchen. There she found her parents sitting at the table, engrossed in deep conversation. When they saw her, they stopped talking and turned toward her with compassionate looks.

"Have a seat," her mother said kindly, pulling out a chair.

Nechama wordlessly obeyed her mother. Then her father said, "Nechama, when Rivky's mother called before, she told me the news about their move. This is coming as a big surprise for Abba and me, and naturally, we have mixed emotions. On the one hand, we're very happy that Mr. Levin was offered such a great job opportunity, but at the same time, we are going to miss the Levins very much. Of course, this will be especially hard on you because your only classmate is moving away."

Nechama acknowledged her mother's statement with a nod, and her mother went on. "Abba and I are actually in the middle of discussing what this means for you in terms of school. We're trying to figure out the different possibilities that can work for this upcoming year."

Rabbi Greenberg observed the overwhelmed expression on his daughter's face and spoke up. "Don't worry, Nechama. We will do our best to come up with a solution that you will be happy with. Meanwhile, try not to think about it. Why don't you take a shower and go to sleep now? We'll talk more tomorrow."

Nechama, who was drained from the long day, was happy to obey. "Okay, Abba," she said softly, then wished her parents a good night and went upstairs to get ready for bed.

Snuggled under her blanket, Nechama couldn't help but ponder Rivky's move and everything it entailed. At first, she thought she might never fall asleep, but within minutes, her mind began to drift off, and soon she was sleeping soundly.

The next morning, Nechama opened her eyes to the bright sunlight that was streaming through her window. Well-rested, she felt ready to face the day ahead. After saying Modeh Ani, washing *negel vasser* and getting dressed, she went downstairs to have breakfast. The rest of the family was already in the kitchen when Nechama got there.

"Good morning," her mother greeted her cheerily. "I'm happy to see that you slept well. Why don't you sit down and have something to eat while we fill you in on today's plans?"

"We're going to Highland Park," Sarala informed Nechama importantly. "You can go biking with Rachelli and Yossi if you want, while Ima and I have lots of fun looking for adventures. Then we'll have a picnic with yummy blueberry muffins for dessert!"

"That's basically the rundown," her mother smiled amusedly. "How does it sound to you?"

"Sounds good," Nechama approved. She liked bicycle riding on the park's shady trail. She thought about the previous day's sweaty uphill hike with Rivky and asked, "Do you think I can invite Rivky? Maybe joining us for a trip will put her in a better mood."

"Sure," her mother agreed, "that would be fine."

As soon as Nechama finished her bowl of cereal, she reached for the phone and dialed Rivky's number. Waiting for someone to pick up, she held her breath, bracing herself for Rivky's miserable response.

Instead, Rivky answered in a tone that was quite chirpy. "Hello?"

Taken aback, Nechama said, "Rivky? It's me, Nechama."

"Oh, hi, Nechama. What's up?"

"Uh, nothing much. My family's going to Highland Park in about an hour, and I was wondering if you wanted to come along."

"Hmm," Rivky said thoughtfully. "Well, I am kind of busy packing all my stuff, but then again, it wouldn't hurt to take a little break. Yeah, I'll come."

"Do you want to check with your mother first?" Nechama suggested.

"Oh, I'll ask her when I hang up, but I'm sure she'll say yes. I'll see you then."

"Yeah, see you then," Nechama echoed and replaced the phone receiver, reflecting on Rivky's good spirits.

That's Rivky, Nechama mused. You just never know what to expect with her.

During the entire ride to Highland Park, Rivky chattered about her upcoming move. "It's so exciting," she bubbled enthusiastically. "Los Angeles sounds so amazing! For one thing, there are so many *frum* Jews there. There are dozens of shuls! Plus, there are lots of kosher restaurants, too. Just think, you can have your choice of *milchig* or *fleishig*, whichever you prefer."

Nechama listened as Rivky continued. "And there are so many girls in each grade that each grade is divided into two or three classes. Imagine that! You'll never believe how many attractions there are nearby, also! You'll have to come and visit me during vacation, Nechama, and I'll take you all around."

Nechama spent most of the next few hours listening to Rivky rave about L.A. and what a super place it was. Feebly, Nechama attempted to change the subject on several occasions, but she shouldn't have bothered. Rivky was interested in talking about one thing and one thing only.

Thankfully, Rivky was exhausted by the time they got into the car to go home, and neither she nor anyone else talked much on the ride back. Only Sarala kept piping up with her comments, but eventually, she dozed off, and then it was quiet.

Nechama stared out her window reflectively, caught in thought. *So it looks like Rivky has come to terms with moving; in fact, she's acting a lot more upbeat than I'm feeling right now. I can't help but feel concerned, though. Right now, I'm the solitary eighth-grade student left in Woodhaven Hebrew Academy. I don't think the prospect would thrill anyone.*

That evening at supper, Sarala proclaimed, "Abba, did you hear? Rivky Levin's family is moving all the way to Los

Angeles. She's going to have lots and lots of new friends, and she's going to have tons of fun."

Her father tried suppressing a chuckle. "Is that so?" he asked as seriously as he could.

"Yup, it is," Sarala verified, nodding sagely. "I heard Rivky say so with my very own ears." Her baby-blue eyes grew wide with pity, and she shook her head sadly. "Poor Nechama," she declared. "She won't have any more friends."

"What are you going to do without Rivky?" Rachelli asked Nechama. She, too, looked sympathetic. "And what's going to happen in school?"

Nechama only shrugged and turned questioningly toward her parents. Rabbi and Mrs. Greenberg exchanged a long, meaningful glance, and then her father said, "Actually, Nechama, Ima and I talked things over some more, and we basically came up with two options. The first is to stay in Woodhaven Hebrew Academy and skip a grade. That means that you and Rachelli would be in the same class, which is something you both have to agree to. It also means that you would have to do lots of independent studying in order to catch up to the ninth-grade level."

"And what's the other option?"

Her father took a deep breath. "The other option," he said, meeting Nechama's eyes squarely with his, "is to attend an out-of-town school. That obviously means living away from home and starting from scratch. So now it's up to you. Those are your alternatives. We will be glad to advise you in your decision, and we will support you when you make up your mind. Ultimately, though, the choice is yours because we want you to do what you feel most comfortable with."

Rachelli was the first to speak. "Wow!" she exclaimed. "This is serious business. And just for the record, I wouldn't mind at all if you wanted to join my class."

"Thanks," Nechama said appreciatively, but in her heart, she knew it was more complicated than that. Being in the same class as Rachelli would mean that she'd be compared to her older sister on a daily basis, and she wasn't sure she was ready for that. On the other hand, it was almost impossible to consider leaving home and learning in a new school. It was one thing to face a new school and community when your family was right there with you, but to meet the challenge all alone? It seemed so daunting to her.

After supper had been cleared, Yossi followed Nechama to her room. "Nechama?" he asked softly.

"Yes?"

"Which option are you going to choose?"

"I don't know," Nechama sighed, then inquired curiously, "Which would you choose?"

"Me? I'd choose the option of staying home, no matter what," Yossi answered without hesitation. "But you know me. I like staying home, and I couldn't think of living somewhere else. You're different, though. Maybe going away to a new school would be better for you." Yossi was quiet for a moment before he added, his freckled face more serious than usual, "I'd really miss you, though."

"I'd miss you, too, Yossi. But there's no need to think about that right now. I haven't made any kind of decision yet."

Lying in bed that night, Nechama kept weighing the pros and cons of her two options. At some points, she would picture herself as a student in an out-of-town school, surrounded by a circle of sweet, friendly girls. But then she'd think of herself going home to a strange house that was not her own, and her stomach would drop. That was when she would revert to the picture of her sitting in her sister's classroom, in the same, old familiar school building that she'd grown up with. She spent a while like that, bouncing back and forth between her choices, until she finally fell asleep.

The next morning Rachelli told Nechama, "Sheva's mother is taking us to the mall soon. Do you want to come along?"

"Yeah, thanks," Nechama said gratefully, eager to divert her mind from the decision at hand. Who cared that she had nothing to shop for? Walking around with Rachelli and Sheva would definitely be more enjoyable than hanging around the house.

When the girls got back home, they were welcomed by the smell of brownies. They followed their noses and found their mother and Sarala busy in the kitchen.

"We were very productive while you two were gone," their mother informed her older daughters when she saw them. "We baked brownies and made lemonade, and now we're in the middle of putting up supper."

"We're making lasagna and French fries," Sarala declared. "And I was a really big help today."

"You definitely were," her mother affirmed. "How was shopping, girls? Did you find anything?"

"I got some pretty hair clips, and I also bought some more film for my camera," Rachelli reported.

"And I just looked around," Nechama said.

"Good for you," smiled her mother. "If either of you are hungry, you can help yourselves to brownies and lemonade. Supper should be ready soon. Nechama, a letter came for you in the mail today. It's on the dining room table."

Nechama quickly finished chewing the brownie in her hand, and then went off to get her letter. A short glance at the return address on the envelope told her that the letter was coming from Lakeview City, and she figured at once that it was from Leah. With interest, Nechama read the letter enclosed.

Dear Nechama,

Hi! How are you? Baruch Hashem, everything here is okay. It's Sunday, and we have the day off from camp, so I am actually really bored right now. I tried calling some friends to get together, but they are all busy going out with their families. My father and Levi are playing basketball in the park, and my mother's in bed with a stomach virus, so there's really nothing much for me to do around here. I started reading one of my books for the second or third time, but then I decided to write to you instead.

I still can't believe the story that happened to us in Thriller Park last week. My family was amazed — at least, my father and Levi were. My mother, to be honest, looked horrified when she heard.

"Leah, I don't think I want you going on any more trips to Thriller Park," she told me.

I got nervous when my mother said that, but my father came to my rescue right away. He told my mother not to worry. "There's practically no chance of this happening again," he said.

Now that it's all over, I actually think the story is kind of funny. My friends are still talking about it. They're pretty proud of themselves. But Hindy is proudest of all. She says, "What did I tell you? I knew that ride wasn't worth going on."

Anyhow, please write back. I would love to hear from you.

Sincerely,
Leah Weiss

Nechama read the letter a second time. *I think I'll write back a letter right now,* she thought. That will give me something to do until suppertime.

Nechama went to her room and sat at her desk with a pen and piece of stationery. She rested her chin on her hands thoughtfully before she started to write.

Dear Leah, she began, and then the words seemed to flow on their own.

Hi! Thanks for your letter.

How are you? I'm fine, Baruch Hashem, but very confused. You see, I just found out that Rivky Levin is moving. Remember I told you that I only have one girl in my class? Well, she's the one — but not anymore, I guess.

So now I have to decide what to do. Either I can skip to ninth grade and be in my sister Rachelli's class, which means lots of extra catch-up work for me, or I can switch to another school, which means living away from home. Right now, I don't have the faintest idea of which of those two choices to pick. There are just so many things that are unclear. Like how would it work out for me to be Rachelli's classmate? Or, if I decide to go away, where will I go? Who will I stay with?

Basically, I have a lot more questions than answers right now. What do you think? Do you have any advice to give me? If you do, I'd love to hear it!

Write back soon.

Sincerely,
Nechama

Folding the letter into an envelope, Nechama marveled at the way that putting her feelings down on paper always made her feel better. Writing the letter had been quite helpful. Still, as she walked to the corner of her block later that afternoon to deposit the letter in the mailbox, she had no clue just how helpful the letter would actually turn out to be.

chapter Three

"Leah, you got a letter!" Levi shouted as he ran through the house in search of his sister. He finally found her out on the patio, where she was working on her summer scrapbook.

"Here, Leah," he said, handing her the letter. "This is for you."

"Thanks," Leah told him, accepting the envelope, which she opened right away.

Eagerly, Leah read Nechama's letter. When she was done, she sat back and contemplated Nechama's predicament. What a sticky situation, Leah thought. I'd hate to be in her shoes right now. I wish I had some smart suggestions for her, but, truthfully, I don't know what I would do if I were in her place.

Leah was still pondering Nechama's dilemma when her mother pulled into the driveway half an hour later. As she emerged from the minivan and approached the patio, Leah looked up from her artwork to greet her.

"Hi, Mommy," she said. "How was your day?" Mrs. Weiss had spent her morning and the early part of her afternoon putting together packages for the Lakeview City Bikur Cholim Committee.

"It was nice. How about yours?"

"It was okay. I finished a few more pages in my scrapbook. And I got a letter."

"A letter? From whom?"

"From Nechama."

"That's nice. It's great that the two of you are actually corresponding."

"Yeah, well, I feel really bad for Nechama."

"Why is that?" her mother asked, a curious expression on her gentle face. She sat down in the lounge chair next to Leah as her daughter answered.

"Nechama wrote to me that the only girl in her class is moving away, and she doesn't know whether to skip a grade or go to a different school. If she does decide to switch schools, she doesn't know which school she'll go to."

"Why doesn't she come here and join your class?"

Leah regarded her mother in amazement. "Mommy, what a great idea! I can't believe I didn't think of it myself! Do you think that Nechama would be able to live with us? That would be perfect! I mean, our house is definitely big enough, and I would finally have someone my own age around here."

"Hold on, Leah. Try not to get too carried away. If Nechama chooses to transfer to a new school, and if she and her parents decide that the school here would be good for her, then it's certainly possible that we would agree to host her. We do have plenty of space, and it's true that another girl's company would probably be nice for you. However, I would have to discuss the issue first with Tatty before we make any offers."

Leah gave a squeal of ecstasy. She was so excited at the prospect of Nechama coming to live with her that she didn't know what to do with herself.

Mrs. Weiss shook her head at Leah's exuberance. "Leah, remember that everything is so questionable and indefinite right now. There's really no point in getting your hopes up high so prematurely."

But her mother's words fell on deaf ears. Leah spent the rest of the afternoon dreaming about Nechama moving in with her as she waited for her father to return home from work. Even while she helped her mother with supper, peeling zucchini and sweet potatoes, her mind was elsewhere.

Mrs. Weiss noticed how preoccupied her daughter was. It wasn't hard to guess the reason for Leah's distractedness.

"Just remember, please don't pounce on Tatty the second he comes home," her mother instructed Leah as she put a pan of chicken and vegetables into the oven to bake. "I don't want you mentioning anything to Tatty before I raise the subject myself. For some reason, I'm feeling unusually tired right now, so I'm going to lie down in bed and try to rest a little. Please look out for Levi while I'm upstairs, okay?"

"No problem, Mommy," replied Leah, who had finished her peeling job and headed out of the kitchen to find Levi.

An hour later, Dr. Weiss stepped in the front door, just as Mrs. Weiss came back downstairs. The oven rang right on schedule, signaling that the chicken was ready.

"Hi, everyone, I'm home!" he called.

"Hi, Yosef," Mrs. Weiss said as she headed into the kitchen.

Dr. Weiss always returned home from work with a big appetite, since he usually didn't eat anything after lunch at noon.

"Let me just put the food out on serving plates, and then we'll be ready to sit down. Do you mind calling Levi? It sounds like he's outside shooting baskets."

"And what about Leah? Where's she?"

"Here I am." Leah had come in so quietly that no one had noticed her appearance.

"Hi, Leah! How's my princess doing today?"

It took all of Leah's control to keep from blurting out everything, but her mother's eyes were on her intently, so she just answered neutrally, "I'm okay."

"That's all?" her father asked in surprise. Leah usually greeted him with a full account of her day. "You're probably just hungry like I am. I'm sure after you eat, you'll be ready to talk more."

But Leah hardly said a word throughout supper. The only thing she wanted to speak about was off-limits until her mother brought it up, so she just listened with half an ear as Levi and her mother filled her father in on their day. Then, when the family had finished the main course, Mrs. Weiss brought a plate of sliced fruit to the table, and everyone helped themselves, except for Leah.

"No dessert, Leah?" Tatty asked with raised eyebrows. "That's not like you. Is everything okay? You've been acting strangely since I came home."

"She's been acting strangely the whole afternoon!" Levi

muttered in a voice that was loud enough for everyone to hear.

Mrs. Weiss shot her son a warning glance, and then cleared her throat and said, "Actually, I can probably help explain Leah's odd behavior."

Dr. Weiss looked in bewilderment from his daughter to his wife. "Apparently, something is going on around here, and I'm in the dark. Please, Yaffa," he told Mrs. Weiss, "enlighten me if you can."

"Today, Leah received a letter from Nechama, the girl she met at Thriller Park. Nechama, it seems, is in a quandary right now because her only classmate is moving away. That leaves Nechama with two possibilities. Either she can join the grade above her, or she can transfer to a different school. I actually suggested to Leah that maybe Nechama would consider coming here to school, and we discussed the option of her boarding with us."

"Hmm," Dr. Weiss said at first, as he processed the information that he had just heard.

"So what do you think?" Leah asked eagerly, her eyes shining expectantly.

"I think," Dr. Weiss answered slowly, "that the idea definitely has merit. But I also think that Mommy and I have to discuss this more by ourselves before we make a final decision." Observing his daughter's face fall with disappointment, he added with a wink, "Don't worry, Leah. We'll try to be as quick about this as possible. I'm getting the distinct feeling that you won't be able to hold out for too much longer."

Later that evening, Leah, dressed in her nightgown and

ready for bed, went to wish her parents a good night. They were relaxing in the living room.

"Good night, Mommy and Tatty. I'm going to sleep now."

"Good night, princess," her father smiled.

"Good night, *zeeskeit*," her mother said affectionately.

Leah turned to go, when her father stopped her. "One second, Leah."

Leah turned back around with a questioning look. Inside, her heart started beating faster.

"Don't you want to know what we decided?" her father inquired teasingly.

"Of course, I do!"

"Well, Mommy and I talked it over, and we'll be happy to offer Nechama a home if she needs it. Should Nechama decide to come here for school, we think that hosting her would work out well for both of you girls."

"Oh, thank you!" Leah cried delightfully. "I can't wait to write to Nechama and let her know."

"Just a minute, Leah," her mother said. "Tatty and I think that it would be best if we contacted Nechama's parents and spoke to them directly. If you give us her address, I'll call information tomorrow for their number and try reaching her mother at home."

"Okay, I guess that makes sense," Leah conceded. Then she informed her parents, "I'm so excited! I don't know how I'll be able to fall asleep tonight."

Immediately, her mother looked concerned. "Leah, please make sure you get some rest; otherwise, you'll feel exhausted during camp tomorrow."

"I'll try," Leah promised, though she knew for a fact that it wouldn't be easy.

"Leah, can you please pass the glue?"

Leah was startled by Raizy's impatient tone. "Here," she said, adding indignantly, "There's no need to get so uptight."

"You're right. I'm sorry," Raizy apologized. "It's just that that was the third time I asked you the same question. What's with you, Leah? You seem to be somewhere else today. What are you so busy thinking about?"

Leah jumped on this opportunity to confide her news. "Do you remember Nechama?" she queried.

"Of course I do! She's the girl we met by the Ferris wheel at Thriller Park. But what does that have to do with this?"

"Just listen. I took down her address and wrote her a letter, and then she wrote me a letter back. To make a long story short, she may need to find a new school because right now she's the only one in her class, and this morning my mother's supposed to be calling her mother to tell her that if she wants to come to our school, she can stay at my house!"

Raizy's eyes grew wide. "Are you serious?" she asked in amazement.

Her exclamation drew the attention of a few girls nearby.

"What are you talking about?" demanded Leiba. Brown-haired, freckle-faced Leiba always liked to know everything that was going on, and she was great at sniffing out the latest scoop.

Raizy gave Leah a questioning glance as if to say "Is it okay if I tell?" Leah, who was glad to spread the word, shrugged back as if to answer, "Sure, I don't see why not."

Having received this silent sign of permission, Raizy proceeded to make an announcement loud enough for all the girls in the bunk to hear. Her proclamation was met by quite a stir.

"I hope she comes," declared Feige, who had been one of the girls to meet Nechama at the amusement park. "She seems really nice."

"Yeah, that was the impression I got, too," Raizy confirmed.

Slender, dark-skinned Elana, who had joined the class in the middle of sixth grade, thought, *It would be nice to get in a new girl*, but, as usual, she kept her opinion to herself.

"I don't know," Leiba declared doubtfully. "I don't think it's such a great idea to switch schools in eighth grade."

"It may not be a great idea," said down-to-earth Hindy, "but it doesn't sound like she has much of a choice. For her, this may make the most sense."

"And besides, if she does join our class, we'll make sure that she feels welcome right away," Miriam asserted. Wide-eyed, pink-cheeked Miriam was known for her kind-heartedness and her eagerness to help others.

"Well, make sure to let us know what happens after your mother calls," said Raizy.

"Don't worry, I will," Leah promised.

When Leah flew into her house that afternoon, her mother was sitting on the couch, skimming through a cookbook.

"Hello, Leah."

"Hi, Mommy. So did you call her?"

"I did."

"And what did she say?" Leah asked, bursting with curiosity.

"At first, my phone call caught Mrs. Greenberg off-guard. She said she was very surprised by my unexpected offer and very touched, as well. She wanted to talk things over with her husband, so she called me back later to ask if she and Nechama could come next week to see the school and meet us."

"So what did you say?" Leah asked eagerly.

"What do you think I said?" her mother retorted with a smile. "Naturally, I said that we would host them with pleasure, and I gave Mrs. Greenberg the number to the school so she could make the necessary arrangements."

"Oh, thank you, Mommy! This is just too good to be true! I have to call my friends right away and tell them."

Mrs. Weiss raised her eyebrows doubtfully. "I don't know if it's wise to spread the news before it's finalized. In any case, I'm going out to visit Tanta Bracha in a few minutes, and you're welcome to join me if you'd like."

For a second, Leah wavered. On the one hand, she really wanted to call her friends and update them on Nechama's upcoming trip to town, but on the other hand, she always had a nice time when she went to see Tanta Bracha.

"Okay, I'll go with you," Leah decided.

"We'll leave in a few minutes. I'm just going to go upstairs for a bit, first. In the meanwhile, please pick some flowers for Tanta Bracha from the garden. You know how much she loves flowers."

"Sure, Mommy."

Outside in the backyard, Leah chose her bouquet carefully. She looked for the brightest, most interesting flowers because they reminded her of Tanta Bracha. Tanta Bracha was no one's real aunt, actually, but with her loving, nurturing personality, she had somehow earned that affectionate title by the people in her community. When Leah had been younger, Tanta Bracha had babysat for her, and since then, the Weisses had always kept up with her, dropping by to say hello and often having her over for Shabbos.

Leah's thoughts were interrupted by the sound of the back door closing and her mother's approaching footsteps.

"All set?" asked her mother.

"Yup," Leah replied, and the two of them walked to the minivan.

"You did a nice job picking flowers," Mrs. Weiss complimented her daughter, eyeing the colorful bouquet with approval.

"Thanks," Leah said. "I had fun picking them. Do you think that before Nechama and her mother come, I can pick some more to put in a vase in their room?"

"I don't see why not. Mrs. Greenberg just called again, by the way. She set up a meeting with Mrs. Perelman for next Tuesday, so she and Nechama will be coming on Monday evening and driving home the next day."

"I can't wait!" Leah exclaimed. "I really hope they like our school. Did Mrs. Greenberg tell you what other schools they're looking into?"

"She actually said that this is their best option, so far," her mother admitted. "For one, it's relatively close to them, and Nechama would even have the option of taking the train home for Shabbos. Also, this is the only place where Nechama has been offered a house to stay at."

Mrs. Weiss and Leah got into the minivan, and before they knew it they were walking up the cobblestone path to Tanta Bracha's small, pretty house. Leah rang the bell. Moments later, the door was flung open, and Tanta Bracha greeted them with a brilliant smile. A colorful Israeli kerchief covered her hair, and an apron was tied over the flairy, yellow dress she wore.

"Hello, hello!" she warmly welcomed her guests. "What a wonderful surprise! Come in and have a seat in the living room."

"It smells delicious in here," Mrs. Weiss remarked as she and Leah breathed in the sweet aroma of fresh pastries.

"I've spent the morning baking," Tanta Bracha explained. "Tomorrow the Shiffs are making an *upsherinish* for their son Motty, so I offered to bring over some cake and cookies for the simcha."

"You're incredible," Mrs. Weiss began, but Tanta Bracha dismissed Mrs. Weiss's praise with a wave.

"Oh, please," she said, "it's no big deal. I'm happy to fill my time with good things." Saying so, she turned to Leah. "Leah, it's so nice to see you. You look beautiful, as usual, and you've gotten great color from the sun. Those flowers in your hand are for me, I presume?"

Leah nodded, holding out the bouquet to her hostess.

"Thank you, sweetheart," Tanta Bracha said, sniffing the

blossoms as she accepted them. "These are so pretty. Excuse me for a minute while I put them in water."

Tanta Bracha disappeared into the kitchen, returning with a vase, which she set on the coffee table right before them. "There. Now I can enjoy them as we talk. So, tell me, Leah, how are you? You look like you're bursting with good news. Come on, sweetheart, spill the beans."

Leah didn't need a second invitation. "Tanta Bracha, you'll never believe what happened," and with that, she launched into a detailed report of her meeting with Nechama, their correspondence, Nechama's problem and her solution.

"Amazing, amazing," Tanta Bracha kept muttering, listening attentively to Leah's story. When it was over, Tanta Bracha exclaimed, "Good for you, Leah! It will be so special for you to have a live-in friend. Yaffa, it's very kind of you and Yosef to agree to take Nechama in, but, of course, I'm not surprised. Everyone knows you and your husband have hearts of gold. Nechama is really lucky to stay with such a fine family."

Mrs. Weiss blushed and said, "So far nothing's definite. The Greenbergs still have to make their decision."

"Mark my words," Tanta Bracha declared, winking reassuringly at Leah, "as soon as they meet you, they'll be sold. Just you wait and see."

On Monday evening, Leah hardly ate any supper. She was too excited. Later, she tried distracting herself with a book, but she gave up because it was impossible for her to concentrate.

Instead, she went to join Levi, who'd been outside on the lookout for his family's visitors since he'd been dismissed from the supper table.

"Do you think they'll ever get here?" Levi queried when Leah came out.

"Of course, they will. They should be here any minute."

"I don't know. I've been standing out here forever, and they still haven't come."

"Maybe they got stuck in traffic or something like that. I'm sure they'll be here soon."

"I sure hope so because Mommy's going to call me in to go to bed soon, and I want to see them when they come."

"Why are you so eager to see them?"

Levi looked insulted by the question. "What do you mean? For the past week, all everyone's been talking about is this Nechama Greenberg and her mother. Of course, I want to see them. And besides, I'm curious to meet this girl who may be moving into my house."

Leah realized her brother had a point. "That makes sense," she conceded. Noticing a gray minivan driving slowly in their direction, Leah squinted to get a better look. "Hey, I think that's them. Want to go inside and tell Mommy and Tatty that they're here?"

Levi obligingly scrambled to his feet and dashed into the house to notify his parents of the Greenbergs' arrival. By the time Nechama and her mother got out of their car and walked up the steps, the whole Weiss family was already standing there to welcome them.

"Hi, you must be Mrs. Greenberg," Mrs. Weiss smiled at the pleasant-looking woman in front of her. Mrs. Greenberg, with her big blue eyes and easy smile, was a plumper, more matronly version of her daughter. "And you must be Nechama. I'm Yaffa Weiss, this is my husband Dr. Yosef Weiss and these are our children, Leah and Levi."

"Thank you so much for having us. We're really so grateful."

"Come in, come in," Dr. Weiss urged the newcomers. "Let me take your bags to your room while Yaffa gives you something to eat and drink."

As Mrs. Weiss led the group inside, she asked, "Can I serve you supper?"

"Oh, no thanks. We took food with us and ate on the way."

"So please sit down, and I'll bring out drinks and fruit."

While Mrs. Weiss went into the kitchen to get some light refreshments, Leah sat with the Greenbergs around the dining room table. It was awkward at first because Leah wasn't sure what to say, but Mrs. Greenberg quickly broke the silence.

"Leah, please tell me about your school. How many girls are there in your class?"

By the time Mrs. Weiss returned to the table with a pitcher of water and a bowl of berries, a discussion of Lakeview Girls' Yeshiva was already in full swing. After a while, when the conversation got more technical, Nechama and Leah left their mothers to talk alone while they headed up to Leah's room.

"Oh, wow, your room is really nice. It almost feels like a hotel in here." Nechama surveyed her surroundings, taking in the plush rose carpets, the matching floral linen and the hand-painted furniture.

"Thanks. My parents did it over for me as a birthday present last year. If you come live with us, we can just pull out the other bed, and there's plenty of extra space in my dressers for your stuff, too. That is," Leah hurried to add, "only if you wanted to sleep in my room, of course. Otherwise, we have a really nice guest bedroom on this floor, too."

"Are you kidding? Of course, I'd love to share a room with you. That would just be part of the fun, wouldn't it?"

Glad to see that Nechama seemed to share her vision of friendship and bonding, Leah laughed. "It would be like having a sleepover party every night. I'm so excited when I think about it!"

"Me, too. At least, sometimes I am. Other times, I'm nervous. It's pretty scary to go away from home and switch to a strange school for eighth grade."

"That's true," Leah admitted. "I don't know if I would have the courage to do a thing like that!"

"I don't really have much of a choice, though. In my mind, I'm trying not to focus on all the challenges. Instead, I tell myself that everything will work out okay if I come here."

"It will. Don't worry," Leah promised. "You'll see, the girls in my class are really nice, and my family will really try to make you feel comfortable in our house."

"Thanks. Your parents look very sweet. They must be because what other kind of people would agree to have a stranger come live with them?"

Just then, the girls heard their mothers approaching. Mrs. Weiss and Mrs. Greenberg stood at the doorway to Leah's room, and Mrs. Greenberg said, "I hate to interrupt, Nechama, but we have to be up early tomorrow for our meeting with Mrs. Perelman. I think we should call it a night and get ready for bed."

"Okay, Ima," Nechama said, and she and Leah reluctantly wished each other a good night.

Mrs. Greenberg noticed the girls' hesitation to part. "Remember," she tried comforting them, "if the meeting tomorrow goes well, you'll have many, many more hours to spend together talking."

Those words brought a smile to everyone's face, and on that cheerful note, Nechama and her mother went off to sleep.

"So that's it? Nechama's really coming? It's final?" Leah's eyes shone with ecstasy as she spoke to her mother.

"That's what Mrs. Greenberg just called to say. She'll be driving back here the day before school starts to settle Nechama in."

"So what are we going to do now?"

"What do you mean?"

"I don't know," Leah admitted. "I was just thinking that maybe we should celebrate or something."

"What did you have in mind, exactly?" her mother question-ed patiently.

For a second, Leah was stumped. It didn't make sense to throw a party, have a cake or go out to eat, which was the way the family usually commemorated special occasions. "Maybe," she suggested after a moment's thought, "we could prepare the room for Nechama so that she'll feel at home here. For example, we could buy a frame for her to hang a picture of her family in."

"That would be nice," Mrs. Weiss agreed. "We could also drive to the mall one day and pick up some cute knick-knacks before Nechama arrives."

"Why don't we go now? We still have a couple of hours before Tatty comes home and we eat supper."

"I'm sorry, Leah, but I'm too tired to go out right now. I think I'm going to go upstairs and lie down a little bit. Hopefully, we can go to the stores tomorrow."

Leah swallowed her disappointment. The next afternoon, though, she was nothing but cheerful as she rode home from the mall with her mother. They had bought all kinds of little surprises for Nechama, including a custom-designed plaque to hang on her door that said "Nechama and Leah's Room."

In the passenger seat, Leah proudly studied the painted wooden sign and declared, "This is going to be the greatest thing ever, sharing a room with Nechama. I can just see it now. She's going to be like the sister I've always dreamed about."

Mrs. Weiss's expression turned serious as she stole a glance at her daughter. "Leah," she said, returning her gaze to the road, "I also have positive feelings about Nechama coming to live with us. She seems like a fine girl coming from a solid family, and I'm sure you two will get along beautifully. However, I want to tell you now that living with another person is not usually all smooth sailing; there's bound to be some bumps along the way."

Mrs. Weiss saw the blank look on Leah's face, and she hurried to elaborate. "What I mean to say is, over the year, different issues and challenges are likely to come up, and I just want you to remember to always act honestly and with sensitivity. And, of course, if you ever need our help, Tatty and I are always here for you."

Leah listened to her mother's words, but only with half an ear. Bumps? Issues? Challenges? Maybe with other people who lived together, but not with her and Nechama. No way.

CHAPTER Four

The night before school started, Nechama fell asleep a lot later than she should have. First, she and Leah had been talking for a while, and then, even after they'd grown quiet and Leah's breathing had gotten soft and even, Nechama still remained wide awake.

She thought about her day and her saying good-bye to her family. In her mind, she replayed her last few minutes at home.

Her parents and siblings all gathered around her. Even Avraham, a close family friend who was like the Greenbergs' grandfather, was there to wish Nechama farewell and give her some advice and spending money before she left.

"Good luck, Leah," Avraham told her in a voice full of care and affection. "I'm sure it won't be easy to be in a new school without your family, but I'll tell you what people told me when I first began to keep Torah and mitzvos. They said, 'All beginnings are hard,' but, G-d willing, you'll adjust with time and see that all the difficulties paid off."

Then Abba kissed her on her head and gave her more words of encouragement.

"Everything will be good, Nechama," he reassured her. "I am certain that it won't take long for you to settle in to your new place. And remember, call whenever you need to talk – you know our number."

Rachelli gave Nechama a tight hug. "Bye, Nechama, I'll miss you. I'm already counting down till the next time you come home."

"Me, too," Sarala chimed in, adding, "Don't forget to bring home special treats from the bakery there!"

Yossi watched Nechama get into the car with big, sad eyes. He didn't say much, but as Mrs. Greenberg drove off, Nechama looked back and saw Yossi still standing in his spot and waving.

Then, at the Weisses' house, after Ima helped Nechama unpack her things and get organized, it was time to say good-bye to her mother, as well. Seeing her mother leave was difficult, and Nechama had to blink away the tears from her eyes before going back into the Weisses' house.

The rest of the evening was okay. The Weisses were really nice to her, and she and Leah had fun getting their backpacks ready for school. After that, Nechama showered, using the new puff that Leah had gotten for her. Once in bed, Leah gave her a full run-down on the teachers and classmates she would meet the next day. Then Leah drifted off, leaving Nechama alone with her thoughts.

Lying there in a strange bed and unfamiliar surroundings, Nechama felt lonely and scared. She missed her family, though the Weisses were trying so hard to include her and make her feel welcome in their home. Nechama thought back to the note she'd found on her bed. Scrawled in a messy handwriting, it had said, "I'm happy you're here. I hope you like it in our house. From Levi." Nechama smiled at the memory, and with that peaceful thought, she finally dozed off.

Nechama and Leah were not the only ones to arrive early for their first day at school. When they entered their classroom, several girls were already there and went over to Nechama to introduce themselves.

Raizy was the first to talk. "Hi, I'm Raizy. I don't know if you remember, but we already met at Thriller Park."

"Yeah, I remember," Nechama replied with an easy smile.

"And I'm Leiba. I was also there."

"Me, too," Feige chimed in. "My name's Feige."

"And I'm Miriam. We should have worn name cards for you! Don't be embarrassed to ask us for our names again. And if you need anything, I'd be more than happy to help."

"Thanks," Nechama answered appreciatively.

Leah noticed that Nechama was beginning to look overwhelmed by the crowd that had gathered around them, and after the last few girls told Nechama their names, Leah pulled her gently by the hand and said, "Come, let's find good seats while they're still left."

The bell rang soon after that, and Mrs. Solomon, the eighth-grade homeroom teacher, walked in. Petite, with a natural-looking wavy *sheitel* and a warm smile, Mrs. Solomon seemed youthful and charismatic. She gave a brief overview on the subjects she would be teaching and then continued, "As your main *mechaneches*, besides teaching you, I will also be acting as an advisor for all of your special eighth-grade projects. That includes your graduation trip and all the fundraising you'll need to do for it. From what I understand, you already had class elections at the end of last year, am I right?"

The eighth graders nodded.

"I was told that you chose Raizy as your president and Feige as your vice-president, so I will be working together with them and all of you in order to ensure that everything runs as smoothly and effectively as possible. I will be meeting with Raizy and Feige after school today to come up with some general plans and ideas. Afterward, you girls should get together so that Raizy and Feige can let you in on everything we've decided and you can give them your input and suggestions.

"From my experience, the sooner you get started on planning your projects, the better. That way, you'll have enough time to raise the money you need. So good luck, girls, and you should be hearing more details shortly. Remember, the participation of each and every girl is essential for your success."

Mrs. Solomon's words excited the girls, and at lunchtime, her talk was the main topic of conversation.

"I really hope our class makes enough money to cover our entire trip," Leiba said loudly. "My sister's class didn't raise enough money, and they each had to pay an extra fifty dollars in order to go on the trip."

"Didn't you listen to Mrs. Solomon's speech?" Hindy

reproached her. "She said that as long as we start now, and all of us do our share, we'll raise the amount of money that we need."

"I wonder what kind of fundraisers we'll be working on this year," mused Miriam. "I, for one, would love to do some kind of bake sale."

"Well, Feige and I are sitting down with Mrs. Solomon after school to set our goals, so we'd actually like to hold a class meeting tomorrow night to discuss details with the class," Raizy announced.

"Where's it going to be?" Leiba wanted to know.

"You can have the meeting in my house," Miriam volunteered. Miriam was an only child who'd been born to her parents when they were older. Being the sociable person she was, with no company at home besides her parents, she had friends over regularly and liked to host class gatherings.

"Okay, so that's where it will be. Listen up, everyone," Raizy declared in a loud voice. "Tomorrow night at seven o'clock, we'll be getting together at Miriam's house. Please make sure to be there because we're counting on all of you!"

"So what do you think of school so far?" Leah asked Nechama as the two of them walked home.

"I liked it today," Nechama admitted. "The girls were friendly, and the teachers seemed very nice, especially Mrs. Solomon. I'm glad she's going to be our homeroom teacher."

"Yeah, me, too. Everyone knows how great she is. Not only

are her classes interesting, but she also does fun projects with her students every year. And I heard that the eighth graders always have a blast with her on the graduation trip."

"There's definitely a lot more happening in Lakeview Girls' Yeshiva than in my school back home." Nechama paused as she covered a yawn.

"Are you tired?" Leah asked in concern.

"I guess so. It took me a while to fall asleep last night."

"Oh." Leah looked disappointed. "I was thinking that we would take a walk to the main avenue, go shopping for school supplies and then stop for ice cream, but you're probably too exhausted for that." Though the truth was that Nechama had really been looking forward to unwinding with a book when she got home, she didn't want to let Leah down. "No, I'm up to going out with you. I'll just try to go to sleep early tonight."

"Great!" Leah exclaimed, breaking out into a smile of relief. "Let's go home and get something to eat before we head out."

That night, Nechama's eyes closed as soon as her head hit the pillow. It had been a full day, and she was completely wiped out.

"It's so nice to be able to walk to school," Nechama remarked the next morning as she and Leah headed out under the sunny blue sky. "In Woodhaven, my school was a fifteen-minute drive from my house."

"It's nice to be able to walk to school with company," Leah replied appreciatively. "I mean, walking alone is fine, but it gets boring sometimes. I was always so jealous of the girls who had sisters to walk with. But that's history now, thanks to you."

"I guess this is a treat for both of us, then," Nechama surmised.

In the comfortable silence that followed, Nechama thought to herself, *I'm really lucky to have Leah as a friend. She is being so kind to me, and she makes me feel like I'm the one doing her a favor by staying in her house.*

The second day of school passed by quickly. Nechama realized that her classmates and surroundings were becoming more familiar to her, and that was reassuring. Still, she was glad that Leah was at her side, making sure that she was taken care of at all times.

When Mrs. Weinberg, the last teacher of the day, dismissed the girls, Nechama and Leah hastened to organize their belongings and head home. As they made their way out of the classroom, Miriam approached them.

"Leah," she asked, her almond-shaped eyes sparkling with their usual impish glint, "do you and Nechama want to come shopping with me to get nosh for our meeting tonight?"

"Sorry, Miriam," Leah answered regretfully, "but Nechama and I already had plans to stop at the Knit and Bead Shop and make earrings. Maybe next time."

"Yeah, maybe next time," Miriam echoed, clearly hurt. As the only other girl in the class with no siblings close to her age, she shared a common bond with Leah, and the two of them had always come through for each other when needed. Until now, that was.

Nechama, sensing the tension, suggested, "Maybe we can go to Knit and Bead another day?"

But Leah wouldn't hear of it. "No, we should really go today. Remember, I already told you that the woman who works there on Wednesdays is very artistic, and she can help us design our jewelry. Miriam, you understand, don't you?"

Miriam nodded halfheartedly, but Leah didn't notice. She was too busy nudging Nechama along.

Leah and Nechama arrived at the class meeting at seven o'clock sharp, wearing the earrings they had made that afternoon. When they entered Miriam's house, there was a festive atmosphere in the air. Music was playing, and the table was laden with an assorted array of nosh and food. Girls were chatting and giggling, and it sounded more like a party than a meeting.

"Yumm!" Feige proclaimed as she helped herself to a chocolate Danish.

"Miriam, it looks like you prepared for an army," Hindy observed. "I'm feeling full just looking at all the food you have out."

"What tape is playing?" Leiba wanted to know. "I don't think I've heard it before."

Elana, who was standing near Leiba, said in a quiet voice, "I think it's the latest Chevi Chein album."

"It is," Miriam confirmed. "It just came out a couple of weeks ago."

"It's really good," Leah commented.

"All of Chevi Chein's tapes are good," Hindy declared. "She has a great voice, and her songs are catchy, too."

Raizy stood up and cleared her throat. "I hate to do this," she said, "but we really have to get down to business. We have a lot to cover tonight, so I hereby call this meeting to order."

"Yes, ma'am," Miriam saluted humorously, and the room got quiet as the girls focused their attention on Raizy and Feige.

"As you all know," Feige began, "we have a lot of money to raise, so we're going to need to organize several big fundraising events over the year. Committees of different girls will oversee each of these events, but, of course, they will count on the rest of us for our help and participation. Together with Mrs. Solomon, Raizy and I have come up with approximate dates for our major fundraisers, and tonight we'll set up the committees so everyone can start brainstorming about the details of their specific projects." Feige took a breath and motioned for Raizy to continue.

Raizy consulted the paper she held in her hand and said, "Okay, we'll be having an event after the Sukkos break, then a Chanukah program and then another program Purim time, and our last big fundraiser will be right before Pesach. That one's usually a carnival on Sunday to entertain the kids while their parents clean for Pesach at home. So what we need to do now is form groups for each committee, and then we'll discuss other ways that we can earn money during the year, as well."

Following Raizy's words, the eighth graders broke out into

discussions as they decided which committees they were most interested in joining.

"Let's do the Purim program," Leah suggested to Nechama. "That's always a fun event, and everyone has a good time."

"Sure," Nechama replied agreeably. "It's all the same to me."

"Okay," Leah informed Raizy above the din, "Nechama and I want to be on the committee for the Purim *chagiga*."

"I want to sign up for the Chanukah event," Leiba said loudly.

"Hold it," Feige instructed, holding up her hand. "Let's do this in an orderly way. Anyone who wants to be part of the committee for the first fundraiser right after Yom Tov, please raise your hand."

When Feige asked who wanted to be part of the Purim program committee, Nechama and Leah answered in the affirmative. So did Miriam and Hindy.

Once all the committees were finalized, the conversation turned to ideas for smaller fundraisers. The eighth graders discussed raffles, garage sales, pizza day and a variety of other suggestions.

"Oh, my goodness!" Hindy suddenly burst out. "It's already nine o'clock. I better go home now."

There was a murmur of agreement as several other girls rose to leave, too. "I didn't realize it was so late!" Leiba cried. "I hope my mother's not nervous."

"Come, we'd better head out, too," Leah told Nechama. "Don't forget, I still want to show you my photo albums."

"Yeah, I can't wait to see them," Nechama replied. "I'm curious to see how you looked when you were younger."

"Let me tell you, there are some really funny shots of me," Leah confessed with a giggle. "Some of them are quite embarrassing, actually."

"They can't be worse than the pictures of me when I was a kid," Nechama reassured her.

The two of them laughed as they walked together under the clear starry sky, completely oblivious to Feige, who was still at Miriam's house wondering where they had gone.

"Where's Leah?" Feige asked the girls who were still around. She lived a few houses down from Leah, and the two of them usually walked home together after class gatherings.

"Oh, she's not here anymore," Miriam answered, adding with a trace of bitterness, "She already left with Nechama."

"I can't believe that today is Thursday!" Leah exclaimed as she and Nechama got ready for school that morning.

"Why? What's so special about Thursday?" Nechama asked.

"I don't know how I forgot to tell you. Things were so busy around here this past week that it completely slipped my mind, but every Thursday there are Israeli dance classes at the JCC, and I always go."

"Israeli dance classes?" asked Nechama with interest. "That sounds like fun."

"Do you like dancing?"

"Uh, I don't know. I haven't really had the chance to find out. There are no dancing classes for girls in Woodhaven."

"Then you must come with me tonight. Even though I'm

not a great dancer, I always have a good time, and so do all the other girls who go."

"You don't have to convince me. I definitely want to go and see what it's all about."

But when Nechama and Leah got back from school that day, they found a forlorn-looking Levi sitting on the front stoops.

"What's wrong?" Leah asked her brother.

"Mommy promised that she'd take me out to the pizza shop for supper tonight, but now she's not feeling well and she says she's not up to it," Levi explained in a voice full of self-pity. "I waited for this all week, and now I'm not even going."

"That's too bad," said Leah. "Maybe Mommy will take you next week."

Nechama felt sorry for Levi. He was so upset. Spontaneously, she asked, "Why don't I take you to the pizza shop? Would you like that?"

Levi considered this for a minute, and then said, "Yeah, why not? Let me go upstairs and ask my mother for money."

Leah was surprised by Nechama's generous offer. Somewhat unenthusiastically, she said, "Let me just take a quick drink, and I'll be ready to go."

"That's okay, Leah, I'll take Levi by myself," Nechama said. "I didn't mean for you to come along, also."

"Yeah, but he's my brother," Leah insisted. "There's no reason that you have to take him to the pizza shop alone."

"I really don't mind," Nechama said truthfully. "And I know how much you wanted to go to the dance class tonight. So Levi and I will go out for pizza by ourselves, and that's the end of that."

Leah tried arguing, but Nechama wouldn't hear another word about it. As soon as Levi returned with a ten-dollar bill from his mother and a message that Nechama should use the money to pay for both of them, Levi and Nechama waved good-bye and started on their way.

Levi was in a good mood as he walked alongside Nechama, and Nechama was in high spirits, too. She was happy that she'd been able to cheer up Levi, and taking him out made her feel like a big sister again. As much as she liked the Weisses, she still missed her family and the special role she played in looking after her two younger siblings.

In fact, Nechama was enjoying herself so much that when she saw Levi look longingly at the park on their way home, she suggested, "Why don't we stop for a few minutes so you can play a little?"

In response, Levi shot her an expression of gratitude and dashed off to climb on the monkey bars. Watching him run around reminded her of Yossi, and she smiled.

By the time Nechama and Levi got to the Weisses' house, Leah was already back from her dance class. "Hi," she greeted them. "You were gone for a while. Did you have a nice time at the pizza shop?"

"Yeah, we did," Nechama replied.

"I wish that my mother had given you money to bring back pizza for all of us," Leah said. "My father's coming home soon, and supper's not made. My mother is still upstairs sleeping, and I don't want to wake her up."

"So why don't we make supper?"

"Us?" Leah asked blankly. "But how can we? I don't know the first thing about making supper!"

"Well, I don't know how to make anything fancy, either, but I do know how to prepare a few simple dishes. Let's make pasta, scrambled eggs and salad. That's easy enough, and it's definitely better than nothing."

"Okay, sure. Just tell me what to do, and I'll get to work."

Fifteen minutes later, when Mrs. Weiss entered the kitchen, she was shocked by the scene that welcomed her. The eggs were ready, the salad was dressed in a bowl and a pot of pasta was bubbling on the fire.

"I don't believe it, girls!" she declared. "I woke up a minute ago and realized that I had slept for a lot longer than I'd meant to. Right away, I panicked because Tatty will be home any minute, and I hadn't done a thing for supper. Then I thought I smelled some food cooking, and I came downstairs. Nechama and Leah, I'm amazed by what you've done. Thank you so much!"

"Nechama gets the credit," Leah said. "She was the one who came up with the idea and showed me what to do."

"Yeah, but you helped a lot," Nechama interjected. "I couldn't have done it without you."

"Well, I'm grateful to both of you," Mrs. Weiss said. "And I see you've already set the table, too." Mrs. Weiss shook her head in self-recrimination. "I'm so embarrassed by my carelessness. This has never happened before! Please accept my apologies, Nechama. I'm sorry."

"You don't have to be, really," Nechama protested. "I like

working in the kitchen. I help out with supper all the time in my house."

Shortly after, Dr. Weiss walked through the front door, and Nechama and the Weisses sat down to a simple but satisfying meal. Mrs. Weiss told her husband the story of how supper had come to be, concluding, "As good a job as the girls did, though, supper will remain my domain. I don't expect them to have to do this again."

Dr. Weiss observed the glow of contentment on Nechama's face. Sensing that she hadn't been this happy since she'd moved to their house, he objected, "I disagree. Now that we've seen how capable Nechama and Leah are in the kitchen, I think you should include them regularly in your supper preparations. Allowing them to help out will be beneficial to everyone."

And the pleased expression that appeared on Nechama's face following Dr. Weiss's statement only reinforced his opinion.

chapter Five

Leah was in seventh heaven. Having Nechama as a boarder was just as wonderful as she'd anticipated, and maybe even more. Nechama was so sweet and full of fun, and the more time the two of them spent together, the more they discovered their similarities. It thrilled them to find out how many things they had in common.

"I can't believe you also don't like chocolate," Leah declared to Nechama as Mrs. Weiss served pudding pie after Shabbos lunch. "People think I'm crazy when I tell them."

"I agree," Dr. Weiss spoke up with a smile. "You ladies don't know what you're missing by turning down this dessert."

"So where is the Bnos gathering today?" Mrs. Weiss asked the girls.

"It's at Elana's house," Leah answered, "but I don't know if we're going to go."

"Why not?" her father questioned with raised eyebrows. "You always go to the Bnos gatherings."

"Well, we'll see. Nechama and I are going to learn something together, and we'll take it from there."

As it turned out, the girls never made it to the gathering.

After Shabbos, Raizy called to find out why they'd missed it.

"I don't know. We were just having a good time hanging out in the house," Leah told her.

"Oh. Well, tomorrow a few of us are going bowling. Want to come?"

"Nechama and I are actually going shopping downtown tomorrow, but thanks for asking."

"Yeah, well, *gut voch*, then," Raizy said, bringing the conversation to an abrupt close.

"*Gut voch*. See you on Monday."

On Tuesday after school, when Leah and Nechama got home, they found the house quiet and empty. Upon closer inspection of the kitchen, they found a note hanging on the fridge. Written in Mrs. Weiss's neat handwriting, it read, "Hi, girls. I had to go out for an unexpected appointment, so I dropped Levi off at a friend. Tatty will be picking me up on his way back from work, and we will stop to buy supper before we come home."

"An unexpected appointment," Leah mused out loud. "I wonder what that's all about. In any case, I hope my parents take out from a *milchig* restaurant. I'm in the mood for a pasta and cheese dish."

"So let's make one ourselves," suggested Nechama.

"But how can we? I mean, I don't know how. Do you?"

"No, but that's not a big deal. We'll take out your mother's cookbooks and look up a recipe for *milchig* pasta and a side dish or two. All we have to do is follow the instructions, and if there's anything we don't understand, I can always call my mother for help. See if you can reach your mother on her cell phone now to ask her for permission to make supper, and if she agrees, we'll get started."

Obediently, Leah dialed her mother's number, and Mrs. Weiss, with a little coaxing, gave her consent to the girls' request. "Just be careful," she warned, "and please clean up after yourselves."

With that taken care of, Nechama made a beeline for the shelf of cookbooks and took down a few that she had seen in her own house. She began skimming the table of contents in one of them, and soon she was studying the dairy section. Leah peered over her shoulder, and soon she, too, was caught up in the process of deciding on a menu.

"Should we make a dessert, too?" Nechama asked.

"Why not?" Leah answered. "I think if we're doing this, we should do it right. Let's do a main dish, a side dish, a salad and a dessert. What do you say?"

"Sounds good to me. Okay, let's figure out what we're going to make so we can write up a list of ingredients and see if we're missing anything."

After a quick trip to the grocery store for some missing ingredients, the girls got down to work. Leah seasoned fresh salmon while Nechama cooked up a spicy sauce for the pasta. Nechama sautéed vegetables while Leah prepared a salad dressing.

"Let's hurry, so we can surprise my mother and father when they get home," Leah urged.

"Okay. Then why don't you set the table while I finish up in the kitchen? If you can find tall candles to put into your mother's glass candlesticks, then we can dim the lights in the dining room, and it will look really fancy."

Leah and Nechama were just putting the food out on serving plates when they heard the rest of the Weiss family walk in.

"Mmm, something smells good," Mrs. Weiss declared.

"What's going on around here?" Levi asked loudly. "It looks as if the lights in the dining room aren't working."

"They've been dimmed, actually, and the candlelight looks lovely. It looks and smells as if we've entered an elegant restaurant," Dr. Weiss remarked, jokingly adding, "Are you certain we're in the right place?"

"You sure are," said Leah as she and Nechama stepped into the dining room from the kitchen. "Tonight, we are treating you to a gourmet dinner."

Leah's parents couldn't get over what the girls had done. Throughout the meal, they kept showering Leah and Nechama with praise.

"Who would have ever thought that we have two of the most talented chefs residing under our very own roof?" Dr. Weiss asked his wife after dessert had been served.

Mrs. Weiss smiled. "Leah and Nechama, you've really outdone yourselves," she told them. "Thank you for a delicious supper."

"You're welcome," they said, with smiles that reflected their feelings of satisfaction and pride.

That night, as they got into bed, the girls were still in a good mood from their successful dinner. "Did you see how shocked your parents were?" Nechama asked Leah. "They were not expecting such a fancy meal at all!"

"Of course not! I mean, before last week, I never cooked a thing in my life. But today I saw that cooking can really be fun."

In fact, Leah thought to herself once the girls had wished each other a good night, *practically everything is fun when Nechama's around. Studying for tests, walking to school, doing chores … you name it, when I'm doing it with Nechama, we have a good time.*

On Thursday in school, when Leah and Nechama sat down at a table to eat lunch together, Leah said, "Remember, Nechama, tonight there's dance class, and this time, you're coming with me."

"Don't worry, I was planning on it already. I'm really excited, actually."

"What are you talking about?" asked Feige, who had slipped into a seat beside them.

"Dance class," Leah replied.

"Oh, are you going tonight?" Feige inquired.

"Yeah," Leah answered shortly, then turned back to Nechama and said, "Listen, we must stop and get bottles of water on our way home. While we're at the grocery, we should also stock up on more honey pretzels. We finished the last pack yesterday, and you know how much we really like them."

Leah continued talking about various other snacks the girls should pick up while they were at the store, and Feige, feeling excluded from the conversation, turned to speak to the girls sitting on her other side.

The dance class that night was a big hit. Observing Nechama during the session, Leah was able to tell that her friend was really enjoying it. Although Nechama was a beginner, she caught on to the steps quickly, and she carried them off easily and with grace.

"You dance well," Leah complimented Nechama after the class.

"I just followed the teacher's instructions," Nechama answered modestly. "Thanks for bringing me along. I had such a good time. I think I'll be joining you every week."

"That's what I was hoping," Leah admitted. Changing the subject, she asked, "Did you pack yet for tomorrow?"

"No, but I've made a list of everything I need to take home with me for Shabbos," Nechama replied. "I'm a little nervous about going on the train. I've never done it before."

"I did it once last year. It's not bad, really."

"I'll take your word for it."

The next day, Leah and Levi joined Mrs. Weiss and Nechama for the ride to the train station. Mrs. Weiss helped Nechama buy a ticket, and then the Weisses escorted Nechama to her train.

"Nechama, are you sure you have everything you need?" Mrs. Weiss checked anxiously.

Nechama nodded.

"I noticed you didn't eat much when you came home from school today, so please be sure to eat the sandwich I made for you. I put some fruit and water in your bag, too. And don't forget that if there's an emergency, you have our toll-free number that you can call."

"Thanks," Nechama smiled. Mrs. Weiss looked more nervous than she was.

"I guess that's it," Mrs. Weiss said reluctantly. "Okay, then, have a safe trip, and please call us when you get home."

"I will, Mrs. Weiss. Thanks for everything and good Shabbos," Nechama replied.

"Bye, Nechama," said Leah. "I'll miss you."

"Bye, Leah. Have a good Shabbos."

When the Weisses got back to their house, Leah had a funny feeling inside. Nechama had left just minutes ago, but already the house seemed emptier.

Over Shabbos, Leah realized how accustomed she'd gotten to Nechama's company. There were so many moments when she wished Nechama were there to share a joke, an observation or just a smile.

"You look like you've lost your other half," Dr. Weiss teased his daughter. "Why don't you go to the Bnos gathering and get together with your friends?"

But during the afternoon, it started to pour, and Leah opted to stay at home and curl up with a book, instead. By the time Shabbos was over, though, Leah was bored of reading and wanted to get out. She decided to call a friend and make plans to go somewhere on Sunday.

She first tried Miriam. "Hi, Miriam, want to do something together tomorrow?"

"No, tomorrow I'll be busy," was Miriam's cool response.

"Okay, *gut voch*," Leah said. After she hung up, she dialed Raizy's number.

"Raizy, do you want to go somewhere with me tomorrow?" she asked when Raizy came to the phone.

"Uh, no, I can't," Raizy answered evasively, and then the two of them said good-bye.

Let me call Feige, Leah thought. *Maybe I'll have better luck with her.*

But Feige also turned down Leah, and so did Leiba. Feeling disappointed by her lack of success at finding a partner to spend the next day with, she decided to give Hindy a shot.

"Sorry, Leah," Hindy told her, "but a bunch of us already have plans to go swimming at the community center."

"Really?" asked Leah bewildered. "But why didn't anyone tell me that when I called them?"

Hindy sighed. "I don't know how to say this to you, but I think some people are getting pretty hurt and annoyed by the way you've been acting lately."

"What do you mean?"

"Well, ever since Nechama has come, you haven't been very sociable," Hindy explained frankly. "You've been acting like she and you are the only ones who exist, and no one else. When girls come over to you and try to be friendly, you basically ignore them. So now do you understand why no one told you about our plans for tomorrow?"

For a few seconds, Leah couldn't speak. She felt as if she'd been slapped across the face.

"Leah, are you still there?" There was compassion in Hindy's voice as she added, "I'm sorry for being so blunt, but I just wanted you to know what's going on. Still, I think you should join us tomorrow. Meet me at my corner, and we'll walk together to the community center. I'll tell the girls that you're coming. Just make sure to act like your old, normal self and everything will be fine."

Leah managed to say thanks and good night, and then she returned the phone to its base, tears stinging the corners of her eyes. Once she had calmed down a bit, she thought about Hindy's words and realized the truth in them. Although it hadn't been intentional, she had gotten so caught up with Nechama that she'd neglected all of her other friends.

It wasn't easy for Leah to put aside her emotions and look at her actions objectively, but when she did, she had to admit that by sticking so closely to Nechama, she'd been doing a disservice to everyone else. Now that Hindy had opened her eyes to the situation, it was time to let go of Nechama a bit and open their circle of friendship to include others.

Leah ruefully thought back to the speech her mother had given her before Nechama had moved in. Though she hadn't taken her mother's words to heart then, now she began to appreciate the wisdom in what her mother had said.

It has been only two weeks since Nechama has come, Leah thought to herself, *and I'm already facing one of those hurdles Mommy was describing. I think Mommy would be proud of the way I'm handling it, though. I've learned an important lesson tonight, and I'm going to be really careful from now on to be more considerate of others.*

The next week in school, Leah observed the positive results of her changed attitude. Besides the fact that her friends were glad to have her back, Nechama was a lot more comfortable in school once she began building friendships with all of her new classmates.

"You know," Nechama confided thoughtfully one evening as she and Leah were relaxing on the couch, "I'm really starting to appreciate being part of such a big class. It was overwhelming at first, but now I like the fact that I'm surrounded by so many different girls." While Nechama was talking, the phone rang, and a minute later, Mrs. Weiss walked into the living room with the cordless phone in her hand.

"Girls," she said, "Tanta Bracha's working on centerpieces for the kollel's *melava malka*, and she wants to know if you'd be available to help her this evening."

"Sure," Leah agreed, and as Mrs. Weiss informed Tanta Bracha that she would drive the girls over after supper, Leah told Nechama, "Wait until you meet Tanta Bracha. Everyone loves her. She must be sixty or seventy, but she acts like she's still a young lady."

Tanta Bracha was on the porch when the girls got to her house. She was seated at a table that overflowed with art supplies, and she smiled broadly as Leah and Nechama approached.

"Hi, Leah," Tanta Bracha said. Turning to Nechama, she declared, "You must be Nechama. Welcome to town. How do you like Lakeview City so far?"

"It's very nice," Nechama answered.

"It is," Tanta Bracha agreed, her eyes twinkling as she added, "especially when you're staying with one of the best families in the neighborhood. Okay, girls, please pull up chairs for yourselves, and I'll show you what I need you to do. I hope you don't mind working outside. The weather's just so perfect now that I thought it would be a shame to stay indoors."

"Yeah, but I heard it's supposed to get cooler over the weekend," Leah commented.

"Oh, don't mention another word about that. Right now, let's just enjoy this beautiful weather while we have it. Well, girls, the theme of the *melava malka* is 'A Garden of Torah,' so for centerpieces, we're making Torahs standing in flat Styrofoam circles that we'll decorate to look like gardens."

"That sounds so pretty," Leah said.

"Thank you. I actually thought the idea was a good one, too. There's just one problem, though. I still haven't figured out how to transform these Styrofoam pieces into gardens. Do either of you have any ideas?"

"How about covering them with origami flowers?" Nechama suggested.

"Origami flowers sound lovely," Tanta Bracha approved enthusiastically. "Do you know how to make them?"

"Actually, I just learned how over the summer when my sister Rachelli and I took out a library book on origami. Here, I'll show you." Nechama proceeded to masterfully turn a piece of bright pink paper into a pretty flower.

"That's amazing. You really know what you're doing. Can

you demonstrate that for us slowly so Leah and I can learn how to make those flowers, too?"

It wasn't long before Tanta Bracha and Leah had caught on to Nechama's instructions. Before long, the three of them were busy creating origami blossoms. They talked as they worked, and conversation flowed easily, as it always did with Tanta Bracha.

"An incredible story happened to me today," Tanta Bracha told them. "It all started when my neighbor, Mrs. Hurwitz, called me this morning. She asked if I had an extra bag of sugar to lend her or, if not, whether I was going to the grocery store sometime this morning. Now, I didn't have a bag of sugar for her, and, the truth is, I hadn't planned on making a trip to the grocery store until tomorrow. However, I figured I might as well help out Mrs. Hurwitz if I could, so I decided to do my Shabbos shopping a day early and pick up the sugar she needed.

"I headed out to the store and pulled into the parking lot. It was fairly empty, though I did pass one older lady on my way into the store. She was standing by her cart, and she was kind of resting her head on the handlebar. Like I said, I walked right past her, but then a flash of concern shot through me. I decided to turn back and check if the lady was okay."

Leah and Nechama listened with interest to Tanta Bracha's story. "Well, was she?" asked Leah.

"As a matter of fact, she wasn't. She told me that as she was walking back to her car, she suddenly felt very faint. She didn't know what it was, but it may have been the heat. I wanted to know how I could be of assistance to her, and she asked if I could please load her bags into the car because she just didn't have the energy to do it herself. I gladly obliged. When I finished, she said she was feeling better and up to driving home. Before we parted, she thanked me profusely. She was extremely appreciative to me, while I just felt so honored to have been chosen as Hashem's messenger to help her."

"Wow!" exclaimed Nechama.

"Yes," agreed Tanta Bracha, "isn't it amazing the way Hashem works? Every moment, people go about their business without realizing that everything they do is part of a bigger picture. Hashem, though, is behind it all, making sure that each of the pieces falls into place. It's called *hashgacha pratis*. Not always are we aware of how our actions play a role in Hashem's master plan, but today I was lucky enough to see it clearly."

"So you mean this is going on around us all the time, and we have no way of knowing?" Leah asked.

"Not necessarily. The more you look out for it, the more you're likely to see it," Tanta Bracha answered.

"I think I understand what you're saying," Nechama nodded, a thoughtful expression crossing her face. "Like even the fact that you called us to help with your centerpieces, and you didn't know how to design the bases, and I had learned how to make origami flowers this past summer – all these pieces came together so that we could make these pretty gardens for the *melava malka*."

"Exactly!" Tanta Bracha exclaimed, clearly delighted that Nechama had grasped the meaning of her words. "And like I just explained, if you hadn't been looking out for the *hashgacha pratis* of it all, you'd never have thought twice about it!"

"I guess even the fact that Nechama and I came here and got to hear your story was part of Hashem's plan. That way, you were able to teach us this lesson," Leah piped up with a smile.

Tanta Bracha broke out into her deep, mirthful laughter. "It looks like you girls have really gotten the message. I'm glad to be in the company of such bright, charming young ladies."

When the trio finally completed all their work, Nechama stretched and remarked in a tone of satisfaction, "Look at that! We're all done."

"It seems that we are," Tanta Bracha agreed, but there was a hint of regret in her voice as she spoke. "I guess that means that it's time for the two of you to go home. I've really enjoyed your company, you know, and I hope you'll visit again soon."

Leah and Nechama both promised her that they would. When Dr. Weiss drove up in his car, they thanked Tanta Bracha, who stood waving at them from her doorway until they could no longer see her.

"Isn't she special?" Leah asked.

"She really is," Nechama nodded, continuing thoughtfully, "I feel bad for her, though. It must be hard for her to live all alone, especially since she's someone who loves people so much."

The girls' conversation was cut short by their arrival at the Weisses' house. When they walked inside, they found the first floor quiet and empty.

"Where's everybody?" Leah asked her father.

"Levi went to sleep, and Mommy did, too, because she was feeling kind of knocked out. She did make you milkshakes before she went to bed, though, and they're waiting for you in the fridge."

As the girls headed to the kitchen to enjoy their evening treat, Leah couldn't help but feel a pang of worry. *I wonder what's up with Mommy,* she thought. *Lately, she's been feeling sick and tired a lot. I really hope everything's okay.*

chapter Six

"Bye, Mrs. Weiss. Bye, Leah. I'll call you when I get home," Nechama told them as she got out of the minivan at the train station, pulling her small wheelie suitcase behind her.

"Bye, Nechama. See you after Sukkos," Leah called behind her.

This was Nechama's third time going home by herself, so she was able to find her train without any trouble. Nechama settled into her seat and took out the book she had borrowed from Leah for the ride. Leah had recommended it, and Nechama looked forward to reading it. Opening to the first page, Nechama noticed that the train was quickly filling up. She had never traveled during rush hour before, and she wasn't used to the crowd.

Watching more and more people walk through her car, Nechama realized that she would probably have to share her double seat with someone else. Sure enough, only moments before the train pulled out, a teenaged girl with straight, white-blond hair and fair skin entered her car huffing. Her pale blue eyes landed on the empty place near Nechama, and, still breathing heavily, she slid into the available spot.

"Boy, am I glad I made it," she told Nechama as the train

started moving. "I thought I was going to miss this train for sure."

Nechama smiled politely at the girl, without continuing the conversation. It was obvious that she and the stranger beside her had little in common, and besides, she was eager to begin reading. She started her book again but her new seating companion interrupted.

"I'm Natalie," she said. "What's your name?"

"Nechama," Nechama answered.

"Say that again, please," Natalie requested affably, and when Nechama did, she asked, "I've never heard of that name before. What kind of name is it?"

"It's a Jewish name," Nechama explained. "It means comfort in Hebrew."

"Oh, are you Jewish?" Natalie questioned with open curiosity.

Nechama nodded, and Natalie said, "That's neat. So am I, but my family's not religious at all. I guess yours is, right?"

Nechama nodded again, and Natalie asked, "Does that mean you go to a special religious school?"

"Yeah. That's actually why I'm on the train now. I board with a family in Lakeview City so that I can go to the school there, and I'm on my way home now for vacation."

"You mean you live away from home? I can't believe your parents let you. You don't look like you're any older than I am, and my parents had a hard enough time letting me make the trip to visit my aunt who just had a baby."

Nechama shrugged. "I'm not saying it's easy for my parents to send me away, but they do it because it's important for them to know that I'm getting a good education."

Natalie whistled softly. "Wow. So what kinds of things do they teach you in your school?"

"Lots of things," Nechama replied. Realizing that Natalie was waiting to hear more, she said, "I don't even know where to begin. Well, for one thing, we learn all about our laws and customs."

"Are there a lot of them?" Natalie asked innocently.

"Well, let's put it this way. We have 613 commandments from G-d, so you can probably imagine that learning about them can keep you pretty busy."

"I'll say! So are you telling me that G-d gave all of the Jews 613 commandments? I've never heard that before. What are these commandments about?"

Nechama and Natalie spent the rest of the ride engaged in discussion. There was no end to Natalie's questions, and Nechama answered them as best as she could, even though there were a couple of times when she had to admit that she was stumped. Natalie was fascinated by everything that Nechama had to say.

Before they knew it, they heard the conductor announce, "Last stop, Woodhaven, coming up now."

"Oh, shucks, I wish I could talk to you longer. All this stuff is so interesting," Natalie declared. "Listen, maybe we could get together some time. Where do you live, Nechama?"

"On Colony Road – do you know where that is?"

"Are you kidding? That's just a few blocks from me. I live on Oak Street. This is too crazy. You must give me your phone number." Natalie fished through her purse, and using the pen and paper she found, she took down Nechama's number.

The train came to a halt, and the girls walked together toward the front of the station's building.

"Are you planning on taking the bus home, too?" Natalie asked Nechama.

"No, my father's coming to pick me up," Nechama replied, and, spontaneously, she offered, "Why don't you come with us? Your house is so close to ours. It really won't be a big deal."

"Thanks, that would be great! I actually wasn't too excited about going on the bus. It's always so crowded at this time of the day."

The girls stepped outside, and Nechama spotted her family's gray minivan right away. "There's my father," she pointed, and she led Natalie toward the car.

As soon as he saw Nechama approach, Rabbi Greenberg jumped out of the car to give his daughter a hug and help her with her suitcase.

"Abba, this is Natalie," Nechama informed him. "I met her on the train, and when I found out that she lives on Oak Street, I told her she could get a ride home with us."

If Rabbi Greenberg was surprised, he didn't show it. He smiled pleasantly at the girl, dressed so differently from his own daughter in a short-sleeved tee shirt and jeans, and held open the door as she and Nechama got into the car.

Once Rabbi Greenberg started driving, Nechama was hardly shocked when Natalie began asking him questions. "Are you a Rabbi?" she wanted to know.

"Yes, I am," Rabbi Greenberg answered, careful not to show his amusement.

"So does that mean you know all of the laws about all of the 613 commandments?" Natalie asked.

Every one of Rabbi Greenberg's responses elicited new questions from Natalie, and Rabbi Greenberg spoke to her with patience and wisdom. As he drove down the familiar streets of their neighborhood, he asked, "Natalie, where exactly on Oak Street do you live?"

Natalie directed Rabbi Greenberg to her house. "There it is, the one with the man trimming bushes in front of it. That's my father. He likes to do all the gardening himself."

As Rabbi Greenberg drove up in front of Natalie's house, her father looked toward them with an expression of surprise. He lay down his garden shears and walked over to the minivan as Natalie got out.

"Hi, Dad, this is Nechama, and this is her father. I got a ride back with them from the train station."

Natalie's father, a short, thin man with a small beard, spoke to Rabbi Greenberg through the open window of the passenger seat. "Hi, I'm Alex Golovyan," he said with a distinct Russian accent. "Thank you very much for driving my daughter home."

"My pleasure," Rabbi Greenberg replied. "I'm Shmuel Greenberg, by the way, and apparently, we're almost neighbors. I live a few blocks down on Colony Road."

"Dad, Nechama's father is a rabbi. I was asking him all sorts of questions about Judaism on the way home, and I was really amazed by all his answers. I could have gone on talking to him for hours."

"Well, you're welcome to visit us at our home and continue our discussion there. Tomorrow evening, we'll actually begin celebrating the festival of Sukkos, which lasts for seven days, and we'd be honored if you would join us for one of the holiday meals."

"That would be awesome!" Natalie exclaimed. Turning to her father with imploring eyes, she pleaded, "Oh, Dad, please say we'll go."

"Natalie, you know I have to consult Mom before I make any plans," Mr. Golovyan reminded his daughter before telling Rabbi Greenberg, "Thank you very much for your kind invitation. Obviously, I cannot accept without first consulting my wife. I will speak to her, and then I will get back to you."

"I already have their number," Natalie informed her father.

"Wonderful," said Mr. Golovyan.

"As soon as my mother gives an answer, I'll call you up and let you know," Natalie said to Nechama and Rabbi Greenberg.

"We look forward to hearing from you," Rabbi Greenberg smiled. "Have a good night."

"You, too," said Mr. Golovyan.

Natalie and Nechama said good-bye, too, and then the Greenbergs were off, driving toward their house and a family that was eagerly awaiting their arrival.

"It is so good to be home," Nechama declared appreciatively amidst all the preparations for Yom Tov the next afternoon.

"Does that mean you're considering moving back?" Rachelli asked hopefully.

"Oh, no," Nechama answered quickly.

"Sounds like you're pretty happy in Lakeview City," her mother observed.

"I am," Nechama confirmed. "My classmates are all nice, and it's great having so many of them. My teachers are nice, too, and, of course, the Weisses are super-nice. But, even so, it's great to be back here for Yom Tov. I've been counting down to Sukkos since school started."

"We've been looking forward to your homecoming, too," Mrs. Greenberg told her daughter. Noticing the stocky, gray-haired cleaning lady standing in the doorway, Mrs. Greenberg asked, "Are you done, Paulina?"

"Yes," Paulina answered in accented English. "I have finished everything you asked."

"Then let me pay you so you can go home and relax a little," Mrs. Greenberg said, handing the cleaning lady an envelope that was lying on the counter. "Here you go, Paulina. Thank you so much. As usual, you've been a lifesaver."

Paulina bashfully waved away Mrs. Greenberg's words of appreciation and wished the family a happy holiday before taking her leave. Once she was gone, Nechama turned to her mother inquisitively.

"What happened to Bertha?" she asked, referring to the woman who had worked as a cleaning lady at the school and in their home for as far back as Nechama could remember.

At the mention of Bertha's name, Mrs. Greenberg smiled affectionately. "The poor woman was getting too old to be doing this kind of work," her mother explained. "In the beginning of the year, when she started having terrible problems with her back, she decided it was finally time to quit. So, sadly, we told her good-bye. Luckily for us, Paulina responded right away to the ad we put in the paper, and she's been a real blessing. She's a hard worker, and she seems eager to please, so we're very grateful to have found her."

The phone rang just as Mrs. Greenberg finished talking, and Nechama reached to pick it up. "Hello?"

"Hi, is Nechama there?"

"This is Nechama."

"Hi, Nechama, it's Natalie. I'm calling to tell you that my family will take you up on your father's kind invitation. Can you please tell me your address and the time you're expecting us?"

Nechama gave her address to Natalie and then consulted her mother about the time they'd be starting the first Yom Tov meal. "We'll see you tonight at about eight o'clock," she told Natalie, adding, "I'm glad you're coming."

"Me, too. It wasn't easy to persuade my mother, but when she saw how much I wanted to join you for the meal, she finally gave in. I was really happy when she said yes. I have so many more questions for you and your father, and I've even started writing them down so I don't forget any of them when I get to your house. Anyhow, I better go now. See you later."

That night, after candle-lighting, a sense of serenity filled the Greenbergs' home.

"Good Yom Tov," Mrs. Greenberg said with a radiant smile after making the bracha on the lights. Lovingly, she kissed each of her children, and then Rabbi Greenberg and Yossi left for shul.

Mrs. Greenberg got comfortable on the couch, and her daughters sat down around her. "So, Nechama, tell us the latest about your life in Lakeview City. Even though we've been talking on the phone, I've been waiting to get the full run-down from you in person."

Nechama was glad to fill her mother and sisters in on the details of the past few weeks she'd spent away from home. They listened in rapt attention as she compared Lakeview Girls' Yeshiva to their school in Woodhaven. She went on to describe all the fundraisers her class had planned so far.

"I'm on the committee for the Purim fundraiser, along with Leah and two other girls I told you about, Hindy and Miriam. We're getting together after we come back from Sukkos vacation to discuss exactly what our program will be."

"Why do you have to meet so early in the year? Purim is still months away," said Rachelli.

"Yeah, that's what I thought, too, but Leah told me that the Purim program is always a big deal, with professional entertainment that has to be arranged way in advance."

"Well, that definitely sounds more exciting than any of the

fundraisers we did last year," Rachelli remarked.

Sarala had been trying to follow the conversation as best as she could. "Do you think we can come?" she wanted to know.

"We'll see," her mother smiled. "We have a long time to think about it. And speaking about time, we better daven and get ready for the meal before our guests arrive."

When Nechama finished davening, she looked out the window and saw the Golovyans walking up the sidewalk. She ran to open the front door.

As the Golovyans stepped into the house, Rabbi Greenberg and Yossi came home from shul, too. Everyone made their introductions.

"I'm Sophya," said Natalie's mother, with a Russian accent that was a little subtler than her husband's.

Watching Mrs. Golovyan extend her hand to shake Mrs. Greenberg's, Nechama observed that Natalie had clearly developed her fair coloring from her mother. The poised Russian woman gave off a very formal impression in her short suit and heels.

"I'm Sarala," Sarala made sure to announce for everyone's information.

"Hello, Sarala," Mr. Golovyan told her. "That's a beautiful dress you're wearing."

"I think so, too," Sarala agreed. Her comment was met with laughter.

"Come, let's go outside to the sukkah," Rabbi Greenberg urged. "I'm sure everyone is hungry, so let's get started. We'll have plenty of time to talk more while we're eating."

Walking to the sukkah, Sarala followed Mr. Golovyan closely. His compliment had definitely won her over.

Rabbi Greenberg made kiddush and then directed everyone to the kitchen to wash their hands for challah. He recited the brachos out loud so that the Golovyans could repeat the words after him. Finally, they were all seated in the sukkah, enjoying the first course of their meal. Sarala made sure to perch herself on the chair right next to Mr. Golovyan. From there, she proceeded to launch into a complete report about her teachers, friends and family.

As soon as everyone began passing around the food, Natalie took the opportunity to resume questioning Rabbi Greenberg. She interrogated him about the reasons for the many customs she noticed taking place, like eating in a sukkah and washing for bread.

Listening to her father, Nechama realized that she, too, was learning things from his answers to Natalie's questions. In fact, it seemed like everyone at the table was enjoying Rabbi Greenberg's explanations, except for Mrs. Golovyan who looked embarrassed about her daughter's curiosity.

"Natalie, I think that's enough for now," she said in a soft but firm tone.

"That's okay," smiled Rabbi Greenberg, who had overheard the comment. "The Torah says, 'A shy person doesn't learn.' I am happy to answer any questions that Natalie has."

Still, sensing that Mrs. Golovyan was uncomfortable, Rabbi Greenberg decided it was time to change the subject. When Rachelli and Nechama cleared the plates and served the soup, he declared, "Natalie, you're asking some very good questions. Let's take a break so I can give them some more thought, and maybe if we don't get to all of them tonight, you'll come over again, and we'll talk some more. For now, let's sing a song. Yossi, do you have any special requests?"

Once the singing was over, Rabbi Greenberg asked Mr. Golovyan about his job, and Mrs. Greenberg began making small talk with Mrs. Golovyan, as well. Rachelli, Nechama and Natalie started a conversation of their own.

Nechama learned that Natalie was a high school freshman like Rachelli. Natalie told the Greenberg sisters that she had been born in Russia but had moved to the United States when she was six months old. She attended the local public school, and the highlight of her week was her Tuesday gymnastics class.

"I just started going to Israeli dance classes in Lakeview," Nechama informed Natalie.

"Israeli dance classes? I've never heard of that before. Are there any around here?"

"No, I don't think so," Rachelli answered, "but if we get together a group of girls who are interested, maybe we could start a class in the neighborhood."

"Let me know if you do, please," Natalie told Rachelli. "It sounds like the kind of thing I'd like to try out."

After the meal was over, the Greenbergs escorted their guests to the door.

"Thank you for your hospitality," Mr. Golovyan told Rabbi and Mrs. Greenberg. "The food was delicious, and we had a pleasant time with you."

"We'll know you mean it if you come again," Rabbi Greenberg answered with a smile.

"If it's up to me, we definitely will!" Natalie enthused.

"Natalie, you're always welcome," Mrs. Greenberg said warmly. "Now that you know where we live, feel free to drop by anytime."

"Especially since I still owe you some answers," Rabbi Greenberg added.

"Don't worry, I'll take you up on it. Nechama, I hope we can get together before you go back to Lakeview. Listen, I'll give you a call in a couple of days. You'll be allowed to answer the phone then, right?"

Nechama nodded. It was impressive how much Natalie had picked up over the brief time they'd known each other.

"Come, Natalie," Mrs. Golovyan told her daughter, taking her by the hand. "It's very late, and you have school tomorrow morning. Good night," she said to the Greenbergs, "and thank you again."

As the Greenberg family cleaned up, they talked about their guests. "Natalie is such a pure *neshamala*," Mrs. Greenberg said. "You can just see how thirsty she is for Yiddishkeit."

"Mr. Golovyan, too, appears receptive," Rabbi Greenberg remarked.

"Yes, but Mrs. Golovyan seems cold to the whole thing," Nechama interjected.

"I noticed that also," Rachelli agreed.

"It could be that the idea of our completely different lifestyle is overwhelming to her," Rabbi Greenberg suggested. "Maybe, with time, she'll warm up to it more."

"We definitely have to invite them over again," Mrs. Greenberg said. "You know, I'm still amazed when I think of how Natalie landed up next to Nechama, of all people on the train. Their meeting was clearly meant to be."

"It's so good to hear your voice, Leah!" Nechama exclaimed when Leah called her on Sunday, the first day of Chol Hamoed. "I was just thinking of you. I was going to call you tonight."

"Well, I guess I beat you to it. Anyway, I'm not going to be home tonight. We're driving to Brooklyn soon to spend the rest of Chol Hamoed and the last days of Yom Tov with my Bubby and Zaidy."

"Oh, really? I didn't realize your family was planning on going away."

"Neither did we, until my father convinced my mother last night. He said that a change of scenery would be good for all of us, and he made arrangements for another doctor to cover for him at work."

"So are you excited?"

"You bet I am, especially since my Bubby just called to tell us that she bought us all tickets for the big Chevi Chein concert tomorrow. I can't wait to hear Chevi Chein sing live."

"Wow, sounds like a nice thing to do on Chol Hamoed."

"Yeah. So how are you keeping busy?"

"Well, today Rachelli and I are going to Paint Party, which is one of those places where you paint your own pottery. Actually, Natalie should be here any minute to pick us up."

"Natalie? Who's that?"

"Oh, I forgot that you don't even know who Natalie is! I met her on the train coming home, but it seems like I've known her for a while already. One second, there's the doorbell. It must be Natalie. Listen, I have to go now, but I'll fill you in on everything when I get back to your house."

Hanging up, Nechama saw that Natalie and Rachelli were both waiting for her, so she grabbed her jacket, and the three of them called good-bye to Mrs. Greenberg.

"Bye, girls, enjoy," she answered.

At Paint Party, each of the girls chose a clay dish to decorate, and for the first few minutes, they were all quiet as they concentrated on their work. After a short while, Natalie pulled out a chocolate bar from her purse and asked, "Either of you want a piece?"

"No, thanks," Rachelli and Nechama answered, almost in unison.

Upon hearing the sisters' quick, uniform refusal, Natalie's face took on a look of understanding. "Oh, is this candy not kosher?"

Both Nechama and Rachelli were surprised by Natalie's question. How did she know what kosher was?

Natalie saw their reaction, and she laughed. "I've been doing a lot of research on Judaism these past couple of days," she explained. "After we were over for the holiday meal, I went to the library and took out a few books. Since then, I've spent most of my free time reading, so I've learned quite a bit."

Seeing that her new friends were listening to her attentively, Natalie continued, "Actually, you may think I'm strange, but when I was at your house, I felt something special that I'd never felt before. As soon as I walked through your door, I had this sense of peace and joy. Your family was so happy and comfortable with what they were doing, and that made a big impression on me.

"Before going to sleep that night, I decided that I needed to find out more about your lifestyle, and that's what I did. Everything I've been reading has been interesting to me. Truthfully, I would really like to study more with a tutor, but my mother is not supportive of this new interest at all and would never agree to pay for that."

Rachelli, who was inspired by Natalie's sincere words, said, "If you'd like, I would be more than happy to get together with you and teach you whatever I can."

"Are you serious?" Natalie asked, jumping at Rachelli's offer.

"Of course, I am."

Natalie rewarded Rachelli with a radiant smile and said, "In that case, when can we have our first session?"

After they left Paint Party, Nechama and Rachelli walked Natalie home. They waited until she got into her house, and then they continued toward their own block.

"You know, Rachelli, I'm jealous of you that you'll be learning with Natalie and teaching her more about Yiddishkeit," Nechama admitted to her older sister. "It makes me feel bad about living in Lakeview City. If I were here, I'd be able to help Natalie out, too."

"Well, just remember that all this only started because you met Natalie on the ride back from Lakeview City," Rachelli answered. "If you hadn't been going to school away from home, we wouldn't even know who Natalie was."

"I guess you're right, but I still wish there was more I could do for her now that I do know her."

"There is," Rachelli insisted. "You can keep in touch with her while you're away, and when you come home for Shabbos and vacations, you can spend time with Natalie then."

Mollified by Rachelli's suggestions, Nechama asked, "Do you think that one day Natalie will actually be *frum*?"

"Who knows?" Rachelli replied. "I definitely hope so. Judging from the way she's talking now, it sounds possible, but I think a lot depends on whether her mother changes her attitude."

"Why are you leaving already?" Sarala complained with a pout. "You just got here."

Nechama understood what Sarala was saying because she felt the same exact way herself. Sukkos had passed by too quickly, and now it was time to return to Lakeview City.

"Before you know it, Nechama will be back. Just wait and see how the next two weeks will fly by," Mrs. Greenberg declared, attempting to cheer up the sad-looking group around her.

"They'd better!" exclaimed Rachelli. "I don't know how I'm going to get used to not having Nechama around all over again."

Realizing that extending the good-byes would only make things more difficult for Nechama, Rabbi Greenberg decided to cut them short. "Okay, Nechama, let's head out to the station now so that we don't miss the train," her father suggested.

The Greenberg family walked Nechama to their minivan. As she got in, Yossi shoved a bag into her hands. Nechama looked down and recognized it as the bag of nosh he had collected in shul on Simchas Torah.

"Thanks, Yossi, but you should really keep this for yourself. You worked hard to get it," Nechama told him.

"No, that's okay," Yossi answered firmly. "I want you to have it for the ride, in case you get hungry on the way."

Less than half an hour later, Nechama was seated on the train, trying as hard as she could to keep herself from crying. Mustering all of her courage, she forced herself to take her mind off her family and the nice time they'd had together over Yom Tov. Instead, she focused on Lakeview City, and all the good things that awaited her there.

CHAPTER Seven

"You know, Mommy, even though it was only our first day back at school, it feels like we never left. Sukkos vacation seems like ages behind us," Leah told her mother as she and Nechama helped themselves to drinks and crackers in the kitchen.

"That's how it always is," smiled Mrs. Weiss. "We bounce back to real life very quickly. That reminds me. Tomorrow afternoon I have a doctor's appointment at five o'clock. Do you think you can walk home straight after school and be here to watch Levi until I get back?"

"Sure," Leah agreed, then asked, "What's wrong, Mommy? Are you still feeling sick?"

"No, Leah, everything's fine. I'm just going for a routine check-up," her mother answered quickly.

Leah wasn't sure whether she was imagining it, but she thought her mother sounded a little uncomfortable as she responded. Leah tried to push away the uneasy feeling in her stomach and decided not to probe further.

"We better hurry up and start our homework," Leah told Nechama. "You'd never guess it was only our first day back by the amount of assignments we already have!"

At school the next day, Raizy slipped into the seat across from Nechama and Leah at lunch. "Can you believe the weather?" Raizy exclaimed. "In just a few days, it's gotten so chilly, and it hasn't stopped raining, either."

"It's all in the spirit of Cheshvan," Nechama joked.

"That's easy for you to say because you don't mind the rain," Leah told her friend.

"You don't?" Raizy asked incredulously.

"No, I actually like it," Nechama admitted.

"Really? Even when you don't see the sun for days, and everything is wet and slippery wherever you go?" Raizy asked, and when Nechama nodded, she shrugged and said, "Okay, then I'm glad at least one person is enjoying this weather."

"Raizy, are you organizing any projects for the month of Cheshvan?" Leah wanted to know.

"Yes. As a matter of fact, Feige and I just met with Mrs. Solomon during recess, and we decided to hand something out in honor of *Yud Zayin* Cheshvan, when the *Mabul* started."

"If you need any help with that, Nechama and I are available," Leah volunteered.

"Thanks. I'll let you know when we decide exactly what we're doing. Meanwhile, though, I have to change the Student Council bulletin board before Rosh Chodesh. Do you think you'd be able to stay after school today to help me take down the old decorations and put up new ones?"

"I can't because I have to baby-sit my brother," Leah said.

Turning to Nechama, she added, "But, Nechama, you can stay with Raizy if you want."

"I'd love to help you, Raizy," Nechama said.

When the final dismissal bell rang later that day, Leah said good-bye to Nechama. Stepping outside, she opened her umbrella and hurried to catch up with some classmates who were ahead of her. It felt strange to be walking home without Nechama beside her.

"Where's Nechama?" Mrs. Weiss asked when Leah walked into the house alone.

"She stayed to help Raizy set up the Student Council bulletin board," Leah replied.

"Oh, okay. Now, Leah, there's chicken and rice in the oven. Please take them out in an hour when the oven bell rings. And the emergency numbers are hanging on the fridge."

"I know that already, Mommy," Leah reminded her mother patiently.

"Okay, so I'm going to go now, or I'll be late. Bye, Leah. Bye, Levi. I'll see you later."

After their mother had left, Levi complained, "I'm so bored. I can't play outside because it's raining, and there's nothing to do inside."

"Do you want to play a board game with me?" Leah asked. Levi's eyes lit up at the suggestion.

"Yeah. Let's play Monopoly."

Leah suppressed a groan. Monopoly always took forever, but the truth was, with Nechama away, she really didn't have anything better to do.

Once Leah and Levi started to play, Leah found herself actually getting caught up in the game, and she was surprised when she heard the ring of the oven bell.

"Wow, that hour really flew by. Everyone will probably be home soon. Let's play for another fifteen minutes, and then you can help me set the table for supper," Leah told Levi.

Levi agreed to Leah's plan. As the two of them put out the plates and cutlery, Leah glanced at the kitchen clock. "It's almost six already. I wonder what's taking Nechama so long at school."

Leah and Levi's parents arrived home soon after. "Thanks for setting the table," Mrs. Weiss told them appreciatively. "Where's Nechama? Is she still not back?"

"No, she hasn't come home yet," Leah confirmed.

Her mother immediately looked concerned. "That's odd. You said she and Raizy stayed at school just to put up a bulletin board. She should have been back by now for sure. Do you think we should call the school? Or maybe we should try Raizy's house."

"I think," Dr. Weiss said calmly, "that we should wait a few more minutes before we do anything. Maybe the bulletin board took longer than expected. Or maybe the girls stopped off somewhere on their way home. If Nechama still hasn't come by six-thirty, then we'll decide what to do."

A sense of tension hung over the room as the next couple of minutes slowly passed. At about a quarter past six, the whole family was startled by the sound of a key unlocking the front door, and they were even more surprised by Nechama's pale, shaken appearance when she walked in.

"Nechama, what happened?" Mrs. Weiss gasped.

"It's a long story, but basically, Raizy broke her foot while we were at school, and the ambulance just drove her to the hospital."

"How did Raizy break her foot?" Leah asked.

Nechama started to answer, but Dr. Weiss cut her off. "Nechama, before you say another word, I think you first need to take a drink and have something to eat. Let's sit down for supper, and when you're feeling a little better, you'll tell us more."

Gratefully, Nechama sat down by the dining room table and accepted the plate of food that Mrs. Weiss handed her. The smell of the chicken and rice made her realize how hungry she was. She hadn't eaten anything since lunch.

Once Nechama had filled the hole in her stomach, she shared her story with the Weisses. "You already know that I stayed after school to help Raizy with the bulletin board. By the time we were finished, the only one left in the building was the janitor who was mopping the floors. We got all our stuff together, and as we started going downstairs, Raizy realized that she had forgotten something in the classroom. I waited for her on the landing as she ran back. She was in such a rush to leave already that she didn't notice that the steps were still a little wet, and as she reached the top of the staircase, she slipped and came tumbling all the way down to the bottom."

"Ouch! That must have been terrifying for you to watch!" Leah burst out.

"It was," Nechama agreed. "At first, I didn't know what to do. Raizy started crying in pain, and she told me she couldn't move. I knew I had to get help right away. The janitor had already left, so no one else was in the building. I went to the pay phone and called 9-1-1. I waited with Raizy till an ambulance came, and as soon as the EMTs saw her and heard what had happened, they said she must have broken her right leg, the one she had landed on. They put her on a stretcher and called her parents. Her mother drove over right away so that she could ride together with Raizy to the hospital, and that's when I left and came home."

"What a horrible experience," Mrs. Weiss sympathized. "Poor Raizy, and you must be drained, too. I think you should do your homework right away so that you can go to sleep early tonight. You look like you could use some extra rest."

Nechama was exhausted. She hardly said a word as she and Leah completed their homework that evening, and as the girls got into bed, she was clearly not in the mood for their usual chattering.

Chiding herself for feeling disappointed, Leah thought, *It only makes sense that Nechama's too tired to talk after all she's been through today. By tomorrow, everything will be back to normal.*

The next morning, the girls overslept, and Mrs. Weiss had to drive them to school so that they wouldn't be late. When they got to their classroom, Nechama was like a celebrity. Everyone gathered around her between classes and during recess and lunch to hear her first-hand report of Raizy's accident. Although Nechama wasn't interested in repeating the story and all of its details, she wasn't comfortable refusing to answer her friends' questions.

That whole day, Leah watched as girls surrounded Nechama and interrogated her. Even as the two of them walked home together, they were flanked by students from some of the younger classes who wanted to know more about Raizy's fall.

Leah stayed on the sidelines, feeling almost abandoned by her roommate. She comforted herself by thinking, *At least I'll get a chance to talk to Nechama when we get home.*

Soon after the girls got home, though, Nechama told Leah she was going to call Raizy and see how she was doing. Nechama spent a while on the phone, and after she hung up, she said, "If it's okay with your mother, I think I'm going to visit Raizy after supper."

For a moment, Leah contemplated asking Nechama if she could go along, but then she reconsidered. After all, Nechama hadn't invited her to join. Maybe she wanted to spend time alone with Raizy.

While Nechama was away, Leah wandered around the house aimlessly. Her mother had gone upstairs to lie down – again – and her father had taken Levi to shul for Mincha and Maariv. When the silence was broken by the phone ringing, Leah hurried to pick it up, grateful for the distraction.

"Hello?"

"Hello, is Mrs. Weiss there?" asked the lady on the other end.

"She's not available right now. Can I take a message?"

"I'm calling from Dr. Reisner's office to let her know that we got back the results of her blood test. We're closing now, but please tell her to call here first thing tomorrow morning."

"Okay," Leah answered, scared by the woman's serious, businesslike tone.

Leah wrote "Mommy, call Dr. Reisner's office first thing in the morning" on the family's message board, and she could no longer push away the fears that had been gnawing at her for a while. Leah thought over the situation. For over a month already, her mother hadn't been acting herself. Usually, her mother was active and energetic. Lately, though, she hadn't been feeling very well, and she'd been spending an awful lot of time in bed. Then there were the recent doctor appointments, and now this strange phone call about blood test results. What in the world was going on?

Leah wished she could confide in someone, but whom could she talk to? It was clear that she couldn't speak to her parents. They were obviously trying to hide the situation from her because they hadn't mentioned a word about it, and even when Leah had questioned her mother, she had acted as if nothing was amiss.

Nechama, naturally, was Leah's next option. Leah decided to open her heart to Nechama later that night, when the two girls would be in bed, and the room would be dark. But when Nechama got home, she seemed preoccupied with her own thoughts, and although Leah tried starting a conversation with her more than once, Nechama responded with short, distracted answers.

Never mind, Leah thought. *I'll just wait until tomorrow to discuss my worries with Nechama.*

"Does anyone know when Raizy's coming back to school?" Miriam posed her question to the class at large. "I tried calling her last night, but no one picked up."

"Yeah, it was hard to get through last night," Leiba confirmed. "I called a few times before someone answered. Raizy told me she's coming back on Monday."

"Let's make a welcome-back party for her at recess," Miriam suggested. Miriam was always looking for excuses for celebration.

"That's a good idea," said Feige, "but how are we going to arrange it exactly? Should everyone bring in their own nosh, or should we all give money to one or two girls who will be in charge of buying all the food?"

"I think everyone should chip in a dollar, and I can be the one to go shopping for nosh and paper goods," Leiba volunteered. As someone who considered herself to be one of Raizy's closest friends, she was eager to put herself in charge of the party.

"I'll help you if you want," Nechama offered.

"Okay," Leiba agreed, and with that, it was finalized.

Nechama spent her lunch break with Leiba so the two of them could figure out all the details of the party. Leah sat with Hindy and Feige and tried not to feel left out as she watched Nechama and Leiba talk animatedly together.

Even as Leah and Nechama walked home together, all

Nechama spoke about was Raizy's party. "You know, we should probably make Raizy a big welcome-back card. When I call Leiba later, I'll discuss that with her. We need to add a sheet of oak tag to our list of things to buy. We also have to decide whether we should get cupcakes or donuts. What do you think, Leah?"

I'll tell you what I think. I think that you should stop getting so caught up with Raizy and her party and pay attention to me for a little bit is what Leah wanted to say, but what actually came out of her mouth was, "I don't know. I guess either one is fine."

By the end of the evening, Leah didn't want to hear another word about Raizy's party. Quite frankly, she thought Nechama was getting way too carried away.

"Can you help me make up a poem to put on Raizy's card?" Nechama asked Leah when the two of them were in their nightgowns and preparing for bed.

"Sorry, but I'm not really up to writing now," Leah turned her down. "It's been a long day, and I'm ready to go to sleep."

"Okay. Good night, then," Nechama said good-naturedly. "I hope you don't mind if I keep the desk lamp on so that I can try to work on the poem myself."

"No, not at all," Leah answered stiffly, and then she proceeded to get under her covers and fall asleep.

"Don't you just love Shabbos?" asked Nechama after Mrs. Weiss had *bentched licht*.

Leah was pleasantly surprised by Nechama's question. It had been a while since Nechama had said anything that didn't involve Raizy or her party. Inwardly, Leah breathed a sigh of relief. She hoped this was a sign that things were returning to normal.

And for a while, it seemed like they were. Leah and Nechama sang the tefillos of Kabbalas Shabbos together like they usually did, and they shared *divrei Torah* and class news with the family and their guests at the Shabbos table.

The girls talked for a long time in bed, too. Leah was tempted to bring up her concerns about her mother, but she held herself back. She didn't want to put a damper on the sense of amiable cheerfulness that had just been restored between her and Nechama.

Tomorrow, she promised herself. After we've spent the day together, then I'll open up to Nechama.

The next morning when Leah woke up, her heart felt lighter than it had in a while. She and Nechama went to shul and then enjoyed Shabbos lunch afterward.

As the girls helped clear the table after the meal, Leah asked, "Nechama, do you want to review for our *chumash* test before we go to Bnos?"

"Actually, I think I'm going to go visit Raizy now," Nechama announced, explaining, "She's cooped up in her house because she can't go anywhere with her crutches on Shabbos. I'm sure she'll be glad to have company. Want to come along?"

When she heard Nechama mention Raizy's name, Leah froze. Even when Nechama added, as an afterthought, the invitation for Leah to join her, she still couldn't shake off the resentment that pinched her heart.

"No, thanks," Leah said coldly. "I'll just stay home and look over my *chumash* notes by myself."

"Okay, then, I'll meet you at Bnos," Nechama answered and left soon after.

Over the next few days, Leah's bitter feelings kept growing. It was as if Nechama had practically forgotten that she existed. Nechama seemed to not remember that Leah was the one who'd been her original connection to Lakeview City, and that Leah was the one who was her hostess and closest in-town friend.

Instead, Nechama had ungratefully abandoned her to befriend Raizy. When Raizy returned to school, Nechama was constantly at her side, making sure that she could get around with her crutches. After school, Nechama spent a lot of time at Raizy's house, helping her catch up on the material that she'd missed.

Even when Leah and Nechama were together, Leah acted very coolly to Nechama. She kept waiting for Nechama to apologize, but Nechama seemed not to even realize that Leah was hurt.

One day, during recess, Nechama said to Leah, "I'm going home with Raizy to study with her for the *chumash* test tomorrow. Do you want to come, too?"

"No, thanks," Leah answered in the indifferent tone she'd started using with Nechama.

"So do you mind telling your mother not to expect me home

till about seven? I'll be eating supper there, too."

"Fine, I'll tell her."

"See you later. Good luck studying. Maybe we can review a little more together when I get home."

"Maybe. We'll see."

Nechama went to wait with Raizy for a ride home, and Leah walked out of the school building with Miriam.

"I'm so nervous for the *chumash* test tomorrow," Miriam told Leah. "I've been studying since Shabbos, but I still don't feel like I know the material well enough. There are so many *meforshim*, and some of them are kind of hard. How about you? Are you prepared for the test?"

"Kind of, but I still need to look things over again tonight."

"You're so lucky. I wish I had your brains," Miriam sighed. "Sometimes I wonder what it would be like to be smarter. Life would be a lot easier, that's for sure. I guess I just have to be thankful for what I've got, right?"

"Yeah," Leah agreed distractedly.

"Leah, is everything alright? You've been pretty quiet. Is something bothering you?"

"No, I'm just a little tired," Leah replied, but her excuse sounded lame.

Realizing that Leah didn't want to share her problem, Miriam let the matter drop. She tactfully changed the subject and kept up a one-sided conversation until they got to her corner and had to part ways.

When Leah let herself into her house, she saw that no one else was home. In the kitchen, she found a note from her mother that read, "Hi, girls! Levi and I are out shopping. We'll be back soon."

With no one to talk to, Leah decided to get down to studying right away. After pouring herself a drink, she went to the living room and took out a *chumash* and her notes. She had a hard time concentrating, though. When the phone rang after a few minutes, she was still staring at the first *pasuk*.

"Hello?" Leah said.

Her greeting was met with a message. "This is a recording from Health Plus Pharmacy to let you know that your prescription is ready."

Prescription? thought Leah as she hung up. *It must be for Mommy because Levi, Tatty and I have all been feeling perfectly fine. I wonder why Mommy is trying to cover up her sickness, though. Maybe it's serious, and she doesn't want Levi and me to know because she doesn't want to worry us. That must be it. Mommy is always trying to make sure that Levi and I don't get scared or nervous.*

But scared and nervous is exactly how Leah felt. When Mrs. Weiss returned with Levi, Leah took a close look at her mother and noticed how pale and queasy she looked.

"I'm going upstairs to my room for a bit," her mother said.

"Are you sick?" Leah asked, trying to sound nonchalant.

"Not at all," her mother answered quickly. "I'm just tired and need to lie down a little."

Mrs. Weiss turned to go, but Leah called after her, "Mommy, one second."

"Yes?"

"The pharmacy called to say that there's a prescription that's ready."

"Thanks," her mother nodded and then left the room.

Mrs. Weiss had just gone up to her room when the phone rang again. Levi picked it up, and from his side of the conversation, Leah was able to tell right away that it was their Bubby calling. After a few minutes, Levi said, "Hold on, let me go see if mommy's up."

Dropping the phone, Levi ran upstairs to tell his mother that she had a phone call. A little while later, Leah noticed that the phone was still dangling. Levi must have gotten caught up with something elsewhere and forgotten that he'd left the phone hanging.

Leah went to return it to its cradle, first checking to make sure that her mother had picked up and that her grandmother wasn't still waiting. Listening for a moment, she heard her mother say, "The doctor wants to see me tomorrow for another check-up."

As tempted as she was to continue listening to the conversation, Leah forced herself to hang up. Her heart was pounding, though, and with a sinking feeling she knew her suspicions had been correct. Something was definitely going on with her mother.

Nechama came home later, chirpy and cheerful. She gave Leah an animated report of her evening at Raizy's house and filled Leah in on all that she and Raizy had discussed. When she'd finished her detailed account, she asked Leah, "So how have you been?"

Leah responded with a muttered, "Fine."

"So do you want to review the *chumash* one last time together?" Nechama asked.

"No, that's okay. I'm not really in the mood."

"Are you sure? We could test each other and make it fun," Nechama offered.

"No, I'm just going to take a shower now and go to sleep."

It was quiet in the girls' room after that. Getting into her nightgown, Leah thought about the situation between her and Nechama. Not in her wildest dreams would she have imagined that this would be the way things would turn out.

"Good night," she told Nechama as she got into bed.

"One second," Nechama said, sitting down on her own bed so that she was facing Leah.

"What?" Leah asked, a hint of impatience in her voice.

"You tell me what," Nechama answered, looking Leah straight in the eye.

"What are you talking about?"

"I'm talking about what's going on between us right now. Things just haven't been the same the past few days."

"Oh, you mean you've noticed?" Leah asked sarcastically.

"Of course, I've noticed. At first, I thought maybe it was my imagination, or maybe you just needed some time to yourself, but when you continued giving me the cold shoulder for a few days, I decided to speak to you and find out why you're acting like this to me."

"Well, how would you feel if your good friend suddenly dropped you for someone else?" Leah replied, feeling as if a dam had been let loose within her. "How would you feel if all that your roommate ever talked about was her new friend, and all she wanted to do was spend time with her new friend, and all she seemed interested in anymore was her new friend? Tell me, how would you feel then?"

There were tears in Leah's eyes as she questioned Nechama, and there were tears in Nechama's eyes as she answered. "Leah, I can't believe you felt like I was dropping you. I would never want to lose your friendship. You mean too much to me. I'm so sorry you thought I was choosing Raizy over you. That's not the case at all. Of course, I like Raizy, and I'm happy to be her friend, but nothing could take the place of the special friendship I have with you."

"So then why have you been spending so much time with Raizy?" Leah demanded.

"I don't know what to tell you," Nechama admitted, looking a little confused herself. "I think that because I was with Raizy when she fell, I feel a little responsible for what happened and for making sure that she gets better. So I've been throwing myself into helping Raizy as best as I could, not realizing how this was affecting you. I'm sorry, Leah. Will you please forgive me?"

"Of course, I will," smiled Leah. Now that Nechama had explained her behavior and had apologized, Leah was only too happy to make up. "I've missed you, you know."

"Me, too," Nechama replied. "I'm glad this is all cleared up. You don't know how worried I was getting. Just thinking that we'd go to sleep another night without one of our long talks made me want to cry."

"So what are you waiting for?" Leah laughed. "Get into pajamas and let's talk!"

Leah and Nechama chatted until very late that night. It was as if they were making up for lost time. At one point, Leah found herself sharing her concerns about her mother's health.

"I don't know what's going on exactly," Leah said, "but whatever it is, it doesn't sound good. Why is my mother having all these doctor appointments and check-ups? And why does she need to take blood tests and medicine? I'm so scared that it might be something very serious. Otherwise, why is she trying to keep it a secret from me?"

"I don't know, Leah," Nechama answered sympathetically. "I understand why you're nervous, but maybe everything's under control. Maybe your mother was sick, so she went to the doctor, and she had to take blood tests to see what the problem was. Maybe the doctor figured out what was wrong, and the medicine she's taking will make her all better. It just might be as simple as all that."

"I hope so," Leah said. "I really hope so."

"Look, hopefully, that's the case. Let's start saying extra Tehillim for your mother to have a *refuah shelaima*, and if it still looks like she's not feeling well in a few days, we'll figure out what to do then."

"Yeah, I guess that makes sense. You know, Nechama, I feel so much better now that I spoke to you about this." There was a comfortable silence between the girls before Leah continued, "I'm so glad that we're friends. It's so reassuring to know that I can share everything with you."

"I feel the same way," Nechama answered sincerely, and then asked, "Can you believe that all this started because of a Ferris wheel ride?"

Leah laughed. "When you put it that way, it is pretty amazing. I mean, just think of how everything worked out. Right after we met, you found out that Rivky was moving away, you wrote to me about it and then my mother suggested that you come live with us. It's exactly what Tanta Bracha was explaining to us when we were at her house. Hashem was clearly behind everything that happened."

"That's for sure," Nechama agreed. Softly, she marveled, "It's that incredible jigsaw puzzle of *hashgacha pratis!*"

CHAPTER Eight

Mrs. Solomon was in the middle of a parsha lesson, and the only sound that could be heard in the classroom was her animated voice. The eighth graders sat in rapt attention as their teacher talked about Avraham and his incredible *chessed*.

"You know, girls," Mrs. Solomon told her students, an earnest look on her face, "I feel that in school a lot of stress is put on the academics, while *middos* are not given the proper attention they deserve. That's why I've decided that at this point, as we're discussing the amazing kindness of Avraham, it would be an appropriate time to launch a mini-*chessed* campaign. In the upcoming month, each girl will be responsible for doing an hour of *chessed* a week. I've come up with a list of possibilities that you can choose from, and by Friday, I expect all of you to let me know what it is you'll be doing as your *chessed* project."

A few girls had their hands raised, and Mrs. Solomon paused to answer questions.

"Yes, Miriam?"

"Can we pair up with other girls for this *chessed* assignment?"

"It depends on what you choose to do. In just a minute, I'll read the list of choices to you, but you'll see, some things you can do with a partner or two, while others you need to do alone. For instance, visiting a hospital or old age home is something that a few girls can do together, while tutoring a child or acting as a 'big sister' to a younger girl is something you would have to do by yourself."

As Mrs. Solomon continued to answer questions, Nechama's mind was racing. She was excited by this new assignment, and she thought about which type of *chessed* she would like to commit to.

At recess, Leah and Nechama sat together on a bench outside and ate their snack. "So what do you think, Nechama? Doesn't the *chessed* campaign sound like fun?"

"It does," Nechama replied. "I can't figure out what I want to do. I like a lot of the choices that Mrs. Solomon gave us."

"I know what you're saying. I also had a hard time making up my mind."

"So you mean you've already decided what you want to do?"

Leah nodded, then added sheepishly, "And I was actually hoping that you would agree to work together with me."

Nechama smiled. "Well, what do you want to do?"

"I thought it would be nice to visit an old age home. There's a Jewish one in close walking distance from my house, so we wouldn't even have to worry about how to get there."

"Visit an old age home?" Nechama asked uncertainly. "That wasn't really one of my top picks. I've always been kind of scared of old age homes."

Leah looked surprised. "Why would you be scared? I go every once in a while with my mother or Tanta Bracha, and the old people are always thrilled to see us. They're so lonely and bored, and visitors make such a difference in their day. I'm telling you, every time that I go, I leave feeling like a million dollars. It's such a big mitzvah."

"Okay, I guess I'll do it," Nechama relented, not sounding completely sure about her decision. "Hopefully, it will work out okay."

"Of course, it will!" Leah assured her, adding, "Look, we can always switch to something else if you're really not happy."

"Are you two talking about Mrs. Solomon's *chessed* assignment?" asked Raizy, who had come to join them on the bench.

"Yeah, did you decide yet what you want to do?" asked Leah.

"I'm not a hundred percent sure, but I think I want to visit an old age home. My neighbor just went to live in an old age home recently, and I know how much she enjoys it when my family goes to see her."

"If that's the case, then why don't you join our group? Nechama and I are planning to visit an old age home, too."

"Oh, really?" Raizy said, looking pleased. "So count me in. Let's tell Mrs. Solomon what we've decided when we see her at lunch."

At lunch, Mrs. Solomon was bombarded by eighth graders who had made their selection. Nechama, Leah and Raizy waited until it was their turn to talk to their teacher, and she smiled when she heard their choice.

"Visiting older people is a very big *chessed*, and I'm sure you'll enjoy yourselves in the process," Mrs. Solomon told them. "There's actually only one other girl who approached me to express interest in going to an old age home, so I think it would be best if the four of you joined together as one team. Please be sure to tell Elana that you'll be working with her, and *hatzlacha* to you all."

That night, as Nechama described her class's *chessed* project to her mother on the phone, Mrs. Greenberg didn't seem as attentive as usual. After Nechama talked for a couple of minutes without hearing much of a response from her mother, she suddenly stopped mid-sentence.

"Ima, what's wrong?" she asked in concern.

"Is it that obvious that I'm upset?" her mother sighed. "I guess I'm really disturbed by what happened today."

"Why? What happened today?" Nechama inquired, holding her breath.

"This morning, Abba went to school early to take care of some things before everyone else arrived. When he got to the building, he was horrified to see that a huge black swastika had been painted on the front glass doors, along with the words 'Dirty Jews.' Luckily, there was enough time to call Paulina and the janitor, who cleaned up before any students came, but still, it was a scare for us. We've never had anything like this before!"

"Who could have done it?" Nechama wondered, hurt and angry that someone could have been so mean and hateful. "Did you call the police?"

"We did, though we asked them to please try to keep their investigation as quiet as possible. Obviously, this is a very sensitive issue. On the one hand, we would like to get to the bottom of it and find the perpetrator, but on the other hand, we want to keep the episode as secret as possible. We don't want parents to get frightened for no reason."

Nechama understood her parents' predicament. "I sure hope that this case gets solved very soon."

"Me, too," her mother answered sincerely. "With Hashem's help, it will."

"I can't believe it's Thursday already!" Nechama told Leah as they were walking home from school.

"Yeah, I know," Leah agreed. "It seems like the week just started, and now it's almost Shabbos."

"Well, I'm happy about that. I'm looking forward to going home tomorrow."

Leah couldn't help the pang she felt at Nechama's words. "I know it's not nice of me, but I have such mixed feelings about the Shabbosim when you go home. As happy as I am for you that you get to spend time with your family, I also feel kind of sad because I know how lonely things are for me when you're away."

Nechama understood. "I have an idea that might help you."

"Really? What is it?" Leah wanted to know.

"Why don't you come home with me the next time I go for Shabbos? That way, you won't be lonely, plus you'll get to meet my family. I'm sure my parents won't mind. In fact, they'll probably be thrilled to have you."

Leah's face brightened at Nechama's suggestion. "Are you serious? That would be so much fun. As soon as you make sure that your parents let, I'll ask my parents for permission."

Nechama was pleased by Leah's eager reaction to her proposal. "It's a shame I didn't think of this earlier, otherwise you could have come home with me this week! But I guess that gives us more time to plan and get excited."

By then, the girls had reached the Weisses' house. They walked straight into the kitchen. Pouring a glass of water for herself and Nechama, Leah declared, "That's strange. I wonder where my mother is. Thursday afternoon she's usually in the kitchen preparing for Shabbos, but I don't see any sign of her or Shabbos food."

"That's because she's lying down upstairs," Levi's voice piped up from the kitchen entrance where he'd suddenly appeared.

"Oh, Levi, you scared me for a minute!" exclaimed Leah. "I didn't see you when I walked in."

"Yeah, well, I was in the family room playing on the computer," Levi explained.

"So why is Mommy upstairs?" Leah wanted to know. A worried tone had crept into her voice as she asked the question.

"I don't know," shrugged Levi. "She's probably resting. Lately, she rests all the time."

"Yeah, but she always starts preparing for Shabbos on Thursday. Today, it doesn't look like she's done a thing so far. Did Mommy look sick?" Leah inquired, trying not to sound as nervous as she felt. She didn't want to let Levi in on her fears.

"I don't know," Levi answered again. "I think she was mainly tired. She told me she was going to stay in bed till the night and that if any of us needed anything, that's where we could find her."

Leah started to panic. "But how are we going to have food for Shabbos? How will anything get done if Mommy's in bed?"

Nechama also had bad feelings about Levi's report. It was true that since she'd moved in with the Weisses, Mrs. Weiss had spent quite a bit of time resting in her room, but even so, it was very unlike her not to have Shabbos organized by Thursday afternoon.

Nechama was ready to reassure Leah and to offer to cook some food for Shabbos, too, when Levi said, "I heard Mommy giving Tatty a shopping list over the phone. She told him to buy everything we need for Shabbos – challah, salad, chicken – everything. And she said we're not having any guests this week, either. So I don't think you have to worry."

Levi's words only made the girls worry even more. Sensing some sort of tension, but not really understanding what it was about, Levi tried to change the conversation. "Hey, don't you guys need to leave soon to go to your dance class?"

Leah and Nechama exchanged a look before Leah answered as lightly as she could, "I don't know if I'm in the mood of going this week. I think I'll go up first to check on Mommy before I decide."

"Well, whatever. I'm going to go back to my computer game. By the way, Mommy said to tell you that Tatty's bringing home pizza for supper."

Once Leah and Nechama were alone, and Levi was out of earshot, Leah turned to Nechama anxiously. "What do you think this is all about?"

As much as Nechama wished that she could comfort Leah and tell her there was no need to worry, she had to admit that something was clearly amiss. "I don't know," she answered honestly. "Maybe your mother's just very tired. Or maybe she has a virus that will be over in a day or two."

Leah was clearly dubious. "I don't know. After the way my mother's been feeling for the past month, it only makes sense that her condition is a little more serious than that. I'm going to go to my mother and see for myself."

But when Leah knocked lightly on her mother's door, there was no response. Afraid of waking her mother, Leah walked away.

Nechama was disturbed to see Leah so upset, and she wondered if a distraction would be a good idea for her friend. "Leah, being that your mother's asleep, and there's nothing we can do for her right now, do you think that maybe we should go to the dance class? It might help you get your mind off what's going on."

After a moment's deliberation, Leah said, "I guess you have a point. Okay, let's get our stuff together quickly. We'll be late if we don't hurry."

During the class, Nechama observed Leah. Although Leah was dancing with everyone else, her heart was clearly not into it that evening. *Poor Leah*, Nechama thought to herself, full of pity for her friend. *I hope all this gets worked out very soon.*

Nechama's train got delayed a bit, so she didn't get home until an hour before Shabbos. After pecking her mother on her cheek and then saying a quick hello to her siblings, she dashed into the shower to hurriedly get ready.

Following candle-lighting, Mrs. Greenberg and the girls settled in on the couch, and Nechama felt herself relax for what seemed like the first time that day. Finally! She loved this chance to catch up with her family on everything that was going on at home.

"Ima," she asked, "whatever happened with the police investigation into the vandalism at the school?"

Her mother, who looked reluctant to go into details in front of Sarala, answered briefly, "Nothing came up, but *baruch Hashem*, we haven't had any more excitement so it seems like that just may be the end of that."

Somewhat relieved, Nechama dropped the subject. Noticing the extra table settings, she asked, "Who's eating over tonight?"

"The Korfs," Ima answered, adding as an afterthought, "And, of course, Avraham and Natalie."

"Natalie? That's nice. I'm glad it worked out that I'm home the same Shabbos she's over."

With a smile, Rachelli replied, "It would be pretty hard for you not to be home on a Shabbos when Natalie's here. She's become a regular like Avraham, who really admires her, by the way. She comes over practically every week, and she stays for a lot more than just the meals. She'll probably be here any minute now, actually."

As if on cue, right then there was a knock on the door. Rachelli jumped up to let Natalie in.

"Good Shabbos," Natalie called out cheerfully when she entered.

"Good Shabbos," Mrs. Greenberg, Nechama and Sarala all answered together.

As Natalie pulled up a chair for herself, Nechama was surprised by her appearance. Natalie was dressed in a modest sweater and long skirt, and tights covered her legs. She looked like a typical *frum* girl.

Natalie noticed Nechama eyeing her, and she laughed. "So what do you think?" she asked, beaming proudly. "How do you like my new look?"

"It's amazing!" Nechama replied with honest enthusiasm.

"Yeah, I'm pretty excited about it myself," Natalie admitted. "Since I met your family, I was impressed by the refined way that you all dressed. When your parents gave me a full explanation of the laws of *tznius*, I decided that this was a mitzvah I wanted to start keeping. There was no way that my mother was going to sponsor a whole new wardrobe when, in her opinion, I have a closet full of perfectly fine clothes already, so I took most of the money from my savings account, and Rachelli joined me last Sunday for a day-long shopping spree."

"Wow!" Nechama exclaimed in disbelief. "That is so special. And you two must have had so much fun shopping. I wish I could have been there." Nechama turned to Rachelli and asked, "Why didn't you tell me any of this when I spoke to you on the phone?"

Before Rachelli could answer, Natalie explained. "It's my fault. I made Rachelli promise not to breathe a word to you. I wanted to surprise you when I saw you."

"Then I guess your plan worked," Nechama replied. "Wow. I still can't believe you went ahead, dumped all of your old clothes and bought *tznius* ones instead. It's incredible."

"We're all in awe," declared Mrs. Greenberg, regarding Natalie warmly.

Embarrassed by all the attention, Natalie made an attempt to change the subject. "Do you think we should start preparing the salads?" she asked. "The men will probably be home soon."

"That's a good point," Mrs. Greenberg said. "Let's daven Kabbalas Shabbos, and then we'll get to work in the kitchen."

As the girls cut vegetables, Nechama talked about all the extracurricular activities that were going on at school. "On Rosh Chodesh Cheshvan, the whole school played a Jeopardy game at lunch. And then, on *Yud Zayin* Cheshvan, the Student Council heads handed out umbrella toothpicks stuck into jellyfish. It was really cute."

Natalie sighed. Longingly, she declared, "I wish I could start going to a normal Jewish school, but right now I just can't see that happening. I don't even want to think of my mother's reaction at the mention of such an idea. As it is, she's so upset about all the religious things I've begun to do. The only reason that she hasn't stopped me so far is because my father keeps calming her down, telling her that I'm a teenager and that she should be glad I'm involved in this and not other things. You know, it's such a shame because if it weren't for my mother, I think my father would also be interested in becoming more religious."

"Do you know why your mother is so against Yiddishkeit?" Rachelli asked.

"Not at all. Whenever I've tried bringing up the question, she closes up and refuses to say a word. Believe me, I'm as curious as you are. There must be a reason for the way my mother feels. It just doesn't make sense that she would be so set against Judaism otherwise."

There was silence as the girls pondered the mystery of Mrs. Golovyan's antagonism. After a few moments, Natalie heaved a deep sigh. "It's frustrating, especially since there are many changes that I would like to make in my life that I just can't because I know they will make my mother so angry. I just keep davening to Hashem to help me and fix this whole situation. In my heart, I know that one day He will."

CHAPTER Nine

"I am so inspired by her," Nechama declared passionately to her friends as the four of them made their way to the Jewish Center for the Elderly, or the JCE as most people called it.

Nechama, Leah, Raizy and Elana were all bundled up in their winter coats as they walked together briskly. Though it was cold and windy outside, weather wasn't on the girls' minds as they listened raptly to Nechama describe Natalie's transformation.

"Since Shabbos, I haven't been able to think of much else besides Natalie. Just imagine completely turning your life around like that in weeks! It takes real strength and courage, and it makes me feel so embarrassed. I mean, how many times have I tried making a simple change like being more careful not to speak *lashon hara?* And here's this girl, who's the same age as we are, who has gone ahead and made not one, but many, drastic changes, like it's the most natural thing in the world! I just can't get over it."

"Natalie sounds like an amazing girl," Raizy declared. "I wish I could meet her."

"You'll just have to come to my house one Shabbos.

Then, you'll have a chance to see her for yourself," Nechama answered.

"That would be nice," said Raizy. "Look, there's the JCE building."

"Finally!" exclaimed Leah in relief. "My fingers are starting to feel frostbitten, even though I'm wearing gloves."

"Yeah, and my ears feel numb, too," added Nechama.

"Same here," Raizy chimed in. Turning to Elana, the only one of the foursome who hadn't spoken up, she asked, "How about you?"

"Let's just say I'm really happy that we don't have to walk a minute longer," Elana responded softly, a smile on her face.

Laughing, the girls entered the doors to the old age home. They were greeted by a blast of warm air.

"It sure feels toasty in here," said Leah. "It's nice to be inside."

Nechama wasn't so sure she agreed. As soon as she walked into the JCE, she recognized the old age home smell, and she started to get nervous. "How did I ever agree to this?" she wondered, and in an undertone, she muttered to Leah, "Now that I'm here, I'm beginning to regret my choice of *chessed*."

"Just give it a chance," Leah told Nechama. "Let's see if you change your mind in a couple of hours."

Despite Leah's reassurances, Nechama hesitantly trailed behind her friends as they entered the central recreation room where many of the residents were gathered. Quietly, she watched as the girls smiled at the elderly people and cheerfully conversed with them. The residents were clearly delighted by their unexpected guests.

"It's wonderful to see such beautiful young ladies!" exclaimed one woman. "Thank you so much for coming."

The people around her echoed her feelings. They were all so happy to see the girls. In fact, the girls' presence seemed to visibly brighten their mood.

Observing all of this, Nechama gradually warmed up. After a few minutes, she began approaching residents herself, asking them how they were and listening to them as they answered.

After spending some time in the recreation room, the girls proceeded to visit people in their private rooms. Some of the elderly men and women were sleeping, and a few were busy with other guests, but most were thrilled when the foursome walked in.

"Here, let me show you pictures of my *eineklach*," a plump man in a wheelchair told the girls, and his face shone as they complimented him on his beautiful grandchildren.

"*B'li ayin hara*, they really are something special," he told them. "I only wish they lived closer. They are a plane ride away, so I only get to see them once or twice year. Still, I'm thankful for even that. You know, there are some people here who never get visitors at all. It's as if their families have forgotten about them, and they're all alone in the world." The man shook his head sadly. "That's why it's so nice when you girls come. It makes us all feel as if there are people who still care about us."

These words moved Nechama and made her realize even more the importance of the mitzvah that she was doing. As the girls peeked into the last room of the old age home an hour or two later, they saw a round-faced woman wearing a curly, reddish *sheitel*. The lady was on the phone, so the girls got ready to turn away, but the woman stopped them.

"Girls, please don't go anywhere!" she called out to them in a loud, accented voice. As the girls stood waiting at the doorway, she said into the phone, "I will call you back in a little while. I have special visitors here now, and I must talk to them."

With that, the lady hung up and turned to the girls with a wide smile. "Please, *maidelach*, come in. What a treat this is. I love it when young ladies like you stop by. So, tell me, what are your names?"

The girls took turns introducing themselves, and then the lady said, "I see none of you asked me my name, but I'll tell it to you, anyways. My name is Bella Jacobovitz, and I'm sure you can tell that I am a lot older than you. Do you know, I am already in my eighties! In a few weeks, I will be turning eighty-five."

"Wow, happy birthday!" Raizy interjected.

"Thank you," Bella replied. "I want you to know that at my age, most people stop celebrating birthdays. They don't think that getting older is a reason to be happy. Not me, though. Every year, I make a little party with my friends here because I know that each day is a bracha from Hashem, and so I'm thankful for every birthday."

"That's great," Leah remarked, with sincere admiration in her voice. "I think we all wish we can be like that when we're you're age!"

"Don't worry, you have a long time to work on it," Mrs. Jacobovitz laughed, and then she urged the girls, "Nu? Aren't you going to sing for me? Many times when the girls come, they sing."

Nechama, Leah, Elana and Raizy all looked at one another and shrugged. "Why not?" was the unspoken conclusion amongst them, and Nechama asked, "Is there any specific song you have in mind?"

"I'm not picky," said Mrs. Jacobovitz. "Any song you sing will be good."

At Raizy's suggestion, the girls sang one of the hit songs from the latest Chevi Chein album, and the elderly lady clapped her hands the whole time. "That was wonderful!" she beamed when they finished. "How about one more?"

So the girls obliged their new friend, and when they were done with their second song, Mrs. Jacobovitz told them, "Thank you so much! You girls really have beautiful voices. You remind me of my niece Yocheved. I never get tired of hearing her sing. That's one reason I wait for her visits. You girls live a little closer than she does, though. Will you come back soon?"

"We will," they promised together.

"Okay, don't forget," Mrs. Jacobovitz said, wagging a finger at them in mock consternation. "I'm waiting."

The girls' spirits were high as they made their way home.

"So how was it? Was it as hard as you expected?" Leah asked Nechama. Leah was quite sure what Nechama's answer would be, but she wanted the satisfaction of hearing Nechama admit it out loud.

"Okay, okay," Nechama laughed sheepishly, knowing what

was going on in Leah's mind. "You were right, and I was wrong. I really had a nice time today."

"So are you ready to go back?" Leah questioned.

"I don't think I have much of a choice," Nechama replied. "Didn't I tell Mrs. Jacobovitz that I'd come again?"

"Good point," Leah conceded. She turned to her three friends and asked, "So when should we make our next trip to the JCE?"

"Sunday works well for me," Raizy answered.

"For us, too," Leah answered, speaking on behalf of herself and Nechama. "How about you, Elana?"

"Sunday should be fine," said Elana.

"Great," Raizy declared. "Then let's just leave it at next week, same time."

When the girls reached the Weisses' block, they said good-bye, and Nechama and Leah headed toward their house. The two of them walked at a quick pace, eager to already be inside their warm, cozy home.

"You know what I'm in the mood for?" Nechama asked. "A cup of hot cocoa with marshmallows melted on top."

"Mmmm, that sounds perfect," Leah remarked, her eyes growing dreamy at the thought. "I'm sure my mother will be happy to help us make hot cocoa, and I think we also have marshmallows in the pantry. Maybe my mother will even agree to light the fire in the fireplace. That would be the best."

Nechama and Leah exchanged excited grins as they ran up the path to the Weisses' front door. Imagining themselves sprawled in front of the dancing fireplace, sipping on their warm drinks, they could hardly contain themselves as Leah rang the bell.

"That's funny," Leah said after ringing the bell for the second time. "My mother didn't say anything about leaving the house while we were away. Maybe she's resting or something."

Leah dug her key out of her bag and let herself and Nechama in. The lights were all out, and the house seemed deserted.

In the kitchen, the girls found a note hanging on the fridge. "Hi, girls!" it read. "Please call us on Tatty's cell phone."

A knot forming in her stomach, Leah reached for the phone. Stopping only a second to pull off her gloves, she dialed her father's cell phone number with trembling fingers.

Feeling her friend's fear, Nechama held her breath as she watched Leah and waited for Dr. Weiss to pick up.

"Tatty?" Leah asked when she heard her father's voice on the other end. "Where are you?" She was quiet for a moment, and then her face became drained of color. "The hospital?" she asked, her voice small and frightened. "What are you doing in the hospital?"

"Mommy was feeling weak," her father answered in a calm, well-controlled tone. "The doctor's office is closed because it's Sunday, so I took Mommy to the emergency room just to check things out, and *baruch Hashem*, it looks as if everything is okay. We should be checking out of here shortly, and we hope to be home in an hour or so."

There was a moment of silence as Leah's mind registered what her father was telling her. She was so stunned – and scared – that she couldn't find her voice.

"Leah? Are you there?"

"Yeah, I am," Leah answered with difficulty.

"Leah, I want you to listen to me carefully. I know you're really nervous, but I'm telling you that there is really no reason for you to worry. All of the tests that Mommy took came out fine, and the doctors said that she is okay. She just has to rest a bit and take it easy, and within days, she should be back to herself."

Leah didn't answer. There were tears in her eyes as her father spoke. No matter what he said, he couldn't convince her that everything was perfectly normal when it so obviously was not.

Dr. Weiss sighed. He realized how shaken his daughter was, and his mind worked quickly to come up with a way to calm her down. "Leah, I'll tell you this much," he said. "The doctors advised Mommy to spend the next couple of days in bed to regain her strength, but you know how hard that will be for Mommy. She likes to be busy doing things all the time. I would really appreciate it if you and Nechama could work on some sort of care package for Mommy to keep her entertained for a while. If you need to, you can even take some cash from the envelope in the kitchen drawer and use the money to buy some things on the avenue. Okay? Can I count on you for that, Leah?"

"Yeah," Leah answered, "I guess so." After all, how could she turn down her father?

Hanging up the phone, Leah met Nechama's wide, empathetic gaze. "I'm sure you've picked up on what's happening. My father took my mother to the hospital because she wasn't feeling well. They're coming home soon, and my father's trying to convince me that everything's really all right, but I know better than that. I mean, how can everything be all right if my mother had to be rushed to the emergency room this afternoon? I know that something's going on because my mother hasn't been herself for weeks already."

Leah's eyes started to fill with tears, and she breathed deeply so that she could continue talking. "My father asked if we could put together a care package for my mother to keep her busy in bed for a while because she needs to rest up when she comes home. He said we could go out and buy things if we wanted to. What do you think?"

Grateful for the opportunity to actually do something productive at that point, Nechama said, "I'm happy to help however I can." Realizing that her mind was a lot clearer than Leah's, she took charge straightaway. "Let's start by making a list of things we can put in your mother's basket."

Nechama pulled out a pen and notepad from the supply drawer, and she began jotting down ideas. "First of all, we should get stuff for your mother to read. But we need to get other things, too. Hmmm, let's see … does your mother like writing?"

Leah shrugged. "She writes letters and cards pretty often, so I guess she doesn't mind it."

"Okay, then we'll get her a pen and some stationery. What else does your mother like doing that she can do in bed? Can you think of anything?"

Truthfully, it was very difficult for Leah to think right then, but she did her best to try and help Nechama, who was, after all, trying to help her. "You know, my mother does enjoy crossword puzzles, so maybe we can find a book of them for her."

Nechama wrote that down. "Okay, anything else?"

As hard as Leah tried to brainstorm more, her mind was a blank. "No, I'm sorry," she said apologetically. "My brain is just not working very well now."

"Of course not!" Nechama responded, full of understanding. "Don't feel bad about it for a second. But tell me, does your mother like to knit at all?"

"I don't think she even knows how to knit. Once in a while, she sews things that have to be fixed."

"Never mind that, then. I think we should hurry out to the stores now and see what we can find. Are you ready to go?"

Almost an hour later, the girls returned home after a successful shopping spree. In the Judaica store, they'd found a couple of magazines, a book of Jewish brainteasers and a CD of Torah lectures. In the pharmacy, they'd gotten a stationery pack and a mini-sewing kit (just in case Mrs. Weiss had to catch up on any mending). And they'd also bought a box of Mrs. Weiss's favorite chocolates just for good measure.

Leah and Nechama were in their room arranging the items in a basket when the Weisses returned home. They ran downstairs to welcome everyone home.

"Hi, girls," Mrs. Weiss greeted them. As bright as she sounded, it was impossible to hide the drained, ill look on her face.

"Hi, Mommy," Leah answered. Hesitantly, she asked, "How are you?"

"*Baruch Hashem*," Mrs. Weiss replied, giving her daughter a faint smile. "I think I'm going to go upstairs to lie down in bed, though, but please feel free to visit me in my room."

"I'm going to go with Mommy to help her settle in," Dr. Weiss announced, "but I'll be back in a few minutes. We brought home pizza for supper, so if you girls don't mind setting the table, we'll eat when I come down."

As the two girls got the table ready for supper, Leah talked to Nechama softly so that Levi wouldn't be able to hear. "It looks like my mother and father aren't planning on letting me know what's really going on. I can't take this anymore. I feel like confronting them once and for all. I'd like to tell them that I know something is wrong and that I wish they would be honest with me. What do you think?"

After deliberating briefly, Nechama declared, "At this point, I think you should try to speak to your parents openly. Now that you have no idea what is really wrong, your head is full of all kinds of scary possibilities. By telling you the truth about your mother's condition, your parents will actually help you feel less worried than you are already."

Nechama's words gave Leah the encouragement she needed. "As soon we finish setting the table, I'll go up and talk to my parents."

"Don't worry about setting the table. I'll take care of it. You go. Good luck."

"Thanks," said Leah.

Her heart beat quickly, and her throat was dry. She walked to her parents' bedroom. As she stood outside, mustering the courage to knock on their door, she heard them talking.

"Yaffa, it's obvious that Leah is suspicious. I think it's time that we talk to her openly."

"Do you really think so, Yosef?" Mrs. Weiss asked uncertainly. "I was so hoping that we would be able to spare her any concern."

Unable to hold herself back any longer, Leah knocked on her parents' door. "Ma? Ta? Can I come in?"

In a tone of surprise, Dr. Weiss replied, "Yes, you may."

Before her parents could say a thing, Leah burst out, "Mommy, Tatty, I came up here because I wanted to ask you what's going on. Please don't say it's nothing because I know that's not the truth. I've been worried for so long already, and I can't bear it anymore!"

For a second, her parents were silent. They were taken aback by Leah's heartfelt request.

Her mother was the first to talk. "Oh, Leah, I'm so sorry!" she apologized, her eyes getting watery with tears. "I didn't realize that you picked up on anything, and I can't believe that you were carrying around these worries all this time. Come, have a seat on my bed, and Tatty and I will explain everything."

When Leah was sitting, her mother continued, "Actually, the news we're about to tell you is probably very different than what you expected to hear." And with this, a huge smile broke out across her mother's tired face. "*Baruch Hashem*, I'm expecting a baby."

It took a minute for Leah to register her mother's shocking announcement. As soon as she did, dozens of questions popped into her head. The first one, which she asked in an incredulous tone, was, "Are you serious?"

"I sure am," Mrs. Weiss reassured her daughter.

"Oh, my goodness! That's so exciting! I can't believe it. But I don't understand. I mean, I guess that's why you've been so exhausted, but why were you sick? And why did you need special medicine and blood tests?"

"To tell you the truth," her mother answered, taking Leah's hand in her own, "these first few months of my pregnancy were not smooth sailing, and there were times when Tatty and I were not sure how things would turn out. Some complications came up along the way, but *baruch Hashem* both the baby and I pulled through okay. Then today, I felt really sick, and my doctor advised me to go to the emergency room. The doctors checked me, and *baruch Hashem* everything is under control, although they advised me to stay off my feet for a few days just as an extra precaution."

"Really? Is that the honest truth?"

"It is," her father confirmed with a smile. "So there's really no need for you to worry anymore."

"If that's the case, I am so relieved – and so excited. I can't wait to have another brother or sister! Do you think I can tell Nechama the news, too?"

Her father replied, "We'd have to be pretty heartless to ask you to keep this from Nechama, wouldn't we?" In amusement, he continued, "To answer your question, yes. You can share the news with Nechama, but obviously, please don't tell anyone else for the time being."

Leah didn't wait another second before heading downstairs to Nechama. Nechama, finished with setting the table, was now on the couch, having a difficult time tackling her homework because she was so nervous about Leah's confrontation. As soon as she heard Leah come into the room, she turned toward her friend anxiously. "What happened?" she asked. "Did your parents tell you anything?"

To Nechama's surprise, Leah grinned from ear to ear. "They sure did! And wait till you hear what it was. Just listen to this – my parents told me that my mother is expecting a baby. Now what do you think of that?"

Nechama was ecstatic. Spontaneously, she jumped up to give Leah a tight hug. "Leah, that's wonderful! And here we were, suspecting the worst. *Baruch Hashem*! I'm so happy for you."

"I know! A part of me still can't believe this is true. I've never let myself hope that my mother would have another baby because she always says that she was just so lucky to have Levi and me. But now it looks like Hashem is making another miracle for us, and do you know what?" Leah's voice dropped as she confided in Nechama. "Maybe I'll even get the sister I've always wished for!"

The next day at school, Leah's mind kept drifting. Images of adorable babies kept popping into her head, and she couldn't stop thinking about the fun she would have looking after her new sister or brother. She'd take the baby out for walks, hold her, cuddle her, sing to her, dress her ….

Leah's reverie was interrupted by a note that was surreptitiously placed on her desk. "Earth to Leah!" it read in Nechama's bold, script writing. "If you don't stop daydreaming soon, EVERYONE will be wondering what is going on with you."

Leah realized that Nechama was right, of course. She turned toward her friend, caught her eye and smiled. "Thanks for the tip," she mouthed.

At lunchtime, Leah and Nechama sat together and laughed about Leah's distracted behavior.

"You look like you're in another world this morning!" Nechama remarked humorously.

"Not after the note you sent me!" Leah protested. "I've been trying so hard since then to pay attention."

Nechama giggled. "Maybe so, but you still need improvement if you don't want everyone to get suspicious."

Just then Hindy sat down in the seat across from them and asked, "What are you two laughing about?"

"Nothing, really," Nechama answered quickly. "Just something silly that happened this morning."

Hindy shrugged. "Well, whatever. Listen, I actually wanted to talk to both of you about the Purim fundraiser that we're supposed to be working on. I thought it would be a good idea for us to get together sometime soon and start making plans."

"That's fine with me," said Leah.

"Me, too," Nechama added.

"Good. Look, here comes Miriam. Miriam, come sit down here, okay?"

"Sure," Miriam agreed good-naturedly. Slipping into the chair next to Hindy, Miriam asked, "What's going on?"

"We're discussing the Purim fundraiser that the four of us are in charge of. We were just saying that we should meet one of these days and start planning a program."

"Sounds good to me. So when will we be meeting?"

"Actually, you came just as we were getting to that. Do you have any preferences?" Hindy asked.

"Not at all. I'm really flexible. What about you people?"

"Any day is okay besides for Thursday. We usually go to the Israeli dance class then," Leah answered for herself and Nechama.

"Thursday's not good for me, either, because I have to help my mother with Shabbos. So let's just meet on Wednesday."

"That was pretty simple," Miriam remarked. "Now we have to figure out a place. I'd be happy to host, if no one has any objections."

"Not at all," Hindy said, speaking for all of them. "Your house will probably be the quietest, with no kids around to make noise. I mean, it would be impossible to find a calm spot in my house in the evening."

"I guess that's one of the perks of being an only child," Miriam said ruefully, "even though I usually wish there was more going on at my house. Leah, you found a really good solution. Listen, Nechama, if there's anyone else our age from your community who wants to board here, please let me know, okay?" Miriam was only half-joking.

Nechama smiled understandingly. "Sorry, but there's no one

else our age left in my community. Remember? That's why I came here."

"Yeah, that's right. Oh, well, I guess I'll survive and just be happy that I can provide a quiet place for class gatherings."

"Okay, let's start," Hindy declared as the girls sat around Miriam's living room. She had a pen in her hand and a notepad in her lap, and she looked ready to get down to business.

"So where do we begin?" Leah asked.

"Well, first we need to figure out an exact date for the event. Miriam, do you have a calendar that we can use?"

"Yeah, wait a second while I go get one from the kitchen."

When Miriam returned with the calendar, she handed it to Hindy. Flipping to the page of Adar, Hindy announced, "Purim actually falls out on a Sunday. Do we want to make the gathering *motzei Shabbos*, or do you think Sunday night would be better?"

After some discussion, the girls decided to hold the extravaganza on *motzei Shabbos*.

"So that takes care of that," said Hindy. "Now, for the bigger question – what should our program be? Any ideas?"

"How about a cute comedy skit?" Nechama suggested.

Her proposal was met with three unimpressed stares. "What did I say wrong?" Nechama questioned, not understanding her friends' lack of enthusiasm.

"Nechama," said Hindy, "before we go any further, let me explain to you that the Purim fundraiser is usually something really, really grand. As far back as I can remember, the eighth graders have always arranged some special entertainer to come perform."

"Last year, for instance, there was a Jewish women's dancing group that put on a show and then taught us a couple of dances," Leah told Nechama.

"And the year before that there was a man who did all kinds of mind-reading and magic tricks. At the end, he even showed us how a few of his tricks worked," Miriam added. "It was really interesting."

"Okay, I think I'm starting to get the picture," Nechama smiled. "Now I can understand why a homemade play just wouldn't be a hit. So, does anyone else have an idea?"

"Don't look at me," Miriam said. "I'm never the one with great ideas. How about you, Leah? You're creative. Can you think of anything?"

"Not really," Leah admitted apologetically. "I mean, it seems like all the classes before us have used up all the ideas for entertainers. From the caricaturist they had a couple of years ago to the hypnotist, it seems like there's nothing original left for us."

"I know what you're saying," Hindy replied. "I've been trying to rack my brains for a few days already, and I haven't been able to come up with anything. I was hoping that if we met and put our heads together, we'd be able to think of something."

The foursome spent the next few minutes throwing suggestions back and forth, but it seemed that each proposal was more ridiculous than the next.

"Listen," Hindy finally said in a matter-of-fact voice, "it doesn't look like we're getting anywhere right now. I think we should just call it a night. Why doesn't everyone go home, give it some thought and maybe ask their family for ideas? We can meet again next week and hope for more success then."

There was hardly any talking amongst the girls as they practically ran to the JCE. In an effort to keep as warm as possible, they had covered as much as they could of themselves, including their mouths. Only when necessary did any of the girls make a muffled announcement, which had to be repeated numerous times because all of their ears were blocked by scarves and hats.

Arriving at the old age home, the girls stomped the snow off their boots and removed the layers in which they were swathed.

"Talk about bundling up!" Leah exclaimed with a laugh.

"Even with everything, I still felt cold, though!" Raizy declared.

"It is really bitter out," Elana agreed softly. Her cheeks were flushed from the cold, and there was a lively sparkle in her eyes.

Looking at Elana then, Leah was struck by how pretty her classmate was. *It's funny how I never noticed that before,* Leah mused to herself. *Elana's usually so quiet that I guess I don't really pay too much attention to her.*

Leah's reflections were cut short as her friends headed over to a woman who was wheeling toward them.

"Aren't you girls the ones who were here last week?" the woman inquired.

"We sure are!" Raizy replied brightly.

"It's so nice of you to come back!" the woman said. "People always say they will, but then we don't see them again. You girls are different, though."

"Well, we had such a nice time here last week that we wanted to come see everyone again today!" Nechama replied sincerely.

The girls were not disappointed. They were met by the same joyous reactions as the week before, and they were glad that they had made the trip out again. As they socialized with the elderly residents, they looked forward to their visit with Mrs. Jacobovitz, who was at the end of their round.

Mrs. Jacobovitz's face lit up when she saw them. "Hello, girls!" she called out. "What a wonderful surprise! How are you doing?"

"*Baruch Hashem*," they answered unanimously.

"*Baruch Hashem*, what?" Mrs. Jacobovitz teased them. "You have to be more exact! Tell me about something exciting that is happening. There must be interesting things going on at school, no?"

Leah tried thinking of something to share. The first thing that came to her mind was the Purim fundraiser. Though she and Nechama had been giving lots of thought to the program's content, they were still at a loss for any good ideas.

"One thing that's happening is that Nechama and I are on a committee to decide what to do for a class fundraiser on Purim, and we haven't been able to come up with any entertainment," Leah said.

"What do you mean?" Mrs. Jacobovitz protested. "What better entertainment can there be than the four of you making a concert for everyone?"

The girls laughed.

Mrs. Jacobovitz shook her head. "It seems you think I'm joking, but I'm not. I'm very serious. You have beautiful voices, and everyone will love to hear you."

Not knowing how to respond exactly to Mrs. Jacobovitz's flattering but unrealistic proposal, Nechama said diplomatically, "Girls in our school know us, so it wouldn't be very special for them to hear us singing. They would think it was too plain and ordinary."

Mrs. Jacobovitz nodded thoughtfully. "I see what you're saying. Well, then, I have another plan for you. Why don't you speak to my niece Yocheved? Remember I told you about her? She's the one who sings beautifully. I'm sure she will be happy to help you out and sing for you, especially if she knows you are my friends."

The girls swallowed their smiles. Again, they did not want to offend their friend and blatantly reject her outlandish suggestion.

Diplomatically, Nechama responded, "You know, let's see what comes up. Maybe over the weekend one of the other two girls in our group already came up with another plan."

"Well, if they didn't, don't forget what I told you. And if you're shy, I would be happy to speak to Yocheved for you.

She's coming soon, you know, in honor of my birthday."

Pouncing on this opportunity to change the subject, Raizy asked, "Do you already know how you will be celebrating?"

Thankfully, Raizy's question began a whole new discussion revolving around birthday plans.

As the girls headed out later, Nechama remarked, "Let's make some birthday cards for Mrs. Jacobovitz and give them to her next Sunday when we come."

Leah smiled in amusement. "So does that mean that you're planning on coming back here next week again?"

"I guess so," Nechama replied. "I mean, it feels like the right thing to do. The people here get so excited when we come, and it seems like they're really waiting for our next visit. What do you all think?"

"I think you're right," Raizy answered, and Elana and Leah nodded.

"Okay, then," were Nechama's last words before the foursome braced the bitter outdoors. "Next Sunday it is!"

Rachelli's voice sounded strange when she answered Nechama's phone call.

"Rachelli, what's going on?" Nechama asked right away.

"It's that vandal again. This time he got inside the school building and destroyed several shelves of *sefarim* in the library."

"Oh, no!" Nechama gasped. "Did Ima and Abba speak to the police?"

"They're actually in Abba's study meeting with a policeman right now."

"Wow! This sounds so serious."

"It really is," Rachelli confirmed. "Abba is so nervous that parents will find out and pull their kids out of school, so he's keeping everything top-secret. The only reason I know what I do is because Ima and Abba needed me to distract Yossi and Sarala when the policeman walked in so they wouldn't see him and get wind of what's going on."

Nechama was quiet for a minute as she registered the information that Rachelli had just told her. "Rachelli," she said finally, in a voice that was soft and unsure, "I'm scared."

"We all are," Rachelli admitted. "But Ima and Abba keep on saying that the best thing we can do is say Tehillim and give *tzedaka*. Listen, Nechama, I hate to hang up on you, but I should really go now to check up on the kids and make sure they're still playing together in the playroom."

"Okay, then I guess I'll speak to you later," Nechama said reluctantly, instructing her sister, "Please keep me updated."

"I will," Rachelli promised and then said good-bye.

Nechama returned the phone she had been holding to its cradle, realizing that her hands were trembling slightly. At that moment, she wanted nothing more than to be home with her family. There she was, though, miles away in Lakeview City, filled with fear for their safety. Remembering her parents' words, she put a dollar bill in the *tzedaka* box and whispered several chapters of Tehillim that she knew by heart, davening to Hashem for everything to be cleared up immediately.

"Take a look at that," Leah declared in awe as she stared out of her window.

"The snow is coming down hard," Nechama commented as she joined her friend and peered outside. "I wonder if Hindy and Miriam will be able to come out in this weather."

Nechama was referring to the meeting that their committee had scheduled for that evening at Leah's house. As if on cue, the phone rang, and Mrs. Weiss called up to Leah that the call was for her.

Leah reluctantly left her place and picked up the phone in her bedroom. "Hello?" she said. She was quiet for a minute, and then stated, "Okay, I guess we'll just have to postpone for another day. Let's talk at lunch tomorrow and decide together in person."

After she hung up, Leah turned to Nechama and filled her in. "That was Hindy. Her parents don't think it's safe to drive in this weather, so she's calling Miriam to cancel the meeting for tonight. Wow! Look at the way the snow is piling up. I wonder if we're going to have school tomorrow."

"I wouldn't mind if we didn't," Nechama admitted. "I could use the extra day off to catch up on schoolwork. I'm so behind on my science project, and I haven't even started studying yet for the Halacha test that's coming up."

"I'm sure everyone would appreciate a snow day," Leah said.

"In any case, I hope the weather clears up by Friday."

"Me, too!" declared Leah, smiling at the thought of

their upcoming Shabbos plans. The girls had finally made arrangements for Leah to join Nechama on her trip home, and the two of them were very, very excited.

"Well, if it would just snow inches upon inches tomorrow and then clear up by the end of the week, that would be perfect," Nechama asserted with finality.

Nechama got her snow day. She and Leah were just waking up when Mrs. Weiss peeked her head into their room and told them the good news. With delighted squeals, the two girls snuggled back under their covers to sleep in for another hour, and then, feeling very rested, they got out of bed and leisurely began their morning.

After the girls spent a chunk of time tackling schoolwork, Leah turned to Nechama and remarked, "I'm getting very restless. Are you in the mood to take a break?"

"That sounds like a good idea. What do you have in mind?"

"Well, are you in the mood to make a snowman?" Leah asked.

"A snowman?" Nechama seemed surprised by the suggestion.

"Of course! Why not get some fresh air and put our artistic talents to use at the same time?" Leah urged.

Nechama didn't have the heart to resist. The two of them bundled up in heavy leggings, long skirts, sweatshirts, coats, scarves and gloves. Feeling ready to brace the frost, they headed outdoors. It didn't take long for Nechama to get caught up in the project of sculpting a man out of snow. In fact, the two girls had so much fun that they decided to create a woman, as well. Levi saw them from his window, and he ran out to join them, too.

More than an hour later, when the trio marched back into the house with flushed cheeks and huge grins, Mrs. Weiss was waiting for them in the kitchen.

"Mmm, smells yummy in here!" Levi exclaimed.

"Watching you outside, I thought that you might like something warm to drink when you came in. So as soon as you're ready, you can come get your mugs of hot cocoa. There's also a batch of oatmeal cookies that will be coming out of the oven any minute now."

Dining on the small feast that her mother had prepared, Leah felt happy and relaxed. "I must say," she declared, "snow days are a wonderful thing!"

The next day at school, Miriam was absent.

"It looks like we'll just have to get together next week," Hindy told Nechama and Leah in resignation, "but we seriously have to get down to business. Maybe we can meet on Sunday. Nechama and Leah, what's your schedule? When will you be getting back to town?"

"We should arrive in the early afternoon," Nechama replied, "but we've already made plans to visit the old age home then. Do you want to meet later on in the evening?"

"I guess so," Hindy agreed. "The sooner we take care of this, the better. I'll just make sure it's okay with Miriam, and then

chapter Ten

we'll finalize on a time and place."

"I'm so glad this is finally happening," Nechama told Leah as they sat on the train heading to Nechama's house for Shabbos. "So is my family, for that matter. My mother asked me if there were any particular foods that she could prepare for you, and Sarala spent hours yesterday making a special welcome sign."

Leah smiled. "That's sweet. I can't wait to meet the rest of your family. I've heard so much about them that it almost seems as if I know them already."

"Well, I'm sure you'll recognize everyone as soon as you see them. After all, you see pictures of them all the time."

Nechama's words were proven true. As soon as Leah walked into the Greenbergs' house, she knew exactly who everyone was.

"You must be Sarala," she told the curly-haired girl whose large eyes lit up when she saw her.

"And you must be Leah," Sarala answered in all seriousness.

"I sure am," Leah grinned. Turning to the slim boy who was looking up from a book he'd been reading on the couch, she said, "I guess you're Yossi."

Yossi nodded shyly and said hi with a small smile.

Mrs. Greenberg walked in from the kitchen then, an oven mitt on one of her hands. "I thought I heard you!" she said. "Welcome! Hi, Nechama. Hi, Leah," she greeted the girls, giving each of them a peck on the cheek. "Leah, I'm so glad you've finally made it over, and I hope you make yourself right at home here. As soon as you've put your stuff down upstairs, please come to the kitchen and have something to eat."

Nechama showed Leah the way to the room she shared with Rachelli. Rachelli was there, and she smiled warmly at them and said, "Hi, guys! I'm just getting some stuff together so I can clear out and let you have your privacy over Shabbos."

Leah started to protest that it wasn't necessary, but Rachelli stopped her. "Don't worry, it's not a big deal at all. Besides, Sarala's so excited that I'll be sleeping with her in her room. She's convinced that the two of us are going to have a slumber party tonight."

The girls laughed, and then Rachelli excused herself. "I better run into the shower," she said. "And you better go down and quickly grab a bite to eat. Shabbos is in less than an hour. I can't wait to talk to both of you after candle-lighting, though."

As Rachelli rushed out, Nechama excused herself for a minute and cornered her sister in the hallway.

"Rachelli, any news about the vandal?" she asked in a low voice.

"No, none at all," Rachelli answered, shaking her head regretfully. "But Abba's already ordered new *sefarim* to replace the ones that were ruined, and now that the rest of the week has gone by uneventfully, it seems like he and Ima are really trying to put the bad experience behind them."

Nechama nodded and thanked her sister for the update. "Don't forget to tell me if anything else comes up," she reminded Rachelli, and then she returned to Leah who was waiting for her in the bedroom.

When the sun had set and Shabbos descended, a feeling of serenity enveloped the Greenberg home. Mrs. Greenberg and her daughters had all just settled down in their usual places in the living room when there was a knock at the door.

"Oh, that must be Natalie," said Rachelli.

"Let me get it!" Sarala cried as she jumped to her feet.

Sarala let Natalie in with Mrs. Greenberg's help, and Natalie cheerfully wished everyone a good Shabbos.

"Good Shabbos, Natalie," Rachelli said. "Come sit down. I saved you a spot on the couch."

"Thanks," Natalie replied.

"Natalie, this is my friend Leah," Nechama said.

"Hi, Leah, it's nice to meet you in person. I've heard so much about you."

"Same here," Leah smiled.

"Do you have any other guests coming tonight?" Natalie asked the Greenbergs.

"Not really," Mrs. Greenberg answered. "It's just you, Leah and Avraham."

"Avraham? Who's that?" Leah wanted to know.

"I can't believe I never told you about him," said Nechama. "Avraham is an old family friend. My parents got to know him when Rachelli was a baby. His mother had just passed away, and although he wasn't *frum*, he started coming to shul every day to say kaddish. My father noticed him and began inviting him for Shabbos. Over the year, as Avraham continued davening in shul each day and joining my parents for Shabbos meals, he grew more and more interested in Yiddishkeit. Now he's like our zaidy, and you would never be able to guess that he didn't always keep Torah and mitzvos."

"He's a real inspiration to me," Natalie added. "Whenever I get discouraged in my efforts to become more religious, I can always count on him for words of wisdom and support. He understands exactly where I'm coming from, and he knows just what to say to calm me down and keep me moving in the right direction."

"Avraham is really a very special man," Mrs. Greenberg agreed. "I only wish we could find him a deserving wife."

Nechama was taken aback by her mother's comment. "A wife for Avraham?" she echoed in puzzlement. "But isn't he too old to get married?"

"Not at all," smiled her mother. "Despite his age, Avraham is quite young at heart, and I'm sure he would be delighted to have the company of a wife. Right now, though, I think it's time to stop talking and start davening."

Sarala got herself a siddur just like everyone else, and as she opened it up, she declared, "Tonight I'm going to daven extra hard."

"Why's that, Sarala?" Mrs. Greenberg questioned.

"Because tonight I'm going to daven that Avraham should find a very nice lady that he can marry," was Sarala's sincere reply.

Leah thoroughly enjoyed her Shabbos meal with the Greenbergs and their "extended family." Sitting with them all, she felt a real sense of belonging, and although the meal stretched for quite a few hours, she was still disappointed when it was time to *bentch*.

After the meal, everyone pitched in to clean up. Natalie helped clear the table, and then she got her coat to leave. She expressed her thanks to the Greenbergs for a wonderful meal, as usual, and told Leah, "It was so much fun talking to you. I hope you come again." She laughed and remarked jokingly, "Just listen to me. I guess I feel so comfortable with the Greenbergs that I'm already inviting people to their house."

Mrs. Greenberg good-naturedly interjected, "Natalie, you know you're like family here. And, Leah, so are you. We would love to have you back. Next time, Nechama, you can bring more friends along, too. We're eager to meet the girls you talk about all the time."

"Really?" Nechama asked. "It wouldn't be too much for you?"

"Of course not!" her mother replied.

At this, Nechama and Leah exchanged an excited look. Already, plans for a fun sleepover bash in Woodhaven were forming in their heads.

That night, as they lay in the darkness of Nechama's room, they discussed ideas about their upcoming sleepover.

"Who else should I invite?" Nechama wondered out loud. "What do you think of asking Raizy to come?"

"That's a good idea," Leah approved. "Both of us are close friends with her, and we've been spending a lot of time with her now that we go to the old age home together."

"Do you think I should also invite Elana?"

"Elana?" Leah repeated uncertainly. "I guess you could. What made you think of her?"

"I don't know. I mean, we have been spending a lot of time with her on the way to the old age home. And besides," Nechama continued thoughtfully, "I bet Elana doesn't get asked often to be part of a sleepover party."

"You're probably right," Leah conceded. "I'm sure she'd actually be quite flattered by the invitation."

chapter Eleven

"Then that will be the group," Nechama decided, "and I think that the perfect time to have you all over would be during our mid-winter break. I know it's not for a while, but if you'd all come then, we'd have a few weekdays to hang out together here besides for Shabbos. We could go shopping one day at the mall, and maybe my mother could take us to the science center nearby, too. It would be a lot of fun."

"Nechama, this is sounding better and better by the minute!" Leah exclaimed.

The two friends giggled and continued to whisper together until they finally fell asleep hours later.

"Can you believe this weather?" asked Leah incredulously.

"I know!" Raizy replied. "It feels like spring instead of winter."

"Yeah, who would guess that just a few days ago there was a snowstorm going on here?" Nechama added.

"Well, I, for one, am not complaining," said Leah. "The past few weeks, the walk to the JCE has been brutal. Today, I am really enjoying myself."

"I'm actually looking forward to seeing all the old people again," Raizy remarked. "Some of them are really cute."

"They're beginning to feel like friends," Elana spoke up thoughtfully.

"Especially Mrs. Jacobovitz," Nechama said with a smile. "Visiting her is always so much fun."

"Yeah, and she'll probably be so happy with the cards we made her," Leah declared.

"Look at that!" exclaimed Raizy. "We're already here. The walk seems so much shorter when the weather's pleasant."

The girls began their rounds. In the recreation room, a group of ladies was gathered around socializing, so on the spur of the moment, Raizy, Nechama, Leah and Elana performed a mini-concert of Chanukah songs. Their audience was thrilled, and the elderly women applauded enthusiastically.

"You must come back again and sing more!" entreated one of the residents.

"Don't worry, we will!" the girls assured her, and then they waved good-bye as they moved along.

Nearing Mrs. Jacobovitz's room, the girls heard the sound of youthful laughter floating toward them.

"Mrs. Jacobovitz must have company," observed Leah.

"Then let's just pop in to say hi and give her the birthday cards," suggested Nechama.

The girls stood at Mrs. Jacobovitz's doorway and knocked softly. Mrs. Jacobovitz, who was chatting animatedly with a middle-aged woman wearing an auburn *sheitel* in a sophisticated up-do, looked up and smiled broadly. "Come in, come in!" she urged.

Entering the room, Leah gasped. Before Leah had a chance to explain the shocked expression on her face, Mrs. Jacobovitz said, "Girls, let me introduce you to my niece Yocheved. Yocheved, these are the wonderful girls I've been telling you about."

"Hi, girls, nice to meet you," said Yocheved with a warm smile. "Thanks so much for coming by to visit my great-aunt. It really means a lot to her."

"It's our pleasure," said Raizy, and Nechama and Elana echoed her words. Only Leah was strangely silent.

Leah's friends looked at her curiously. Nechama shot her a piercing stare that clearly demanded, "What is going on?"

Finally, Leah found her voice. Speaking to Yocheved, she stammered, "But, but aren't you Chevi Chein?"

Yocheved's eyes twinkled in amusement, and her smile stretched from ear to ear. "Yes, that's how I'm known professionally. But to my friends and family, I'm just plain old Yocheved."

"Never plain and old!" her great-aunt protested. Turning toward the girls, she said, "Yocheved has a heart of gold, and like I already told you many times, she has a voice that is magnificent. In fact, Yocheved, I even told the girls that you might be able to sing for them in their school. Do you think you could, Yocheved?"

Yocheved hardly seemed fazed by her great-aunt's brazen offer. Lightly, she replied, "I'd be honored to sing for your friends, Tanta Bella, as long as it works out with my schedule."

Raizy, the most daring of the group, asked, "Really? Do you mean that? Because my friends are trying to organize entertainment for a school-wide event for the night of Purim, and it would be so amazing if you could actually sing there!"

"I'm quite sure I'm available then, but why don't I give you my number? You can call me tomorrow evening when I'll be back at home with my calendar so I can double-check to be certain whether I'll be able to come."

When Yocheved handed the girls a notepad paper with her phone number, they thanked her again profusely, but she graciously dismissed their words of gratitude. "Oh, don't mention it," she told them. "When I was two, my mother and Tanta Bella emigrated together from Russia to America, and since then, we have been the only family for each other in this country. Naturally, we are exceptionally close. Tanta Bella is like a second mother to me, so I am happy to help out the girls who have been so kind to her."

Tanta Bella, who'd been following the conversation between Yocheved and the girls, beamed, obviously proud of the hand she had played in the Purim extravaganza's entertainment

CHAPTER Twelve

arrangements. "You see, I told you I had a solution for you!" was the last thing she told the girls before they left that day.

"Who would have ever imagined that Chevi Chein would be Mrs. Jacobovitz's niece?" exclaimed Raizy as the girls walked home.

"And who would have ever imagined that Chevi Chein would be singing at our very own Purim *chagiga?*" Nechama marveled.

"Wait till we tell Hindy and Miriam tonight!" Leah declared. "They are going to be thrilled!"

There was a palpable sense of anticipation running through the whole school that afternoon before the first night of Chanukah. Girls excitedly talked about the Chanukah parties that they had lined up for the week ahead and the plans they'd made for the few days they had off.

Wisely, the teachers had prepared fun lessons for that day because experience had proven that their students had difficulty concentrating at times like this. And who could blame them? They could already smell the crispy latkes, taste the chewy donuts and feel the Chanukah warmth.

When the dismissal bell finally rang, both the teachers and their students breathed huge sighs of relief and made a beeline for the door. Everyone was in a hurry to get home already and begin the Chanukah celebrations.

For Nechama, it felt strange to be spending the first night of Chanukah at a place other than her own home, but she was comforted in knowing that the next morning she would be on her way to spend the rest of Chanukah with her family.

"What are you thinking about, Nechama?" Leah's voice interrupted Nechama's musings.

"What? Oh, nothing. Sorry. Were you saying something?"

"Only about three times," Leah teased, "but never mind. It wasn't that important. I bet you were thinking about being away from home on Chanukah."

Nechama looked at Leah in surprise. "How did you know?"

Leah laughed. "I guess I know you better than you think. I'm sure it's hard for you to be away from your family, but the good thing is, you'll be with them tomorrow. And the other good thing," Leah added, "is that you'll be with us tonight. Chanukah is very special in my home, and I'm happy that you'll at least get a taste of it."

When the girls walked into the house together, the smell of frying latkes welcomed them.

"Oh, yummy!" Leah cried. "My mother makes the best latkes. She makes them out of regular and sweet potatoes together."

"Hi, girls!" Mrs. Weiss greeted them from the kitchen. "Are you ready for Chanukah?"

"You bet!" Leah answered.

"Well, as soon as you hang up your coats and backpacks, you can come and help me finish up these donuts. Levi started the job, but after a couple of minutes, he gave up and escaped to the computer."

Within moments, Leah and Nechama returned to the kitchen. "Okay, Mommy, we're ready. What do you want us to do?"

"See these custard-filled donuts? They have to be covered with this chocolate glaze. And these jelly donuts over here need to be rolled in confectionary sugar."

The girls had just completed their assignment and were licking their fingers clean when Dr. Weiss walked into the house. "Smells like Chanukah in here!" he declared, his face lighting up like a bright menorah.

"There's a good reason for that," smiled Mrs. Weiss.

Dr. Weiss chuckled. "True. Where's Levi? I better call him to come help me set up the menorahs. It's time we get started and let the festivities begin!"

Dr. Weiss called for Levi in his loud, deep voice, and Levi

came running. "Hi, Tatty, are you ready to light the menorah?"

"I am. Are you?"

"Of course! And I can't wait to taste Mommy's latkes and donuts already!"

"Okay, so when we finish preparing our menorahs, we'll drive to pick up Tanta Bracha, and as soon as we come back home, we'll make the brachos and light. How does that sound to you, Yaffa?" Dr. Weiss asked, consulting his wife.

"Perfect," Mrs. Weiss approved.

A quarter of an hour later, Dr. Weiss was ushering Tanta Bracha into the house and gathering his family together to light the menorahs. Once the single flames were burning bright, Mrs. Weiss summoned everyone to be seated around the dining room table.

"Yaffa, you are too much!" Tanta Bracha said. "Just look at this table you've set! Not a detail is missing, from the centerpieces to the napkin rings. I can't believe you're doing this, and in the condition you're in, too!"

"Oh, please!" Mrs. Weiss blushed, waving away Tanta Bracha's compliments.

"I see I'm making you uncomfortable. I won't say anymore," Tanta Bracha conceded, "but I do want you to know that I am very, very impressed."

Once everyone had eaten supper, and their stomachs were positively bursting, the girls cleared the table so that they could play dreidel. They had a fun game, which Mrs. Weiss finally won.

"Now it's time for a bit of music," Dr. Weiss announced, and

Mrs. Weiss proceeded to perch herself at the piano bench and play a Chanukah tune.

As if on cue, Dr. Weiss, Leah and Levi began to sing along. Dr. Weiss's voice was rich and deep, Levi's was sweet and high, and Leah's, which was somewhere in between, harmonized beautifully.

Nechama listened in amazement. She and Tanta Bracha sat on the couch and acted as a very appreciative audience. They clapped and encored all the way through.

When the first medley of songs was over, Nechama voiced her surprise. "I never knew you all were so musical!"

"Oh, it's a well-kept secret," Tanta Bracha winked at Nechama. "The Weisses keep a low profile of this talent of theirs."

"That's not true," Dr. Weiss disagreed. "We just don't have the time to do this as often as we'd like, but on special occasions, we make a point of it."

"In that case, I am especially honored that you invite me to join you on Chanukah year after year."

"Now it's your turn to entertain," Dr. Weiss urged her, and he explained to Nechama, "Chanukah is a special time for Tanta Bracha because it marks the beginning of her journey toward Torah and mitzvos. You see, Tanta Bracha wasn't always religious, and this change in her life actually was brought about through the lights of Chanukah. But I'm talking too much. Tanta Bracha will tell us the whole story herself."

"Not again," Tanta Bracha protested. "You hear my story every year. Surely, you don't want to hear it again."

"Surely, we do," Dr. Weiss retorted. "Hearing your story is

always a highlight of Chanukah. And besides, Nechama is very curious."

"Oh, okay," Tanta Bracha relented, and everyone settled in their places as she began.

"*Baruch Hashem*, I had a very happy, uneventful childhood. My parents were easygoing, and I was a regular, well-behaved kid known to everyone then as Barb. Although we were Jewish, my parents were far more interested in fun and freedom than in any quests for spirituality, so I knew practically nothing about my heritage.

"But then, as I reached my teenage years, I felt something that I couldn't put my finger on, that I couldn't really describe in words. It was a certain emptiness, which I know now was a tug from my neshama pulling me toward the path of truth."

Tanta Bracha went on to describe the sense of dissatisfaction within her that kept gnawing at her. She recounted different approaches she had tried to achieve fulfillment, but how, in the end, she never found real meaning in any of them.

"And then, in my senior year of high school, my parents planned a trip to Paris for their winter break. I had little interest in joining them, so they made arrangements for me to stay with Rebecca Schwartz, a friend of mine.

"The last night that I was at their house, Mr. Schwartz gathered us together to light the menorah.

"'Menorah? What's that?' I asked.

"'Don't you know?' asked Rebecca. 'Tonight is Chanukah, and we light the menorah.'

"Mr. Schwartz took a few moments to share with me the

little history he knew about the holiday. Then he lit the first candle of the menorah. And that's when I burst into tears. The Schwartzes were full of concern. They wanted to know what had happened.

"But, of course, I didn't have anything sensible to say. After all, how could I explain the rush of emotions that filled my heart upon seeing that single candle kindled? How could I explain that watching Mr. Schwartz light the menorah had given me the sense of peace that I'd been missing for so long?

"So I just mumbled some lame sort of excuse about missing my parents, and then, at dinner, I posed question after question to the Schwartzes about the Jewish religion. It soon became very clear to me that they didn't have much information to offer. The next day, when I went home, I tried grilling my parents, but they dismissed my inquiries, telling me not to trouble my mind with such irrelevant religious matters.

"There I was, completely frustrated. Although I'd been momentarily exposed to the light that I'd been searching for, I had no way to pursue it. No one I knew could give me the answers I needed, and the few books I found at the library were dry and very basic. After many futile attempts to learn more about my Jewish heritage, I began to channel my energy into my schoolwork, instead. I threw myself into my studies with even more vigor than before, trying to ignore the fact that the pleasure I got out of learning English and social sciences was a poor substitute for the thrill that I had experienced at the Schwartzes on that Chanukah night."

Tanta Bracha then proceeded to relate how she had

graduated from high school as valedictorian and had continued to achieve in academics as she moved on to college. On the surface, she was leading the ideal life, but underneath it all, despite all of her talents and accomplishments, Tanta Bracha was not satisfied with the way she was living.

During her college years, Tanta Bracha became interested in alternative medicine. For Nechama's benefit, she explained, "That means treating health problems in natural ways, through herbs, vitamins and things like that."

Once she graduated, Tanta Bracha found a job at an exclusive natural spa resort in California. "Life looked good at that point," she admitted. "I was happy with my work. I felt like I was helping people feel good, and I started to believe that perhaps this was it. Perhaps I had actually found the meaning of life. A few years passed like this.

"And then, slowly, that feeling of dissatisfaction began to take hold of me again. The resort I was working at had started off as a small and intimate facility, looking out foremost for the health and good of our clients. As the resort took off and flourished, though, it became like a business. The people in charge seemed more interested in the money they were making than the people they were treating. Watching this change take place, I grew disillusioned, and it occurred to me that, in truth, something had been missing all along. I tried brushing aside my uneasy feelings because facing them would mean making a big change, and I didn't know if I was ready for that.

"Hashem must have seen that I needed an extra push from

above. It was fall, and my boss announced that our company would be hosting a big party for all of its employees in honor of the upcoming non-Jewish holiday. I let her know politely that although it sounded like a nice idea, I personally would not attend because I was a Jew.

"'What do you mean?' my boss asked, clearly displeased. 'The celebration will be a social affair, not a religious one, and we expect all of employees to be there.'

"Although I tried explaining that I still would be uncomfortable participating, my boss refused to hear me out, and she coldly advised me to reconsider.

"In the next couple of months, not a word more was mentioned to me personally about the party. Amongst my colleagues, though, there was a lot of excited talk going on about the big bash, especially as it drew nearer.

"With only a few days left to the celebration, I was summoned to my boss's office. Putting on a smile that didn't quite seem genuine, she stated with forced nonchalance, 'So I presume we will be seeing you on Wednesday evening.'

"'Uh, not really,' I replied without meeting her gaze. Not interested in getting into a whole confrontation, I added meekly, 'Something came up.'

"'Aha, I see,' my boss nodded, making her skepticism and disapproval quite clear. Then, as I turned to make my departure, she added, 'I'm sorry to see that you don't find our company and its events to be such a priority in your life.'

"When the night of the party arrived, I felt miserable. At work, I'd been getting the cold shoulder from my boss as well as from many of my colleagues who, for some reason, seemed to regard my decision not to join the party as a personal insult. Alone in my home, wanting to forget about my unhappy predicament, I decided to go out. Because of the non-Jewish holiday, all of the stores were closed, so I just took a drive around different parts of town.

"In my wanderings, I was surprised to see that, in the distance, there was one store that had all of its lights on. As I got closer, I realized it was a Judaica store, and sure enough, it was open. Spontaneously, I parked my car and walked into the store to explore. Once inside, I was overwhelmed by everything I saw. I didn't know where to go first; there were so many fascinating things that caught my eye.

"The man at the desk must have noticed my uncertainty, and he immediately offered his assistance. It didn't take long for him to find out that I was an assimilated Jew with little knowledge but lots of interest in my religion.

"'You know,' the man, who introduced himself as Yoni, told me, 'tonight is the third night of Chanukah. I actually have to close the store soon so that I can get home to light the menorah for my family, but I would be very happy if you would join me in my house for this ritual and some traditional Chanukah latkes, as well.'

"You can imagine that I was very much taken aback by Yoni's kind invitation. At first, I turned it down, feeling like I didn't want to impose on him or his family, but when Yoni insisted, I gave in."

Tanta Bracha's face glowed as she remembered her evening

with Yoni, his wife Ruthie and their two little children. Again, she'd felt that indescribable rush of emotions as she watched the menorah being lit, but this time, Yoni and Ruthie were able to provide answers for the questions that she asked. As the evening passed, Tanta Bracha knew it was time for her to go. Her gracious hosts had to put their children to bed, and she had stayed for so long already.

Before she left, Yoni and Ruthie urged Tanta Bracha to call them if she ever wanted to talk more. They gave her their number and took down hers, with plans to arrange a date for a Shabbos meal together.

For the rest of the weekend, Tanta Bracha was on a high, but on Monday, when she returned to the spa resort, her bubble was burst. Tanta Bracha was greeted by her boss, who said she had something to discuss with her in her office.

Tanta Bracha sat down nervously, clenching her hands in her lap.

"Barb," her boss told her, "here at the resort, our success is dependent on the devotion of our employees. After observing your attitude and behavior in the past few months, I have discussed the matter with other company leaders and together we have decided that your efforts on behalf of the resort have been less than whole-hearted. We feel that this is no longer the place for you, and we wish you luck in finding a job elsewhere."

Tanta Bracha continued sitting for another moment as the realization that she'd just been fired sank in. The moment the news registered, she jumped up, stammered a flustered good-bye and fled. In a daze, she drove home and entered her apartment just as the phone rang. Without thinking, she picked it up.

"Hello?" Tanta Bracha said in a very low voice.

"Barb, is that you? Why do you sound so strange?"

It was Jan, a friend from college. Jan was very sympathetic as she listened to Tanta Bracha's story.

"You poor thing," Jan said. "Out of a job without any warning. What are you going to do?"

"I don't know. I haven't really had much time to think about it," Tanta Bracha answered. "The truth is that I really don't know where to go from here. I want to find a job that is meaningful, and that could take some time. On the other hand, I need a new source of income right away in order to pay my rent and other bills."

Jan, a generous person by nature, piped up with an offer. "Listen, Barb, why don't you move to New York? You can stay with me in my apartment until you find a job so you don't have to worry about rent until then. Plus, there are plenty of job opportunities around here. I'm sure you'll find something that you'll like."

Tanta Bracha was extremely hesitant about the idea, but Jan urged her to think about it. Over the next couple of months, Jan made a point of calling often and trying to persuade Tanta Bracha to relocate to the east. Tanta Bracha kept resisting, hoping she would find a local job that she would enjoy. However, after extensive research and several interviews, she eventually realized that her options within the area were dismal. Finally, with the approach of spring, Tanta Bracha caved in and told Jan that she'd be packing up and flying out within a couple of weeks.

In the months since Chanukah, Tanta Bracha had spoken to Yoni and Ruthie a few times over the phone, and she'd even enjoyed a wonderful Shabbos dinner with them. In fact, in the back of her mind, they were one of the reasons she would have liked to stay in California. As Tanta Bracha was preparing to move, she meant to call the warm couple and let them know she was leaving, but in all the craziness of her rushed move, she never actually did.

On the flight to New York, Tanta Bracha remembered with a start that she hadn't said good-bye to Yoni and his wife. She felt a stab of guilt at her negligence but comforted herself by thinking, *I'll call them as soon as I get settled. I'll also be sure to ask them if they have any suggestions on how I can continue learning about the topics we'd been discussing.*

When Tanta Bracha unpacked her belongings in Jan's apartment, she wasn't able to find her address book. When weeks went by without any trace of it anywhere, she lost hope of contacting Yoni and Ruthie again.

Meanwhile, Tanta Bracha took a job as a nurse in a dentist's office. Though it wasn't exactly what she was looking for, she figured she would manage with it until she found a job that appealed to her more.

Tanta Bracha's home life was less than perfect, too. Though Jan was ever so sweet and kind, she was also a social butterfly who lived for friends and fun. She spent practically every evening entertaining or going out, and Tanta Bracha was hardly thrilled with the frequent get-togethers that took place in the apartment.

Although she made an effort to befriend Jan's guests, Tanta Bracha couldn't help but feel that she was different from the others. They all seemed to share the same simple goal of enjoying themselves and having a good time, while Tanta Bracha knew in her heart that there was a deeper purpose to life. She'd begun to touch on it with Yoni and Ruthie, but there were so many more questions she wished she could ask them. If only she had their number!

Summer ended, and with fall came the colorful trees and the cooler weather. Soon it was time for sweaters and jackets, and as Tanta Bracha opened one of her boxes of warmer clothes, she was surprised to find her address book lying between two turtlenecks.

"I must have tossed it in without even noticing," Tanta Bracha explained. "As I stood there with my address book in my hands, I immediately turned its pages to find the number for Ruthie and Yoni. I dialed, and my hands practically shook with excitement. I hoped so badly that one of them would be home to answer my call.

"On the second ring, Ruthie picked up, and I apologized for not contacting her before leaving town. I filled her in on all that had happened since we'd last spoken, and when I finished, I asked her for advice.

"'Is there anything you can recommend for me?' I inquired, adding sincerely, 'I want so badly to learn more about the truth and make it a part of my life!'

"Ruthie listed a few possibilities, and then she paused. 'You know,' she said hesitantly, 'I'm not sure if this is something you would consider, but I have a friend who teaches at a seminary in Jerusalem that caters to women with backgrounds like yours. Would you like me to find out more specific information about it?'

"The idea was so outlandish and yet so appealing. I told Ruthie that I would, indeed, like to hear more about the seminary. To make a long story short, I was registered as a student there within several weeks. Not too long after that, I was on a plane to Israel.

"I was in my own world for the whole flight. I couldn't stop thinking about what a big step I was making, and I wondered about the sanity of my rash actions. Riding in the cab from the airport to my new apartment, I tried shaking myself out of my deep introspection. I reminded myself how important it was not to look back.

"Instead, I looked ahead. And when I did, I began to cry tears of relief and joy. There in front of me, through the taxi's dashboard, I was able to see countless menorahs with their burning single candles."

As Tanta Bracha said these words, her eyes glistened with tears. In a voice that was choked with emotion, she softly concluded, "Hashem was letting me know that I was coming home."

Nechama couldn't stop thinking about Tanta Bracha's story. It was one of the most amazing stories she had ever heard.

Though she often slept on the train ride home, that first day of Chanukah was different. Her mind was too busy reviewing different parts of Tanta Bracha's tale, and before she realized it, the train had arrived at her stop.

Rabbi Greenberg was at the station to welcome Nechama. He kissed her head, took her bags and led her to the minivan.

"How was your trip, Nechama?" he asked once he had begun driving.

"It was fine," Nechama answered.

"Restful?" her father asked with a smile.

"Actually, not this time," was Nechama's reply.

"Oh, really? Why not?"

"It's a long story … not my story, someone else's. Tanta Bracha, a family friend of the Weisses, was over last night for a little Chanukah party, and she told the story of how she became *frum*. It was really incredible. I've never heard anything like it, and on the train, I was so caught up thinking about her story that I didn't nap at all."

Nechama's words piqued Rabbi Greenberg's curiosity. "I would love to hear it if you're up to repeating it."

Nechama didn't need another word of encouragement. Her father listened raptly as she recounted Tanta Bracha's tale in full detail. When she was finished, he looked very moved and had to clear his voice before he could talk.

"That is a beautiful story," he softly agreed. "I'm sure the family will really enjoy hearing it, also. You must make sure to tell it to them when we get home."

Nechama nodded. Before long, they pulled up to their

house and walked inside. Nechama was swept up in a sea of embraces as everyone took turns showering her with hugs and affection.

Once things had calmed down a bit and Nechama had helped herself to a snack of peanut butter bars and juice, her mother turned to her and asked, "Are you ready to peel lots of potatoes for latkes?"

"Sure," Nechama replied.

"Okay, then, let's get started. Rachelli, if you don't mind, please combine all the other ingredients in a bowl, and as soon as the potatoes are grated, we'll mix everything together and start frying."

As Nechama got down to work with a peeler in hand, she asked, "Why so many potatoes? Are we having company?"

"Didn't you know?" Sarala questioned, a bit patronizingly. "Natalie and her family are coming tonight for a Chanukah party."

"I actually didn't know," Nechama retorted, a little hurt that she hadn't been informed of this tidbit of news.

"That's because it was a last-minute arrangement," Rachelli hurried to reassure her sister. "We only thought of the idea yesterday, so Ima called last night. We were pleasantly surprised when Mrs. Golovyan accepted the invitation on the spot."

"I guess that's because Chanukah parties are so traditional. They're not too intimidating," Mrs. Greenberg mused thoughtfully. "And with Mrs. Golovyan, I think that's the key. Anything that's too religious seems to throw her off. We really have to be careful to strike just the right balance with her. As much as we want to show her the beauty of Yiddishkeit, we have to be subtle about it so that she doesn't get turned off."

"So what will be doing with the Golovyans tonight?" asked Yossi, who'd been quietly following the conversation.

"That's a good question," answered his mother. For one thing, we'll light the menorah and then have latkes, donuts and some other refreshments that I picked up. We can sing a few songs, and maybe you'd be willing to give a summary of the Chanukah story."

"Okay," Levi consented, an earnest expression on his face. No doubt, he would take his responsibility seriously and prepare in advance exactly what he would say.

"Maybe we can also play a dreidel game," Nechama proposed. "We played one last night at the Weisses and it was a lot of fun."

"That's a good idea," her mother approved. "And then, after that, I think it will be fine if we just sit around and talk."

"Sounds like a nice program to me," Rachelli remarked. "I'm sure it will be a wonderful party."

But the evening that followed proved otherwise.

"Happy Chanukah!" the Greenbergs greeted the Golovyan family when they arrived.

"Happy Chanukah!" the Golovyans wished in return.

Once the Golovyans settled in, Rabbi Greenberg lit the menorah, and then Sarala performed a few of the Chanukah songs that she had learned in school. When she was finished, the Golovyans clapped enthusiastically.

"And now everyone is invited to help themselves to some food before we begin playing a grand dreidel game," Mrs. Greenberg announced.

It wasn't long before everyone was ready to play dreidel. Natalie proudly explained the rules, which she'd only recently learned herself, and then the game started. When Mr. Golovyan finally emerged as the winner, everyone congratulated him good-naturedly, and there was a feeling of merriment and closeness amongst the group.

Observing the others having such a good time, Mrs. Greenberg noted to herself in satisfaction, *It seems like this party is really going well.*

Rabbi Greenberg took that moment to call upon Levi to relate the actual story of Chanukah. Levi, unsurprisingly, did a wonderful job. In his soft, sweet voice, he spoke clearly and sincerely, and his words were well taken.

Rabbi Greenberg took the initiative to elaborate. "The holiday of Chanukah celebrates the eternality of the Jewish nation. Though we are such a minority, and though we've been persecuted time and again, we have survived and are still flourishing."

"It's wondrous, isn't it?" remarked Mr. Golovyan. "The Jewish people's survival seems to defy all laws of nature."

"It's clearly a miracle," Rabbi Greenberg concurred. "There can be no explanation other than G-d's special protection. And yet, the Jewish people themselves play an important part in the continuity of our nation."

"What do you mean?" Mrs. Golovyan wanted to know. Though she was normally aloof to any discussion of religion, the party had warmed her up enough that she was willing to listen to Rabbi Greenberg, albeit a bit warily.

"I mean," Rabbi Greenberg answered evenly, "that the Jewish people's existence is dependent upon the upbringing we give our children. By teaching them the beauty of the Torah, which makes us unique, we ensure that they will continue to follow in its ways and pass it on to their children, as well. We see this in the word of Chanukah itself, for contained within it is the Hebrew word 'chinuch,' which means education."

Natalie had closely followed the conversation between Rabbi Greenberg and her parents. Spurred by Rabbi Greenberg's relevant message and her parents' moment of openness, Natalie spoke to them beseechingly. "Mom, Dad," she said haltingly, "it would really mean a lot to me if I could go to a Jewish school and learn more about our religion. I would like so much to get a real Jewish education."

Natalie's bold request was met by a moment of heavy silence. Her parents, especially her mother, were clearly taken aback, and the color seemed to drain from Mrs. Golovyan's face as she responded with all the control she could muster, "Absolutely not. There is no way that a child of mine will attend a religious school. Once Natalie goes to a religious school, there will be no limit to her observance."

Gently, Mrs. Greenberg asked in a soft voice, "What is wrong if Natalie becomes observant?"

In response to Mrs. Greenberg's question, Mrs. Golovyan's

face crumbled, and tears began to run down her cheeks. Everyone looked alarmed, and Rachelli rushed to bring her a box of tissues.

Dabbing her eyes and trying her best to regain her composure, Mrs. Golovyan began to speak brokenly. "I am sorry for the scene I am causing, but you can tell that this subject of Jewish observance holds a lot of emotion for me. I normally do not discuss this at all, but because of my behavior, I owe you an explanation.

"I was born in Moscow to religious parents. My father passed away months after I was born, the random victim of an anti-Semitic attack on the street. Then, when I was a little girl, my mother fell ill with pneumonia. She was hospitalized, but when the nurses noticed her head covering and style of dress, they neglected her, not wishing to spend the time and effort to care for an Orthodox Jewish patient. Within weeks, she had passed away, leaving me orphaned at the tender age of five.

"My aunt and uncle, who were secular Jews, took me into their home and raised me as their own child. They taught me the importance of assimilation and of blending in with the people around me, telling me numerous times that if not for the foolish religious notions of my parents, I would not have been orphaned. If my father hadn't stood out so conspicuously with his beard, hat and long black coat, and if my mother hadn't worn her kerchief and modest clothing, they would still be alive.

"Even in my youth, I understood well my aunt and uncle's message. Religion meant persecution, and someone who clung to Jewish traditions was making himself or herself a target for suffering. Hearing my aunt and uncle's words, I vowed that religion would never play a part in my life or the life of my children.

"And that is why I am so determined that Natalie does not adopt an observant lifestyle. I never want my daughter to be victimized the way I was because my parents were so naïve."

There was a heavy silence when Mrs. Golovyan finished talking. No one knew what to say. It was clear that Mrs. Golovyan's argument against Yiddishkeit was based on emotion much more than intellect, and emotion was so much more difficult to debate. As an orphan who'd been raised in an anti-Semitic country in an anti-religious home, who could blame her for her prejudices against *frumkeit?*

Mrs. Greenberg realized that now was not the time for preaching or proving points, so, with compassion, she turned to Mrs. Golovyan and said, "It must have been so hard for you, to be left without parents at such a young age. I can't even imagine the pain you must have felt then!"

Mrs. Golovyan nodded but didn't say anything more. It seemed as if she was uncomfortable discussing her tragic experiences any longer and wanted to change the topic.

Feeling that this was the case, Rabbi Greenberg began talking about the snowstorm they were expecting the next day. Conversation followed, but it was awkward and stilted. Although the Greenbergs made a few more attempts to engage the Golovyans in light banter, the atmosphere of fun and good spirits had cooled, and soon after, the Golovyans rose to leave.

"Thank you for having us," Mrs. Golovyan said, a little stiffly.

"Yes, this party was very nice," Mr. Golovyan added.

"You'll have to come again sometime soon," Rabbi Greenberg smiled. "Perhaps for another Shabbos meal."

"Perhaps," answered Mrs. Golovyan noncommittally.

The girls, too, wished one another good night.

"Bye, Rachelli," said Natalie. "Bye, Nechama, it was nice spending time with you."

"See you on Shabbos," Nechama replied.

"I hope so," Natalie responded in a low tone. Glancing cautiously in the direction of her parents who were not in hearing range, she added, "Hopefully, my mother will still let me come after what happened tonight. I guess I just have to daven hard."

When Rabbi Greenberg had closed the door behind the Golovyans, he turned around to his wife with a weary expression.

"That was some party," Mrs. Greenberg said wryly.

"I guess you can say that it didn't go exactly as we'd anticipated," Rabbi Greenberg agreed.

"Well, one thing's for sure. Our little mystery has been solved. Now we know why Mrs. Golovyan is so set against *frumkeit*."

Rabbi Greenberg nodded sadly. "It's such a shame that her impressions are so far from the truth. In her mind, Yiddishkeit means hardship, but in reality, it is so full of joy and meaning. If she would only spend more time in a *frum* environment, she would realize the misconceptions of her belief."

"But how is that ever going to happen," Mrs. Greenberg wondered out loud, "if she is so determined to keep her distance?"

chapter Thirteen

The following week, back home at the Weisses, Leah and Nechama were busy one afternoon getting ready for another visit to the JCE.

Checking the view from the bedroom window, Nechama cried, "Come here, Leah! This looks like a scene from a snow globe."

"You're right," Leah agreed. "It's going to be a hard walk to the old age home."

Mrs. Weiss, who was passing the girls' room right then and overheard their conversation, said, "You girls are still planning on going to the JCE today?"

Leah and Nechama nodded. Mrs. Weiss shook her head in amazement. "Wow, you girls are brave. I do hate to see you walk in this bad weather, though. You know what? I was planning on going out in half an hour to pick up a few things from the grocery store. Let me drive you and your friends to the JCE then."

"Thanks, Mommy!" Leah said gratefully. "I'll call Raizy and Elana and let them know. I'm sure they'll be glad to hear that we have a ride."

Naturally, they were. As they sat in the Weisses' minivan, Mrs. Weiss asked them, "So, girls, what do you do once you get to the old age home?"

"What do you mean?" Leah asked her mother.

"Do you entertain the people in any special way?"

"We talk to them," Raizy explained. "And sometimes we sing songs, especially for Mrs. Jacobovitz, who loves when we sing for her."

"Have you ever considered putting on a show for the ladies there?" Mrs. Weiss proposed.

"A show?" The wheels in Raizy's head were already spinning. Raizy loved the stage, and Mrs. Weiss's suggestion sounded appealing to her. "Now that's a good idea. Like maybe a play, or a dance, or even both. What do you think?" Raizy asked her friends.

"The women at the JCE would probably be thrilled," Nechama commented, warming up to the idea. "And we would have fun preparing, too. We could get together on *motzei Shabbos* and brainstorm some ideas. Maybe we could practice a dance from Thursday's dance class, and then perform it at the JCE on Sunday. Doesn't it sound like fun?"

Nechama and Elana both agreed to the plan. "We are going to have a great time practicing," Nechama predicted enthusiastically.

"It'll give us a taste of what vacation together in Woodhaven is going to be like," Elana added, her eyes sparkling.

Nechama and Leah exchanged a quick, secret look. They were happy with their decision to include Elana in their vacation get-away.

"Oh, don't even get me started on that," Raizy declared dramatically. "Nechama, my family is so sick and tired of hearing me talk about our trip to your house. They threatened to tape my mouth shut if I said another word about it."

From the driver's seat, Mrs. Weiss laughed. "And we thought we were the only ones getting the complete updates on a daily basis!"

The girls all giggled. "Well, it's hard, you know," Leah defended. "We're so excited, but we can't really discuss anything at school because we don't want all the other girls to feel left out, so the only place to talk freely is at home."

"It's perfectly fine," Mrs. Weiss reassured her daughter. "I was just teasing. And here we are. Have a good time."

"Thank you!" the girls unanimously told Mrs. Weiss, and in good spirits, they piled out of the minivan and headed into the old age home.

When Leah and Nechama got home later that afternoon, Mrs. Weiss greeted them and then told Nechama, "Your sister Rachelli called. She asked you to call back as soon as you can."

Nechama's heart sank as she jumped to conclusions for the reason for Rachelli's urgent message. She went upstairs in order to have privacy during her call, and when she got through to her sister, her suspicions were confirmed.

"It looks like the guy is at it again," Rachelli stated dismally. "This time he attacked the office, covering the walls and desks with hate messages. The secretary was the first one to discover the damage, and she called Abba right away. Abba and Ima rushed over, and the three of them got things back into order more or less by the time school started."

"What's Abba going to do about this now?"

"I don't know," Rachelli admitted. "I don't think he himself is sure about that. Meanwhile, he's sworn the secretary to secrecy. He's also filed another quiet report with the police, but I think they're starting to lose patience. They feel like it's time to go ahead with a full-fledged investigation and forget about keeping thinks low-profile, but Abba is trying to hold them off on that for the time being."

"Poor Abba. He must be so nervous."

"I'm sure that inside he is, but you know Abba. On the outside, he looks like his usual calm, controlled self, and no one suspects a thing. Still, I know he must feel scared, and I heard him telling Ima that he's getting a camera put up in the office by tomorrow."

"Maybe that will help us uncover the culprit."

"Hopefully, it will," Rachelli replied. In a motherly tone, she added, "Meanwhile, don't let yourself get carried away with fear because the truth is that all the vandalism that has been done hasn't been seriously dangerous. Abba says it seems like the person behind it is out to scare us, not to hurt us, and Abba's main concern is stopping the attacks before the school loses any students. Right now, let's just daven that with the help of the camera, this mystery will be history very, very soon."

Nechama did her best to take her big sister's words to heart. In the next few days that followed, she spoke to Rachelli every evening to find out if there was any news. As the week went on, Nechama's tension gradually lessened, and thoughts of the vandalism eventually receded to the back of her mind.

On Sunday, it was surprisingly mild as the girls walked to the JCE. They were all dressed in black tops and long black skirts, and they wore matching gold ribbons in their hair, too. Raizy carried a CD player with their dance music inside.

"What did the program director say when you called her?" Raizy asked Leah.

"She was really thankful, actually. She said that the residents are always happy to have entertainment, especially by young people, and she said she'll make sure to have all the women gathered in the recreation room by one o'clock."

Raizy checked her watch. "That means we have exactly seven minutes to get there."

Exactly seven minutes later, the girls were standing before a delighted audience.

"You don't know how excited we are to see you girls perform," one woman loudly confided to them.

"Yes, I've been spreading the word ever since you told me last week," Mrs. Jacobovitz announced importantly. "I made sure to tell everyone that this is one show they won't want to miss!"

"Well, I hope we don't disappoint you!" Raizy answered jokingly, knowing full well that any performance they put on would enrapture their crowd.

The girls took their places, and then Raizy turned on the music. Not surprisingly, more than a minute of enthusiastic applause followed their dance, in addition to requests for an encore.

The girls obliged, feeling happy that their show had been so well received.

"You girls were just wonderful!" gushed a heavy-set lady in a wheelchair.

"I'm already looking forward to seeing the next show you

put on," a frail-looking, gray-haired woman declared.

The elderly women were full of praises, but the girls tried cutting them off by going around and making small talk with the ladies, asking them how they were doing. They made sure to escort Mrs. Jacobovitz back to her room and visit with her privately because she had come to count on her special Sunday afternoon company. That day, in particular, she felt so proud to be flanked by these four budding stars.

On their way out, the girls were stopped by a short woman wearing a pretty hat and a nametag that said "Sharon."

"Hi, I'm Sharon Firestone, and I'm the program coordinator of the JCE," she introduced herself with a friendly smile. "First of all, I want to thank you so much for coming here every week. It means so much to the residents here to see young faces around, and they talk about you all the time. Second of all, I want to express a special thanks for the performance you staged today. The residents enjoyed it so much that I was wondering if I might be able to schedule you for another show."

"Sure," Raizy replied, speaking for the group. "Do you have a specific date in mind?"

"Yes, actually," Sharon admitted. "I took a look at my calendar, and I noticed that Rosh Chodesh Adar falls out on a Sunday. I thought that would be the perfect day for a special program."

"Hmm, Rosh Chodesh Adar," Raizy said, thinking out loud. "That's just a week after our mid-winter vacation. The timing is actually great because we can practice while we're all together at Nechama's house. Do the rest of you agree?"

The others nodded.

"Excellent!" Sharon beamed. "I am really looking forward. In fact, I'm going to go to my office right now and write you in on the calendar."

Leah and Nechama were both reading in their room when the ring of the cordless phone broke the silence. Nechama, who was closer to the phone, reached for it to answer.

"Hello?"

"Nechama, is that you?" came the voice at the other end.

"Natalie! How are you? Long time, no speak," Nechama replied, clearly pleased by her unexpected caller.

"Yeah, well, things have been busy around here. Our teachers have been loading us with work and tests, but right now I couldn't think of studying a minute longer, so I decided to take a break and call you. How are things by you?"

"Good, *baruch Hashem*," Nechama answered, and she proceeded to fill Natalie in on all the latest Lakeview City news.

"You know, I'm actually going to be in Lakeview City this Sunday," Natalie informed Nechama.

"You are?" Nechama asked in surprise. "Why? What do you have to do here in Lakeview City?"

"We're coming to visit my aunt and uncle, and their baby twins. Remember I told you about them the first time we met on the train? I was on my way back from them at the time. Anyhow, we'll be spending the day with them on Sunday, so maybe I'll bump into you or something."

"I doubt it," Nechama said realistically. "Lakeview City is a big place, and your relatives probably live in a different neighborhood. It's such a shame, though, that you'll be right here and we won't even see you. I mean, it would be great if we could get together or if you could come see us at Leah's house, but I guess your parents wouldn't really be too thrilled about that."

"No, probably not," Natalie agreed, adding regretfully, "though I really would love to see you and Leah."

The girls hung up soon after that, and Nechama told Leah the details of her conversation with Natalie.

"It's too bad that she'll be in town and we won't even be able to meet up with her," Nechama said.

"You know, I have an idea," Leah declared, an excited gleam in her eyes. "Why doesn't Natalie come here for Shabbos? She can take the train, and then on Sunday, when her parents drive in, they can pick her up to visit her cousins as planned."

"That's a great idea!" Nechama exclaimed. There was a moment's pause before she continued somewhat skeptically, "Do you think her parents will approve?"

"There's only one way to find out, right? Listen, let me go and make sure it would be okay with my mother, and as soon as we have that cleared, you can call Natalie back right away so she'll have plenty of time to nudge her parents for permission."

By the following evening, it was all arranged. Natalie called to say that Mrs. Golovyan had reluctantly caved in to her daughter's pressure, and she was very much looking forward to spending Shabbos at the Weisses' house.

"The only family I've ever been with for Shabbos has been

yours," she told Nechama, "so it will be so interesting for me to see what Shabbos is like somewhere else."

"Well, Shabbos at the Weisses' house is always beautiful," Nechama said, promising Natalie, "You are going to have a great time here."

Just as Nechama hung up with Natalie, the phone rang again, and Nechama answered.

"Nechama?" asked the shaken voice at the other end.

"Rachelli, what happened?" Nechama questioned in return, knowing even before Rachelli answered.

"The guy struck again."

"Were they able to see anything on the camera?"

"Nothing at all. Apparently, this person is aware that a camera has been put up, and he made sure to do his damage outdoors, away from the camera's view. He sprayed several anti-Semitic messages across the back walls of the building, and no one was allowed to play outside today while the mess was being cleaned."

"So everyone at school knows what happened?" Nechama inquired in dismay.

"Just the teachers," Rachelli replied. "Abba had to tell them, of course, because they were all instructed not to take their classes out for recess. After school, there was an emergency staff meeting, and Abba stressed to everyone there that it's very important not to disclose what happened to anyone else. He also reassured them that he would be doing his best to find the vandal as quickly as possible."

"But how does Abba plan to do that? Even the camera

seems to be of no help."

"For starters, the police have agreed to station one of their men to patrol near the school this week, and in the meantime, I guess they'll just work with whatever leads they already have."

"So all we can do is just wait and see what happens next," Nechama surmised hopelessly.

"And say Tehillim," Rachelli added.

"Right, and say Tehillim," Nechama echoed.

The sisters chatted briefly for a bit longer before bidding each other a subdued good-bye. As Nechama returned the phone to its cradle, it started ringing once more. Suppressing a sigh of annoyance, Nechama lifted the phone to answer.

"Hello?"

"Nechama, what's up?" was the exuberant response to Nechama's greeting.

Although Nechama hadn't heard the caller's voice in months, she recognized it immediately. "Rivky! How are you?"

"*Baruch Hashem.* I couldn't believe it when I called your house and Rachelli told me that you're boarding in Lakeview City. Do you like it there?"

"Yes, I really do. How about you? Are you enjoying California?"

"I sure am! It's great here. I have tons of friends, and there's so much going on. But there's no point in catching up now on the phone, when we'll be seeing each other in a week."

"Are you trying to tell me that you're visiting Woodhaven soon?"

"You got it! My parents have to fly in to take care of some

business with the house, so we are all coming in Wednesday night. I didn't realize that you're not living at home, but, of course, you'll take off a couple of days from school so that we can hang out together on Thursday and Friday."

Rivky hasn't changed a bit, Nechama thought to herself as her friend spoke. It was just like Rivky to assume that Nechama would miss school in order to keep her company. "Rivky, I can't skip two days of school just like that," she started to protest, but Rivky cut her off.

"Don't be ridiculous!" Rivky declared. "There's no way that you're going to let two silly days of school stop you from spending time with a childhood friend who lives across the country. Listen, just ask your parents for permission to come home early for Shabbos. I'm sure they'll agree."

Nechama didn't bother arguing. Not only did she know she would never win with Rivky, but truthfully, right then, the prospect of extra time with her family was very appealing. With all that was going on, she really did want to be at home near her parents and siblings.

"Okay, so I'll call you next week when I get to town," Rivky said. "I can't wait to see you, you know. I mean, all my new friends are great, but there's nothing like a friend who's been with you since you were in diapers. Anyhow, have a good night, and I'll talk to you soon."

Later that evening, when Nechama called her parents and brought up the idea of going home early the following week, they were surprisingly agreeable to the plan. Nechama was sure that they sensed with parental intuition how much she needed to be close to them now.

Once it was finalized that Nechama would, indeed, leave for Woodhaven after school on Wednesday, she found herself very much looking forward to this unexpected opportunity to be with her family. Just the prospect of returning to the security of her own home for a stretch of several days was enough to keep her in a positive frame of mind, despite the frightening issue of the vandal and his spiteful attacks.

Friday afternoon was a little crazy. Natalie arrived at the Weisses' house only minutes before Shabbos. When she rang their bell, everyone breathed a huge sigh of relief. The whole family had been so nervous that she might not make it.

"Come in, come in," Dr. Weiss ushered in their guest. "You have just enough time to eat something before candle-lighting. Just follow me to the kitchen, where my wife will take care of you."

Leah and Nechama flew down the stairs moments later, freshly showered and dressed in their Shabbos robes. "Hi, Natalie," they greeted their friend.

As soon as she'd finished eating, the girls showed Natalie their room, where a cot had been set up for her. Natalie quickly changed her clothes. Then the three of them returned downstairs for candle-lighting and the welcoming of Shabbos.

The Shabbos meal that night lasted for a long time. Tanta Bracha was eating over, and, as usual, she had lots of interesting stories to tell and words to say. Tanta Bracha was a good listener, too, and she insisted on hearing the full account of

Natalie's journey toward Yiddishkeit, even though the others were already familiar with it.

"I'm amazed," Tanta Bracha proclaimed in sincere awe. "You are exceptionally mature for a girl your age, Natalie. I, too, became religious but that was at a much later stage in my life, after years of experience led me to realize that the ultimate truth could be found in Torah and nowhere else. It's incredible that you picked up on this so early on, and what's more, that you had the strength of character to act on this discovery and make huge changes in your life."

Natalie brushed away Tanta Bracha's glowing praise, answering simply, "I guess I'm just lucky that I met Nechama and her family. Once I started spending time with them, it was obvious to me that their way of life was full of a beauty that was missing in mine. I only wish that my parents would understand what I do and be more supportive of the changes I'm making. Most of all, I wish my parents would agree to send me to a religious school because right now I feel kind of stuck where I am."

Everyone's heart went out to Natalie, who was so sincere in her desire to attend a *frum* school and grow in her Yiddishkeit. Tanta Bracha was quick to give her hope. "Don't feel sad or discouraged," she said softly, "because Hashem is looking after you, and He will never let you down. Even though the situation looks so bleak right now, trust Him, and you'll see that He will help you."

After bentching, Mrs. Weiss covered a yawn with her hand. She looked down at her watch and said, "Oh, my! It's so late already. I didn't realize how long we were sitting and talking.

Tanta Bracha, you still have to walk home. Why don't you just sleep here tonight? The guest room is all set up, and I can give you a nightgown and anything else you need."

"Please, Yaffa, that's not necessary at all!" Tanta Bracha replied. "I'm not so tired, and it will be good for me to walk off all that delicious food that I just finished eating."

"So then Yosef and I will walk you home," Mrs. Weiss said.

"I won't allow it," Tanta Bracha responded firmly. "Look at you! You're exhausted – and for a very good reason. Here you are, in your condition, still preparing elaborate, gourmet meals. Yaffa, you have to take it easy and make sure you are getting enough rest. Right now, you belong in bed, and I refuse to let you walk me home."

"Then I will walk you by myself," Dr. Weiss insisted. "It's not safe for you to go alone."

"Tatty, I'll come with you," Leah offered. "I'll be happy to keep you company."

And with that, it was settled. Leah and her father put on their winter coats to escort Tanta Bracha to her house, and Nechama and Natalie stayed behind to help Mrs. Weiss clean up.

"Thank you for that wonderful meal," Natalie told Mrs. Weiss as she dried the dishes, which Mrs. Weiss washed. "I enjoyed it so much."

"Thank you for all that you added to it by being here," Mrs. Weiss answered.

"Oh, you're welcome. I had such a nice time. Everyone was so warm and accepting, and I'm so glad I got to meet Tanta Bracha, too. She seems like such a special person."

"She is!" Mrs. Weiss agreed. "People as kind, caring and wise as she is are definitely hard to find."

"You know," Natalie mused, turning toward Nechama, "she kind of reminds me of Avraham in a way."

"I see what you mean," Nechama nodded. "Now that you mention it, there are a lot of similarities between them."

"Who is this man that you're talking about?" Mrs. Weiss asked curiously.

"Avraham is an old friend of ours," Nechama explained. "My parents helped bring him closer to Yiddishkeit years ago, and since then he's been like family to us. He comes over a lot, and he's always there to help us when needed."

"Oh, that's nice," Mrs. Weiss remarked, and with that the conversation came to an end. As she rinsed the rest of the china, though, her mind seemed preoccupied and there was a thoughtful expression on her face.

On Sunday morning, Natalie left with her parents after profusely thanking the Weisses for their hospitality. Soon after, Raizy and her mother came to pick up Nechama and Leah for a trip to the mall. The girls had plans to spend a few hours shopping before going to visit at the JCE.

"Bye, Mommy!" Leah called to her mother when Raizy's mother beeped outside.

"Bye, girls," Mrs. Weiss called back. "Have a good time. You're going to the old age home straight after, right?"

"Yeah," Leah answered. "We'll be gone for a while. You

probably shouldn't expect us back till about three or four."

"Okay, but make sure to call me if you're running any later than that," Mrs. Weiss instructed, and then the girls were off.

Leah and Nechama were cold, tired and hungry by the time they walked home later that afternoon.

"It feels like we've had a full day," Nechama remarked as they reached their block.

"We have," Leah replied. "We woke up early to see Natalie off, then spent hours walking from store to store in the mall and then went on to spend more time visiting the people at the JCE. I just can't wait to be home already. We'll warm up, have something to eat and just relax."

"That sounds great to me," Nechama approved, just as they reached the front door and rang the bell.

Tanta Bracha answered, catching the girls by surprise.

"Tanta Bracha, I didn't know you were coming today!" Leah exclaimed.

"Neither did I actually, until a short while ago," Tanta Bracha answered candidly.

"Well, then, why are you here?" Leah wanted to know.

"Is that the way to greet a friend?" Tanta Bracha teased with a smile. "Why don't you come into the house, and we'll talk there. You girls look like you're freezing!"

Leah and Nechama obediently stepped inside. Once they'd hung up their coats, Leah turned to Tanta Bracha and asked again, "So why are you here? And where is my mother?"

Tanta Bracha motioned for the girls to sit down on the living room couch with her, and then she explained, "Leah, your mother was having some complications earlier this afternoon, so she and your father went to the hospital to check things out. They called me to see if I could come over and watch you and Levi until they get back because they weren't sure how long they would be."

Leah's face grew fearful. "What kind of complications was my mother having?"

"I'm not sure about the details," Tanta Bracha answered evasively, "but it seems that she'll have to stay at the hospital for a couple of nights while they monitor her. Your father will be home later on, but I told him to take his time and keep your mother company."

Dozens of questions filled Leah's head. She voiced the biggest one. "Will my mother be okay?"

"Of course," Tanta Bracha reassured her. "*Baruch Hashem*, she discovered the problem, and the doctors are taking care of it. As long as she follows their directions and takes it easy now, things should be okay. Of course, saying Tehillim would be helpful, too. Why don't we take a few minutes and recite some *perakim* of Tehillim together?"

After fervently whispering the holy words of Tehillim for several minutes, Leah felt calmer. In a more relaxed frame of mind, she became aware of the hunger that was gnawing at her stomach.

"You know, I'm actually kind of hungry," she remarked out loud. "I think I'll go to the kitchen and find something to eat."

"Actually, supper should be ready any minute," Tanta Bracha

informed her.

"Really? What's for supper?"

"I put up a vegetable soup and ordered pizza, which should be here shortly. I was getting ready to cut up a small salad when the two of you arrived, so if you want to come into the kitchen and help me with that, it will be ready in no time."

Just as Tanta Bracha finished dressing the salad, the delivery-man came with the pizza. Tanta Bracha summoned Levi from the family room, and they all sat down to a tasty supper. Once they were finished, Tanta Bracha suggested that they play a board game or two. Rummikub, Scrabble and Boggle proved to be so much fun that Leah almost forgot why Tanta Bracha was there. Still, every once in a while, an anxious thought would creep into Leah's head as she wondered how her mother was faring.

Levi was already in bed and the girls were already dressed in their nightgowns when Dr. Weiss returned, looking exhausted and disheveled.

"How is Yaffa?" Tanta Bracha immediately inquired with concern.

"*Baruch Hashem*, things are under control," Dr. Weiss responded. "Come, let me drive you home, and I will give you a more detailed account in the car." Turning to Leah, whose worry was unmistakable, he added, "I'll be home in a few minutes, and I'll talk to you then."

True to his word, when he got back home, Leah's father invited her to sit with him at the kitchen table while he drank a cup of coffee and had a serving of cake. "Leah, today Mommy and I got a little scare. It seemed as if the baby might be coming, even though it is really too early for that. We hurried to the hospital where the doctors put Mommy under intensive care, and she will have to stay there for a little bit until the doctors feel that she is completely out of danger. After that, she will come home, but for the next two months, the doctors are prescribing bed rest for her."

"Bed rest for two months?" Leah questioned, her eyes wide.

"Yes," Dr. Weiss confirmed. "Of course, it will be a little inconvenient at times, but still, if that's what it takes to ensure a healthy mother and baby, then it's worth it."

Over the next few days, the Weiss children spent quite a bit of time visiting their mother in the hospital. It was very painful for Leah to see her mother lying there in her flimsy hospital gown, looking so frail and weak. The first time Leah caught sight of her mother like that, she had a hard time keeping back her tears and swallowing the huge lump that had formed in her throat. Throughout the family's visit, Leah hardly said a thing because she was too scared that if she would open her mouth, she wouldn't be able to keep herself from crying.

Even when she went home, Leah was very quiet. It didn't take long for Nechama to realize that Leah needed her space, and the girls spoke very little that night. In school, Leah wasn't able to pay attention to any of the classes. She couldn't stop remembering the vulnerable way her mother had appeared in her hospital bed, and she couldn't shake off the overwhelming sense of pity and concern that she felt for her.

Again that evening at the hospital, Leah was quiet most of the time. When her mother tried drawing her out of her silence by asking her questions about school, Leah responded with very brief answers.

"What's bothering you, Leah?" her father gently inquired on the way home from the hospital.

Leah merely shrugged.

Her father decided not to prod any further, hoping that the issue was one that Leah would iron out by herself with a bit of time. Still, as they pulled up to the house, he made sure to remind his daughter, "Leah, I just want you to know that if there's anything you want to discuss, I'm here for you. And I also want you to know that I understand it's not easy for you having Mommy in the hospital, but it's important to keep in mind that this is just a temporary situation. In a few months, *b'ezras Hashem*, you will have a healthy baby brother or sister, and this whole ordeal will be behind us."

Leah's only response to her father's words was a short nod before she fled from the minivan into the house. She headed straight for her room, where she spent the rest of the night trying to tackle a page of math problems. Finally, she just gave up and went to sleep a lot earlier than her usual bedtime. Nechama saw that Leah was upset but didn't know what to say to her, so she went to sleep herself a few minutes later.

Leah woke up the next morning at six o'clock, an hour before her alarm clock was scheduled to ring. Her attempts to roll over and go back to sleep were unsuccessful, so she just got dressed and went downstairs, where she found her father eating breakfast.

"Good morning," Dr. Weiss greeted his daughter brightly as he looked up from the newspaper he was reading. "Care to join me for some coffee and Danishes?"

"No, thanks," Leah answered. She paused at the kitchen doorway for a moment before asking, "By the way, do you know when Mommy's coming home?"

"I'm not one hundred percent sure, but if things are going well, the doctors may let her go home by this afternoon."

This piece of news cheered Leah up considerably, and that day in school passed a lot more tolerably than the days before. When the final dismissal bell rang, Leah rushed out of school, eager to get home and find out if her mother was there already or at least on her way.

Leah could hardly contain her disappointment at finding out that the doctors had postponed her mother's release for at least another day. Even though her father had told her to remember that all of this was just temporary, it was hard to really see things that way when her mother had been away from home for three days already – and the doctors still didn't know when she'd be back for sure.

The house seemed so different without her mother there. Leah missed her mother's homemade meals, her impeccable housekeeping, her loving good-byes and welcomes whenever the girls left or returned and, most of all, her comforting presence.

In a miserable mood, Leah joined her father and Levi on their evening visit to the hospital. As her father parked the minivan, he turned to Leah. Trying not to sound too sharp, he told her firmly, "Leah, please get rid of your long face and put on a smile while we're with Mommy. It's hard enough for Mommy as it is, and seeing how sad you are will only make things harder. So cheer up, and let's go."

Upon their return home, the Weisses found a note from Nechama on the fridge. "I went out to study," it read. "I'll be back by eight-thirty."

Leah couldn't explain her disappointment at Nechama's disappearance. After all, she'd hardly talked to Nechama in the past couple of days. Still, she realized that there was something nice about having her best friend around even if they weren't conversing much.

Leah trudged up to her room, not sure exactly how she planned on spending the rest of her night. When she turned on her bedroom light, she noticed a piece of paper on her pillow. She picked it up and saw that it was a note from Nechama. Perching herself on top of her bed, Leah started to read.

Dear Leah,

I know that you're going through a hard time right now. It must be very scary and upsetting to have your mother in the hospital, and I understand that you're not up to talking or socializing much these days. I do want to tell you, though, that I'm thinking about you and davening for your mother to feel better every day. I'm also waiting for her to come back home! I also wanted to tell you that whenever you're ready to talk, I'm ready to listen, and if there's anything I can help you with, please don't hesitate to ask.

Love always,
Nechama

Leah read the letter once, twice and then three times before she put it down. She found Nechama's words to be very comforting, and as she sat reflecting, she came up with an idea. There was so much she had bottled up inside of her. She wished she could just let it all out, but talking about her emotions would be too difficult because she would cry as soon as she started. Nechama's note, though, had given her an inspiration. Why not write down everything she wanted to express?

Leah found a pen and piece of paper. She sat down at her desk and began to put her thoughts into words. An hour and two pages later, she lay down her pen and folded her long, heartfelt letter into an envelope and wrote "Mommy" on the front.

Erev Shabbos was more hectic than usual. The Weiss household was busy preparing for Mrs. Weiss's return. A cleaning lady came in the morning to make sure that everything was perfectly neat and tidy, and different women from the community kept stopping by to drop off Shabbos dishes so that the family wouldn't have to worry about cooking meals.

Soon after Leah and Nechama got home from school, Dr. Weiss left to pick up his wife. While he was gone, the girls helped Levi decorate a huge "welcome home" sign, which they hung on the front door. When that was done, the three of them sat down in the living room and waited impatiently.

After what seemed like an endless stretch of time, the sound of the minivan was finally heard pulling into the driveway, and their mother made her long-awaited entrance. Levi ran to her with an excited squeal.

"Just one second," his father cautioned. "First, let's get mommy seated, and then, everyone can greet her properly."

Once Mrs. Weiss was settled on the couch, she gave everyone hugs and kisses. "It's so good to be back," she declared, and the glow on her face showed how much she meant that. "Come, children, before we think about Shabbos and what still has to get done, I want you to please pull up chairs next to me and tell me how you're doing."

That night the Shabbos meal ended early. It had been a long, hard week, and Dr. Weiss thought it would be best for everyone to get a good night's sleep.

Snuggling under her blanket, Leah didn't have the energy to talk much, but before she drifted off, she told Nechama, "It's so wonderful having my mother back. Even though she has to lie down the whole time and can't do all the things she normally does, just the fact that she's here makes the house feel special." Leah paused, thinking. "Oh, and … Nechama?"

"Yes?"

"Thanks for the note. Really, it … helped."

"I'm glad it did. Anyway, that's what friends are for … right?" said Nechama tiredly as she drifted off to sleep.

chapter Fourteen

Standing at the local bus station, shivering in the cold, Nechama checked her watch impatiently. She tried stifling her annoyance as she noted that it was a quarter after one, fifteen minutes later than she and Rivky had arranged to meet. Nechama was ready to go back home when Rivky breathlessly arrived.

"Nechama!" she squealed, enveloping her friend in a tight hug. "It's so good to see you. Sorry I'm late. I lost track of the time. When I realized that it was already one o'clock, I flew out the door and ran all the way here. Oh, it looks like I had good timing. Here's our bus."

Nechama decided not to mention that the bus they needed had actually passed by the station twice already while she had been waiting for Rivky to come. The two girls boarded, paid their fare and found themselves seats.

"You'll never believe what happened to me as I was running to the station," Rivky declared. "I wasn't watching where I was going, and I accidentally bumped into a lady on the avenue who was walking out of the coffee shop. Of course, I apologized right away, but you should have seen how angry she was. I'm telling you, she looked ready to punch me. I said sorry a few more times, but that didn't make a difference. And then, as I turned around to continue on my way, I was shocked by the words that came out of her mouth."

"Why, what did she say?" Nechama asked curiously.

"Watching me go, that lady muttered in a voice full of hatred, 'Dirty Jew!' I couldn't believe my ears. I never heard anyone say something like that before. I'm so upset now that I didn't take a careful look at that woman, or else I would have called the police to report her."

Nechama tried not to laugh. "Rivky, don't you think you're getting a little carried away? I mean, the police aren't really chasing after someone just for making a mean comment."

"Don't you understand, Nechama? This isn't just about a woman who made a mean comment. It's about a woman who's a danger to the community. I'm telling you, there was something very horrible about her. In fact, I wouldn't be surprised if she was a criminal on the loose."

Reluctant to get into a discussion with Rivky about a topic that seemed so ridiculous, Nechama was glad to see the bus pulling up in front of the mall where the girls would be shopping for the next couple of hours. Sure enough, upon entering the mall, Rivky got carried away with the winter clearance sales that were going on, and the subject of her unlucky run-in was quickly forgotten.

On Friday afternoon, Nechama got a call from Rivky. "Nechama, listen to this! I was helping my parents clear out the odds and ends that were left in our house after our move and guess what I found?" Without waiting for Nechama to respond, Rivky continued, "It's the cutest picture of the two of us sitting in a baby pool in my backyard. You must see it!"

"Okay, maybe I'll come over on Shabbos, and you'll show it to me then."

"Are you kidding? You can't wait until Shabbos to see the picture! You've got to take a look at it now."

"But, Rivky, it's *erev Shabbos*. I'm helping out in the kitchen right now, and I can't just pick up and leave."

"In that case, I'm coming over to you. Give me ten minutes, and I'll be there."

No more than ten minutes later, the doorbell rang. Nechama went to let Rivky in. When she opened the front door, she was surprised to see how pale Rivky appeared.

"Rivky, what's the matter? You look like you've just seen a ghost!"

Her voice full of horror, Rivky demanded, "Just tell me one thing – what in the world was that lady doing in your house?" She pointed her finger in the direction of a figure retreating down the block.

"Rivky, calm down. That lady happens to be Paulina, who's taken over Bertha's job of cleaning at the school and our house," Nechama explained.

"Well, that lady also happens to be the one who acted downright nasty to me yesterday," Rivky exclaimed, her eyes flashing angrily at the memory.

"I think you're making a mistake," Nechama told her friend. "Paulina's not that type at all. She's always very polite and respectful."

"She's obviously putting on an act," Rivky declared with certainty. "You see, I told you that lady was dangerous. She's an anti-Semite who's working for a Jewish family; don't tell me that's not super-suspicious. I wouldn't be surprised if she was an undercover agent for the Ku Klux Klan."

"Rivky, you are just way too dramatic!" Nechama said

reproachfully.

"Maybe you're just too naïve," Rivky retorted. "Even though you insist on trusting your terrible cleaning lady, I am not ready to watch her go off just like that."

"Oh, really? So what exactly are you going to do?"

Making a spontaneous decision right then on the spot, Rivky answered, "I'm going to follow that lady and figure out what she's really up to."

"Are you serious?"

"I sure am! Well, are you coming with me or not? She's already at the corner, so we'd better hurry if we don't want to lose her."

Nechama wavered for a moment. Rivky was acting completely insensibly, and Nechama had no interest in accompanying her on her mission to trail Paulina. Still, Nechama thought, maybe she should go along just to make sure that Rivky didn't do anything really irresponsible or unsafe.

Deciding that it was her obligation to keep her friend in check, Nechama said, "Okay, I'm coming." She grabbed her coat from the front closet and called, "Ima, I'm going out with Rivky for a few minutes. I'll be back soon!"

With that, the two girls were off, walking briskly to catch up to Paulina. Maintaining a small distance between themselves and the cleaning lady, they followed her to the main avenue, where she walked down several blocks of stores.

"Come on, Rivky," Nechama tried coaxing her friend, "this isn't taking us anywhere. Let's call it quits for now and choose a better day to continue our detective work."

"Nechama, we can't give up yet. We've just started!" Rivky protested.

Resignedly, Nechama continued walking until Rivky suddenly grabbed her hand. "Look, see! She's going into a store."

Nechama rolled her eyes in exasperation. "She's going into Murray's, for heaven's sake! Everyone goes to Murray's to buy groceries."

"Well, let's see what she buys. Maybe she'll get a lighter or matches to set some Jewish family's house on fire."

But there was hardly anything unusual about the items in Paulina's shopping cart. As the cleaning lady paid for a bunch of bananas, a loaf of bread and two dozen eggs, Nechama whispered to Rivky, "I don't think she's going to burn down anyone's house with those things!"

"Maybe not," Rivky conceded, "but this is only her first stop. Maybe she's headed next to buy a set of knives."

"Even if she is, it's getting late, and we really have to go back home. Please, Rivky, let's turn around now."

"Oh, okay," Rivky agreed reluctantly. "But don't think for a minute that I've changed my mind about that cleaning lady of yours."

As soon as the Shabbos candles were lit, the Greenbergs' home was filled with a sense of tranquility and peace.

"Every week, I'm amazed at how the arrival of Shabbos creates such a wondrous transformation in our house," Mrs.

Greenberg remarked. "Looking at the way we are all sitting on the couch so leisurely and calmly, you would never guess that just minutes ago, we were all madly rushing around looking harried and tense."

"I love these first few minutes after candle-lighting," Rachelli remarked. "As we settle down and relax, I can actually feel the pressures of the week melt away."

"I know what you mean," her mother agreed. Turning to Nechama, she smiled warmly. "Of course, Shabbos is extra special when you're here to spend it with us. We finally get the chance to really catch up. And this week, even though you've been home since Wednesday night, things have been so busy around here that we haven't been able to talk normally. So tell me, how are things in Lakeview City?"

Nechama didn't need any more encouragement to give a fully detailed report on everything that was happening at school. When she stopped to catch her breath, her mother interrupted.

"And how are things in the Weiss house? Is Mrs. Weiss doing okay?"

"*Baruch Hashem*, I think she's doing fine. I mean, life is very different with Mrs. Weiss on bed rest, but together we've come up with a new routine to make sure that everything continues to run smoothly. Dr. Weiss hired a woman who comes daily to help out with cleaning and other errands, and Leah, Levi and I have all been assigned extra chores."

"Good, I'm glad to hear that you're helping," her mother commented approvingly. "It must be very difficult for Mrs.

Weiss to be confined to her bed."

"It is," Nechama nodded. "I've heard her say a few times that she feels so useless. As she lies on the couch and watches us work, she apologizes constantly, but Dr. Weiss always reminds her that this is what she has to do right now in order to give birth to a healthy baby."

"He's one hundred percent right," her mother said, "but I still understand how frustrating this can be sometimes for Mrs. Weiss. Maybe I'll send her some new books to read while she has all this time in bed. You can take them with you when you go back on Sunday."

The mention of returning to Lakeview City on Sunday made Nechama's stomach give a little somersault. Right then, she didn't want to think about leaving home again. For the next day and a half, she was determined to enjoy every minute she had with her family.

"Where is my calendar?" Rabbi Greenberg muttered to himself as he rummaged through his briefcase on *Motzei Shabbos*. "I'm not sure whether I have a meeting scheduled with a prospective parent for tomorrow or the following Sunday."

After searching thoroughly through his briefcase, Rabbi Greenberg sighed. Addressing his wife, who was drying the last dishes from Shabbos, he said, "I must have left my calendar in my office at school. Let me drive over there now, so I can check when my meeting is."

Rabbi Greenberg left the house, and five minutes later the

phone rang. Mrs. Greenberg picked up. "Hello? Oh, hi … did you find your calendar? … What do you mean? … Oh, no! That's awful! … Okay, good luck. Please let me know what happens."

Mrs. Greenberg hung up the phone, the color drained from her face.

Nechama, who'd overheard her mother's side of the conversation, turned to her mother apprehensively. "Ima," she asked quietly, "what did the guy do this time?"

"It seems like the back and side walls of the building have been sprayed with graffiti, and the windows have all been splattered with eggs. Abba called the police right away, and they're already with him at the school, surveying the scene and trying to collect evidence."

"But I don't understand, Ima. Wasn't there a policeman stationed by the building to be on the look-out?"

"There was for a little while, but then at the end of last week, after several days had passed uneventfully, they decided to withdraw the guard from the school area."

Yossi walked into the kitchen then, and Mrs. Greenberg immediately stopped talking. She shot Nechama a warning look, and Nechama understood that her mother was clearly cautioning her not to mention another word about the vandalism in front of her younger brother.

By the time Rabbi Greenberg returned home, Sarala and Yossi were already in bed. Mrs. Greenberg hurried to prepare a cup of coffee for her husband. Rabbi Greenberg accepted the hot beverage gratefully, and between sips, he filled his wife in on what was going on. Rachelli and Nechama sat by the table, too, and quietly listened to what their father had to say.

While Rabbi Greenberg was talking, the phone rang. Mrs. Greenberg hurried to answer it, hoping it might be the police with promising news. After a moment of conversation with the caller, she put the call on hold and turned to her husband anxiously.

"It's a reporter calling from the Woodhaven Tribune. He's heard about the vandalism that took place over the weekend at the school, and he wants to ask you some questions. What should I tell him?"

His face whitening, Rabbi Greenberg answered, "Please tell him I'm not available right now."

After Mrs. Greenberg hung up, Rabbi Greenberg said somberly, "It looks like the media has gotten wind of what's happened, which means there's no way to keep things a secret anymore. I knew that news would leak out eventually, but I was hoping that we would have apprehended the culprit by then. Right now, though, we're still at square one, no closer to uncovering the vandal's identity than on the first day he struck."

"The cops weren't able to find any clues tonight?" Mrs. Greenberg asked.

"It seems like our little terrorist is very good at covering his tracks. In all of their searching, the policemen were only able to find one possible piece of evidence, a grocery receipt lying on the ground near the scene of the crime. They're pretty certain that it was dropped by the vandal because the time shown on the receipt is late Friday afternoon, when everyone at school had already left. Still, it's hardly any help to them. Knowing that the culprit went food shopping at Murray's is not much of a lead."

Nechama listened to her father speak with growing excitement. Is it possible? she wondered. Could it really be?

"Abba," she asked, looking at her father whose eyes were filled with uncharacteristic despair, "do you know what items were listed on the grocery receipt that the policemen found?"

Distractedly, Rabbi Greenberg turned to his daughter. "I do, actually," he responded, "but why do you want to know?"

"I'm just curious if the receipt is for a bunch of bananas, a loaf of bread and two dozen eggs," Nechama said, checking her father's reaction to see if she was completely off the mark.

It didn't seem as if she was. Nechama's answer brought an expression of surprise to Rabbi Greenberg's face. "That's exactly what the receipt was for!" he exclaimed, clearly taken aback.

"Then I'm quite sure I know who our vandal is," Nechama declared with confidence.

"Would anyone care for more pancakes?" Mrs. Greenberg asked the following morning at a celebratory brunch the family was enjoying.

"No, thanks, I'm stuffed," Sarala piped up. "I didn't eat so much yummy food in a while!"

Everyone at the table shared a laugh, and Rabbi Greenberg

said, "I think Sarala speaks for us all." Turning to his wife he added, "Why don't you come sit down and enjoy some of your delicious food yourself?"

Mrs. Greenberg happily found herself a seat at the table and started filling her plate. She shook her head in disbelief. "I'm still so shocked that all this time I didn't suspect Paulina for a second."

"Well, why should you have?" Rachelli asked. "She was always so polite. How could we have known that she was really a Jew-hater?"

"Or that her brother was previously imprisoned for vandalizing a shul in Detroit," Rabbi Greenberg added, "and thought that Paulina working as a cleaning lady would give them the perfect opportunity to continue terrorizing a Jewish community?"

"None of us suspected a thing," Mrs. Greenberg reiterated. "That is, until Rivky showed up in town," she amended, smiling admiringly at Rivky, who'd been invited to the brunch as the guest of honor.

Accepting the praise, Rivky declared, "From the first time I bumped into Paulina, I knew there was something dangerous about her. I could just tell she was up to no good."

"Well, your instincts were definitely correct," observed Rabbi Greenberg. "You acted as a great sleuth."

Only half-jokingly, Rivky responded, "Didn't I tell you? I'm actually considering a career as a detective when I get older."

chapter Fifteen

When Dr. Weiss returned home that night, he found Nechama sweeping the kitchen. "I don't believe my eyes!" he cried in feigned shock. "There's a news-breaking celebrity at work in my very own house!"

"Oh, Ta, stop teasing," Leah told her father.

"But I'm serious," Dr. Weiss protested. "I've read in the paper and heard on the radio how Nechama helped to solve a case that had all the cops stumped. What a story! Nechama, I can't wait to hear all the details firsthand. From the reports, it sounds like there's been quite some action in your little town as of late."

"That's definitely true," Nechama confirmed.

"And from all that I've heard and read, it seems like your father handled the situation with impressive calmness and professionalism. He's emerged as quite the hero."

"I know," Nechama nodded. "It's pretty ironic. All along, my father's main concern had been that these attacks would scare off parents at the school, but now, with all the positive publicity that he's been getting in light of the case's successful conclusion, he's actually gotten a few phone calls from people who are interested in sending their kids to the school."

"That's great," Mrs. Weiss remarked from her place on the couch. "I'm glad some good has come out of all this in the end."

"Well, the bottom line is that one of the mystery's detectives is now busy scrubbing our counters as we talk!" Dr. Weiss declared, obviously not through with teasing Nechama.

"You know already that there's no stopping her," Mrs. Weiss answered in defense. "I've tried telling her and Leah to leave the mess for the cleaning lady tomorrow, but they're just not listening to me."

"Yaffa, I think we just have two very stubborn, very helpful young ladies on our hands," Dr. Weiss informed his wife, adding, "I don't know how we're going to survive without Nechama when she leaves us over winter vacation."

"What about me, Tatty? Did you forget that I'm going home with Nechama then, too?" Leah called jokingly from the kitchen.

Her father didn't answer right away. From her place at the sink where she was washing dishes, Leah noticed her parents exchange a meaningful look before her father responded to her remark.

"Actually, Leah, we were hoping that maybe you would stay home over vacation to continue helping Mommy. Levi also has the week off, so without Mommy to take him around and entertain him, I'm sure your being around would make things a lot easier."

The color drained from Leah's face as her father spoke. She listened to him in disbelief. How could her parents be asking this of her? Didn't they know how she'd been looking forward to this for weeks already? Was it fair of them to expect her to sacrifice the get-away she'd been dreaming about in order to stay home and watch her brother?

When she found her tongue, all Leah could stammer, in a tone of devastation, was, "But – but – I've been waiting to go to Nechama's house for so long."

Her father opened his mouth to respond, but her mother hurried to speak first. "Leah, you're right. Of course, you'll go to Nechama's with your friends. We will manage just fine while you're away, and you'll have the great time that you deserve. I'm sorry that we even brought this up."

And that was that. Over the next couple of weeks, Leah's parents didn't mention again the possibility of her staying home during vacation, but in her heart, Leah thought about it all the time. She couldn't free herself from the guilt she felt.

On the one hand, it would be so awful to miss out on all the fun that she and her friends had been planning so excitedly, and she was especially anticipating this break because life in her house had been a little more stressful than usual lately! On the other hand, though, was she being selfish to put herself before her family? Was staying behind really the right thing to do?

chapter Sixteen

"Now, listen," Miriam said, her big, green eyes regarding her friends earnestly as they sat in Leah's bedroom, "I am putting complete trust in you. As of this very minute, I understand just about nothing about algebra, but I hope that by the time this evening is over, I will be a whiz at it." Noting Nechama and Leah's skeptical reaction, she hastily amended, "Or, at least, I'll know it well enough to pass my midterm tomorrow."

Nechama and Leah laughed. "We'll try our best," Nechama promised.

"Thanks," Miriam replied, "but let me warn you, it's not going to be easy." She heaved a deep sigh. "Midterms are so painful for me. This whole week I'll be counting down, and not just because vacation's around the corner."

Miriam sounded like she was ready to carry on about the agony of midterms for a while, but Leah gently interrupted, "Miriam, maybe we'd better get started, especially if we have such a big job ahead of us."

"You're right," Miriam conceded in resignation, and the studying began.

Leah was in the midst of explaining a complex math example

when Mrs. Weiss called from her room, "Girls, can one of you please pick up the phone?"

Leah motioned for Nechama to take the call so she could continue helping Miriam. Nechama picked up the telephone. "Hello," she said.

"Hi, this is Yocheved Chein – Chevi Chein. How are you?"

Caught off-guard for a moment by this unexpected caller, Nechama stammered, "Oh! *Baruch Hashem*. How are you?"

"*Baruch Hashem*, good. Actually, I was recently informed of some wonderful news. A friend of mine who has been married for many years without children just gave birth to twin boys!"

"Mazel Tov," Nechama said, puzzled by the purpose of Chevi Chein's call. Certainly, the singer hadn't phoned just to chat and share some happy tidings!

As if hearing her silent question, Chevi went on, "Yes, it is a big Mazel Tov, and that is actually why I'm calling. As it turns out, the *pidyon haben* of my friend's firstborn son will be taking place on Purim, and I cannot miss it. After all, this is a simcha I've been waiting for, for so long, to share with her. Unfortunately, this also means I'll have to cancel my performance at your school, but I'm sure you understand."

"Yes, of course," Nechama replied, doing her best to ignore the sense of keen disappointment that she felt.

"I did want to tell you, though, that I'll be in Lakeview City to visit with my great-aunt for a few days during the week after Shavuos," Chevi Chein continued. "If I can make up anything to you at that time, it would truly be my pleasure."

"Thanks," Nechama answered.

"Well, let me know what you decide. Thanks for your understanding, and *hatzlacha rabba* to you and your friends."

Hanging up, Nechama faced her friends who were regarding her with curiosity and were eager to be filled in. "That was Chevi Chein," she told them dully, "and she called to say that she won't be able to sing for us on Purim because she has a *pidyon haben* to go to then."

"Are you serious?" Leah asked, her expression aghast.

"What are we going to do for our event?" Miriam wailed in despair.

"I don't know," Nechama answered, raising her hands helplessly. "Wait until Hindy hears this."

"Let's call her now and tell her," Miriam said.

"No, I think it's better if we finish studying first," Nechama suggested, trying to act calm and sensible. "That way we can get this algebra completely out of the way before we get caught up with our Purim fundraiser."

"Good idea," Miriam admitted.

The girls spent the next hour trying to make sense of all the math formulas and problems, but their hearts weren't into it. When they finally closed their textbooks and set aside their review sheets, Miriam heaved a big sigh.

"I guess my best bet now is to daven really hard before the midterm because otherwise I'm doomed," she declared.

"Oh, come on," Leah told her. "You're being too hard on yourself. You seemed to understand a lot of the examples that we practiced."

"Let's just hope that I'll still remember everything tomorrow," Miriam retorted. "And now, for the next issue at hand," she continued, "who gets the honor of breaking the exciting news to Hindy?"

"I will," Leah volunteered, reaching for the phone.

Hindy reacted to the update in a characteristically down-to-earth manner. "We really have a problem on our hands," she stated. "Purim is in less than a month, which doesn't give us a lot of time to come up with an alternative plan. We need to get down to business right away. I think we should sit together at lunch tomorrow to brainstorm, and, hopefully, we'll think of something."

The next day, news of Chevi Chein's cancellation spread quickly amongst the eighth graders. During recess, Mrs. Solomon called the Purim *chagiga* committee over to her desk.

"Is it true that Chevi Chein won't be able to make it on Purim?" she questioned.

The four girls nodded sadly.

"We're meeting today at lunch to figure out what kind of entertainment we'll have instead," Hindy informed Mrs. Solomon.

"Okay, good luck," Mrs. Solomon wished the group. "And remember, it doesn't have to be something so fancy or exotic. I'm sure that whatever you come up with will turn out to be fun. If you need to resort to a Purim skit or a smaller scale performance, it will hardly be the end of the world."

"I don't know if that's true," Miriam answered skeptically. "After expecting a smashing show by Chevi Chein, something low-key would be a big let-down for everyone."

"Don't worry," Mrs. Solomon reassured the girls. "Everyone will soon get over the fact that Chevi Chein won't be coming, even though it is a big disappointment, to be sure."

Nechama remembered Chevi Chein's offer to sing for the girls after Shavuos, and she relayed the message to Mrs. Solomon. "So I guess if anything's going on during that week at school, she could perform then," Nechama concluded with a shrug.

"That's good to know," Mrs. Solomon mused thoughtfully. "Our annual mother-daughter tea usually takes place around that time, and a mini-concert by Chevi Chein would certainly enhance the affair. Of course, I first have to check with the administration, but if they okay the idea, I think we should go ahead and book Chevi Chein as soon as possible."

At the lunchtime meeting, the Purim *chagiga* committee came up with a list of possible entertainers. Included in the list were entertainers who had already performed at the school in the past, as well as entertainers who didn't sound quite so exciting. However, the girls realized that they were in a fairly desperate situation and were ready to settle for less than they'd originally had in mind. By the time lunch was over, each of the girls had been assigned an entertainer or two to call in the evening in order to check availability over Purim.

"Okay, between us all, we should come up with someone who's able to make it on Purim," Hindy declared hopefully. "Let's just make sure to compare notes tonight and see what our options are."

The girls bentched and were getting ready to return to class when Mrs. Solomon approached and told Nechama, "I got the principal's okay. We're going to schedule our mother-daughter tea for the Sunday after Shavuos, so if you can bring in to school tomorrow Chevi Chein's number, I would appreciate it. That way, I can call her personally to finalize the plans and confirm all the details with her."

"Sure," Nechama nodded agreeably.

As the girls filed out of the cafeteria, Miriam remarked ruefully, "Even if we don't have a clue yet what we're doing for Purim, at least we know that there's a great program planned for the mother-daughter tea after Shavuos!"

That evening, Hindy called Nechama and Leah. "Any luck?" she wanted to know.

"No, not at all," Leah answered dejectedly. "The two people I spoke to were already booked, and Nechama wasn't able to get through to the caricaturist."

"Well, I wasn't too successful, either," Hindy reported. "I talked to the bird show lady, but she charges way more than we can pay, and I left a message for the balloon man, who hasn't gotten back to me yet. I wonder what's going on with Miriam."

"Why don't I conference call her in?" Leah suggested. "Nechama can pick up another phone in my house, and that way we can all discuss this together."

Within minutes, all four girls were on the line. Miriam's calls, like the rest of theirs, hadn't gone well at all; one group of entertainers wasn't available for Purim, and the juggler said his shows were geared to younger children.

"Now what?" Nechama asked. "Where do we go from here?"

"Good question," Hindy answered. "I mean, it's still possible that the balloon man will work out, but I don't think we should count on it. Maybe it's time to start considering homemade entertainment, after all."

"Like a play or a choir?" Miriam inquired.

"Yeah, something like that," Hindy said. "Here's the catch, though. Whatever we decide to do is going to require the help of our friends and a lot of practice, but winter vacation is only a few days away. That means a lot of girls, including Nechama and Leah, are going to be out of town, so we really have only two and half weeks after our break to put together a great performance."

"Wow, the pressure is on!" Nechama remarked.

"It sure is," Hindy replied. "And over vacation, we should all give a lot of thought about what kind of show to put on. Maybe one of us will come up with a really cute, creative plan."

"I hope so," Leah declared. "I really don't want our Purim *chagiga* to flop."

"None of us do," Hindy answered. "So let's really do our best to think of something good!"

chapter Seventeen

"Leah, I think you're forgetting that you're going away for five days, not five months," Nechama teased.

Surveying the piles of clothes and accessories that were stacked in her suitcase and strewn across her bed, Leah laughed. "You're probably right," she admitted, "but how do I know exactly what I'll need?"

"Well, for one you don't need nine sweaters and seven skirts. You also don't need three Shabbos outfits plus your Shabbos robe. And that's just a start."

The two girls giggled as Nechama sifted through everything Leah had set aside for the trip and decided which items were necessary and which were not. As they were working, they got a call from Raizy, who had recently finished with her crutches.

"I don't know what to do," she told Nechama over the phone. "I just can't seem to fit all of my stuff into one suitcase. My mother says I'm packing way too much, but I don't know what to take out."

"Hold on one second," Nechama said. After a quick consultation with Leah, who went to get permission from her mother, Nechama promised Raizy, "Okay, Leah and I will be over soon. As soon as we finish up here with Leah's things, we'll head out to your house and help you get organized."

When Nechama walked into Raizy's room, her eyes nearly popped out of her head. It looked as if Raizy had set aside her entire wardrobe for the trip.

"And I thought Leah was bad!" Nechama exclaimed. "Wow, we really have a job ahead of us."

Going through Raizy's clothing turned out to be a lot of fun. Raizy put on some music, and she brought some refreshments to her room, too. The girls joked around a lot, in a relaxed mood now that vacation had officially begun.

"I can't wait till we're on our way already," Raizy declared. "Just the thought of five whole days of sleepovers and fun puts me in a good mood. This is so much more exciting than spending vacation at home."

Raizy's words caused Leah to feel a stab of guilt. She, too, was looking forward to spending time with her friends instead of staying at home, but unlike Raizy, she had a mother and brother who really needed her help. Before she could start reconsidering her decision, Leah pushed aside her misgivings and joined Nechama and Raizy's conversation about their upcoming performance at the JCE.

"I think putting on a short Purim musical would be nice," Nechama said. "Each of us could dress up as a different character from the Megillah and act out the story of Purim in song."

"That sounds adorable," Raizy responded. "Is there a specific Purim song that you had in mind to use?"

"Actually, I thought we could try to make up an original song over vacation."

Raizy seemed a little skeptical about that. "You really think we can put together a song that's worth singing?"

"Don't worry," Leah told Raizy. "Nechama's very good at writing. The rest of us will just put in our two cents here and there, and we're sure to end up with a great song."

"In that case, I'm all for the plan," Raizy replied. "Meanwhile, Nechama, it looks like you've done a great job with my stuff here. I don't know how, but you've managed to get all of my things neatly into one suitcase."

"It was no big deal," Nechama replied. Turning to Leah, she remarked, "We should probably get going. It's pretty late."

As Raizy escorted her guests to the door, she said, "Thank you so much for coming over to help me. I really appreciate it!" Her eyes glazed over dreamily as she added, "I don't know how I'm going to fall asleep tonight. I'm not sure if I mentioned it yet, but I am so excited for our trip tomorrow!"

"Okay, I think I've got everything," Leah said a bit nervously as she zippered her suitcase closed.

"And even if you forgot something, it's really fine. After all, you're only going to my house, and I can always give you anything you're missing."

"That's true," Leah conceded. "I guess the only thing left to take care of is food. Let's go to the kitchen and see what snacks we can pack for our trip."

While the girls were rummaging through the pantry, the phone rang. Mrs. Weiss picked up the cordless phone that was next to her on the couch.

"Hello?" the girls heard her say. "Oh, hello, Lily. How are you? … Really? I don't believe it! So you're on crutches for the next month? Poor girl! … Well, take it easy, and feel better. Thanks for calling. Good-bye."

"What happened to Lily?" Leah asked as soon as her mother hung up. Lily was the woman who'd been coming to help out around the house.

"She slipped on ice and broke her foot, and now she's in crutches for a while."

"Oh, no! That means she won't be able to come help out anymore. What are you going to do?"

"I guess we'll have to find someone to replace Lily," her mother answered pragmatically, "and until we do, we'll just have to manage on our own."

"That's not going to be so easy!" Leah burst out dismally. "Even when you get someone new to help out, it'll take time to train her in to the job."

"What can I do?" her mother said. Then, as if reading her daughter's mind, she looked Leah in the eye and continued firmly, "Trust me, everything will work out. Right now I want you to go ahead and enjoy your vacation without any worries. Okay?"

"Okay," Leah replied in a tone that was more than a little uncertain.

"Good," Mrs. Weiss nodded satisfied. "I'm glad that's taken care of. Now if you don't mind, can you please pass me the phone book so I can look up the employment agency's number? Maybe they can send someone over today already."

As Leah delivered the phone book to her mother, the phone rang. It was Elana calling to say that she and her mother would be over in fifteen minutes to pick up the girls and drive them to the train station.

"Girls, do you have everything you need?" Mrs. Weiss asked them.

They nodded, and Mrs. Weiss checked, "Leah, do you have enough money? Enough food? Did you remember to pack your toothbrush? And your hairbrush?"

"Yes, Mommy, I have everything," Leah confirmed, and then she and Nechama leapt up the stairs to fetch their luggage.

Minutes later, the girls returned to the living room with all of their baggage in tow. Mrs. Weiss was just ending her conversation with the agency's secretary.

"Well, then, I look forward to meeting Julie in two days, and, of course, if you do find out that someone is available to come over sooner, please let me know …. Thank you very much …. Good-bye."

A car honked outside. Nechama peered through the front window and exclaimed, "It looks like Elana and her mother are here!" She grabbed her backpack and suitcase and turned to her host, "Bye, Mrs. Weiss! See you next week!"

"Good-bye, Nechama. Good-bye, Leah. Don't forget to call when you get in."

"I won't," Leah promised. She bent down to kiss her mother on the cheek, and then, with one last backward glance at her bed-bound mother, she followed Nechama outside.

Raizy was already in the car, and the girls were in very high spirits as they rode to the train station. They giggled and chatted enthusiastically the whole way. Only Leah was strangely quiet.

"What's wrong?" Nechama asked her in an undertone.

"I just feel so bad about leaving my mother like that," Leah softly whispered to Nechama, without talking loud enough for the other girls to hear. "Not only does she have to stay in bed with Levi on her hands the whole time, but it doesn't look like she's going to have any cleaning help, either, for the next few days." Nechama nodded understandingly. "It's not going to be easy for her, that's for sure."

"What are you two talking about?" Raizy asked Leah and Nechama.

"Oh, nothing much," Nechama answered lightly, adding, "Look, do you see? There's the train station straight up ahead."

Elana's mother helped the girls unload their suitcases from the trunk. "Okay, it looks like you're all set to go," she told them with a smile. "Have a safe trip, and enjoy yourselves."

Elana's mother turned to get back into the driver's seat when Leah called after her, "One second, please!"

Questioningly, Elana's mother turned around. "Yes, Leah? Did you forget something?"

"Um, not really. It's just that I was wondering if you could, um, drive me back home."

"Drive you back home?" Elana's mother regarded Leah blankly. So did Raizy and Elana.

"Yeah. I'm sorry, but I just feel like I belong at home during this vacation."

"In that case, let me help you get your stuff back into the car, and then we'll get going," Elana's mother responded without asking any questions.

Leah looked at her friends apologetically. "I'm very sorry about this. I was really excited about spending vacation with all of you, but I really need to be at home now to help my family. So have fun, and I'll call you to see how things are going."

With that, Leah stepped back into the car for the ride home. Her friends waved at her before disappearing into the station building, and sadly Leah waved back. It wasn't easy to watch her friends go while she stayed behind, but she knew that she had made the right decision.

Reading in bed that night, Leah's mind drifted as she wondered what her friends were doing at that moment. Imagining all the fun they were having together, she started to feel sorry for herself until she reminded herself of her family's reaction upon seeing that she'd decided to stay home.

Her mother, shocked at first, had hugged Leah tightly, her eyes shining with love. Her father had beamed with pride as he'd praised his daughter's maturity. Levi, too, had been very pleased by Leah's return, especially when she had offered to take him and a friend to the pizza shop for lunch and then bowling after that.

Thinking back to all the help she had given her parents that day and to the heartfelt thanks they had expressed, Leah realized that she had no regrets about sacrificing her original vacation plans. Too tired to read anymore, she set aside her book and turned off the lamp on her night table. Then she covered herself warmly with her blanket and fell asleep with a peaceful look on her face.

A few hours later, Leah awoke with a start. In a haze, she blinked a few times and sat up in bed. It was dark outside, and although her alarm clock showed that it was four-thirty in the morning, she could hear her parents moving back and forth in the hallway and talking in hushed, urgent tones.

Bewildered by the strange commotion, Leah left her room to investigate. "Mommy, Tatty, what's going on?" she asked her parents, who were both fully dressed.

"Leah, it looks like the baby is acting up again," her father explained, unable to hide the anxiety in his voice. "I'm going to take Mommy to the hospital now so the doctors can try to get things under control again. You'll stay here with Levi, and I'll call you in the morning to let you know what's happening."

"Okay," Leah nodded. Mustering all of her self-discipline, she kept herself from bursting into panicked tears. She knew her parents were counting on her to remain strong and calm, and she wouldn't let them down.

Leah had a hard time falling back asleep after her parents left. After tossing and turning for more than an hour, she finally dozed off, but her dreams were filled with disturbing images of her distressed parents. She was in the middle of a nightmare about her mother being rushed to the hospital in an ambulance when she realized that the shrieking siren sound that pierced her ears actually belonged to the ringing phone.

Hastily, Leah said Modeh Ani and washed her hands before answering. It was her father.

"Tatty, how is Mommy?" Leah asked anxiously.

"*Baruch Hashem*, she and your baby sister are doing well, considering the situation."

"My baby sister?" echoed Leah in confusion.

"Yes, your baby sister," her father repeated. "I'm calling to let you know that just a little while ago, your mother gave birth to a girl."

"But isn't it too early for Mommy to give birth?" Leah asked in a small voice.

"The baby did arrive a month and a half before her expected due date, but there was no stopping her. *Baruch Hashem*, the doctors say she looks good considering her size and premature birth, although, of course, we cannot bring her home with us right away. Instead, she has to stay in an incubator for a month or so. There she'll receive extra care that will help her develop into a completely healthy baby."

Leah had several questions for her father, but she realized that it was not the best time to ask them.

Her father continued, "I'm on the way now to shul so I can daven Shacharis and make a *mishebeirach* for Mommy and the baby. Afterward, I have to stop into my office for a couple of hours, and then I'll come home to pick up you and Levi so we can all go together to visit Mommy and the baby. Meanwhile, please look after Levi and keep him out of trouble, okay?"

"Okay."

"Thank you, Leah," her father said, adding affectionately, "Just wait till the baby finds out what a special big sister she has."

In the evening, Leah called Nechama to share the good news.

"A baby girl!" gasped Nechama in delight. "That means you finally have the sister you've always wished for! Tell me more, Leah. Does she have a name yet? Who does she look like? How is your mother feeling?"

"One question at a time," Leah laughed, and then she tried answering Nechama's queries in order. "First of all, no, the baby doesn't have a name yet. My parents decided to wait until Shabbos to give the name. Second of all, I haven't seen the baby yet because she's in the ICU, and kids are not allowed inside there. But from what my parents have told me, it sounds like she's too tiny to look like anyone yet. She's only three pounds, you know! Third of all, my mother is feeling really good, *baruch Hashem*, and she'll be coming home right after Shabbos."

"Wow! This must be so exciting for you!" Nechama exclaimed, adding, "And to think that you would have missed it all if you'd come with us to Woodhaven."

"I know," Leah agreed softly. "I keep on remembering Tanta Bracha's words about Hashem's big plan. When I first decided to turn back at the train station, I really had my doubts, but now it's clear to see how my decision was such *hashgacha pratis*."

CHAPTER Eighteen

"Leah, I hate to interrupt you, but can you please pass the salad?" her father asked. In amusement, he added, "Girls, you haven't stopped talking since Nechama stepped foot into our house at noon. It looks like you've been separated for ages!"

"But we have," Leah replied, and she meant it. The five days that Nechama had been away had really seemed like ages to her.

"It's just that so much has happened while I've been gone," Nechama explained to Dr. Weiss.

"I can't argue with that," the doctor conceded with a smile.

That being said, the girls returned to their animated conversation. Leah showed Nechama pictures of baby Esther Bracha and declared, "I hope you join us the next time I go to visit her."

"Of course!" Nechama replied. "I can't wait to see Esther Bracha for myself. When are you going next?"

"I'm not sure. I was planning on playing it by ear. You see, my mother goes to the hospital every morning, and then she goes back with my father and Levi in the evening. We're always welcome to go along then also, but I thought we'd choose a night when we don't have too much homework."

"That makes sense," Nechama agreed.

By this time, everyone had finished eating supper, and Nechama and Leah proceeded to clear the table and wash the dishes. As they worked, they continued to chat.

When Leah felt like she'd gone through every single detail of the story of Esther Bracha's surprise birth, she turned to her friend and said, "Nechama, now it's time for you to tell me about your vacation."

The girls finished cleaning the kitchen as Nechama filled Leah in on her stay at home with Raizy and Elana. Doing her best to play down the fun that she'd had in Woodhaven, Nechama told Leah how the girls had spent each day.

"It sounds like you had a really nice time," Leah remarked without a trace of envy.

"We did, even though we missed you, of course," Nechama said sincerely.

"Did you get a chance to work on the Purim song for the JCE?" Leah wanted to know.

"We wrote up the whole thing, actually. Do you want me to sing it for you?"

"Of course!"

"Let me just get the paper from my backpack."

Nechama was back in a minute. Clearing her throat, paper in hand, Nechama started to sing.

When Nechama finished, Leah clapped her hands. "You did a great job. The words are so cute!"

"Thanks," Nechama replied. "I didn't make them up by

myself, though. The others helped, too, especially Elana."

"Elana? I didn't know she was good at that sort of thing."

"I didn't know a lot of things about Elana, either, before our trip to Woodhaven. Even though she's normally so quiet, she really opened up a lot over the time we spent together. As she got more comfortable with Raizy and me, we got to see a really fun side to Elana. She has a good sense of humor, too, and she was the one who thought of most of the funny lines in the song."

"Who would have ever guessed?" Leah mused. "Normally, she seems so shy."

"You know," Nechama declared thoughtfully, "maybe no one really took the time to find out about Elana's qualities. By the time she joined the class in sixth grade, everyone probably had their circle of friends already, and maybe she just got overlooked."

"You're probably right. I remember that when Elana first came to our school, girls tried to befriend her, but because she seemed so shy and quiet, we soon gave up and pretty much left her alone. Looking back, I feel bad that I didn't give her more of a chance."

"It's not too late," Nechama tried comforting her friend. "Now that we know that Elana really has so much to her, and it's just a matter of reaching out a little more to include her, we'll make sure to do just that."

Leah nodded in agreement and then asked, "Nechama, did you discuss ideas for the Purim *chagiga* while you were home?"

"The subject came up once or twice, but no one really had

any great suggestions. I guess you didn't really have any time to think about it, right?"

"Not really," Leah admitted. "We'll see Hindy and Miriam in school tomorrow and find out if any of them had any brilliant ideas."

"I don't know," Nechama said dubiously. "I'm not raising my hopes up too high. I have a feeling we may just end up doing something simple. After all, time is running out, and we have to do something."

"Sunday is going to be a busy day," Nechama declared as she and Leah peeled vegetables for a soup that Mrs. Weiss was preparing for supper. "I promised to have the whole Purim *shpiel* written up by Monday morning so that we could assign parts and start practicing right after school. That's besides the performance that we're scheduled to put on at the old age home."

Mrs. Weiss, who had been listening to the girls talk as she cleaned chicken, perked up. "I can't believe that I forgot that your show was this Sunday!" she cried, wearing a stricken expression.

"Why? What's the big deal?" Leah asked.

"Tatty and I have arranged to meet with the doctors at the hospital this Sunday afternoon to discuss Esther Bracha's development. I was counting on you to watch Levi while we were gone, but now I think I have to make other arrangements. Too bad Tanta Bracha is away for a few days, or else I could have asked her to come over."

"Are you sure? If there's no other choice, then I'll just stay at home."

"No, of course not. I'll just arrange for Levi to play at a friend's house. Levi will be thrilled."

Leah was relieved that the issue had been resolved so easily. So was Nechama.

"Phew!" Nechama said, letting out the breath that she'd been holding nervously. "For a minute there, I was scared that Elana and I would have to sing at the JCE all by ourselves."

"Why? Where will Raizy be?" Mrs. Weiss asked.

"She just found out that she and her family are traveling to New York for the weekend for her cousin's *bris*, so that leaves the three of us to split five roles. That's why I'm really glad that Leah's still able to come along."

"I'm sorry that I had you worried for a second there," Mrs. Weiss apologized with a smile. "I've just been so forgetful these past few weeks. Do you know what I just realized, too? I haven't even heard the Purim song you'll be singing on Sunday! Do me a favor, girls. As soon as you're finished with those vegetables, please sing it for me, okay?"

One look at Levi when he woke up on Sunday morning was enough to confirm that he wasn't feeling well. His cheeks were flushed, and his eyes were teary. Mrs. Weiss hurried to take his temperature. Sure enough, he was running a fever.

"Does that mean I can't go play at Shimmy's house today?" Levi whispered hoarsely.

"I'm afraid so," Mrs. Weiss responded. "I think I'll have to call his mother and arrange for a rain check."

Poor Levi was so sick, he didn't even argue. Instead, he lay back on his pillow with a piteous moan.

As soon as Leah and Nechama heard about Levi's fever, Leah asked, "Does that mean I'll have to stay home and baby-sit for Levi?"

"I'm afraid so," Mrs. Weiss answered. "I'm really sorry, girls. Leah, I know you were looking forward to your show, and, Nechama, I know you were counting on Leah's participation, but I can't think of another alternative at this point."

Hiding her feelings of disappointment, Nechama was quick to say, "That's okay. Elana and I will manage on our own, don't worry." And in her heart, Nechama decided that she really would make the best of the situation.

Later, Nechama, holding a bag with five masks, headed out to meet Elana. When she joined Elana at their usual corner, Nechama said, "It looks like it's just going to be the two of us today."

"Why? What happened to Leah?" Elana asked.

Nechama explained that Leah had to take care of Levi who was sick at home. "Are you nervous about singing this song by ourselves?"

Elana surprised Nechama by answering calmly, "Not at all. The people in the old age home are such an easy audience to please. No matter how we do, they'll be happy and appreciative. So there's really no reason to be nervous."

Nechama was impressed by Elana's mature, easy-going

attitude. Truthfully, Elana was right. "We just have to divide the five characters between the two of us," Nechama said. "Do you have any preferences?"

"Not at all. What about you?"

"The truth is, I do," Nechama admitted. "I was really hoping I could stick to the easy roles of Esther and Mordechai that don't require too much drama."

"Sure," Elana replied agreeably. Teasingly, she added, "I think you just want to cast me as the villain, playing the parts of Vashti, Haman and Achashveirosh."

"No, no, that's not it," Nechama started protesting.

Elana interrupted with a smile. "I know, I was just joking. Seriously, I have no problem being the bad guys."

"Thanks," Nechama said gratefully.

"Don't mention it."

The two girls chatted easily the rest of the way to the JCE. When they got there, Sharon, the program coordinator, walked over to greet them.

"Hi, girls," she said brightly. "Where are your friends?"

"Last-minute things came up for both of them, and they weren't able to make it," Nechama explained. Noticing Sharon's face drop, Nechama quickly continued, "But, of course, Elana and I will go on with the show."

"Oh, terrific, I'm so happy to hear that," Sharon told them appreciatively. "Everyone's already waiting for you in the recreation room, and they would have been devastated if the show was cancelled. Alright, then, are you girls ready to begin?"

"Yes, we are," Elana answered for both of them.

Nechama, whose heart was starting to beat a little faster, marveled at Elana's confidence.

As the two girls stood before the roomful of elderly residents, the appropriate masks already in place on their faces, Elana gave Nechama's hand a tight squeeze. "You'll be fine," she whispered reassuringly. "And in seven minutes, this will all be history."

That being said, Elana began to sing. In a deep voice, she impersonated Achashveirosh expertly and had everyone, including Nechama, enthralled by her comic act. By the time it was Nechama's turn to sing Mordechai's part, Nechama was already at ease, and she pulled off her lines without a problem.

Elana sang next as Vashti, and Nechama was amazed as she watched her sweet, soft-spoken classmate transformed into a hateful, mean-spirited queen. Elana moved on to become wicked, scheming Haman, and Nechama was so entranced that Elana had to nudge her when it was her turn to take over as Esther.

When Nechama and Elana were done, they were met by a loud, enthusiastic round of applause. Their audience begged for more, and the girls sang a round of lively, popular Purim songs on the spot. Afterward, they went around to speak to the residents individually, promising to return on Purim day to deliver *mishloach manos*.

Mrs. Jacobovitz gave each of the girls a big hug. "That was wonderful, just wonderful!" she complimented them. "One of the best Purim acts I've ever seen. Where did you girls get that adorable song?"

"Nechama wrote it," Elana answered.

"Nechama, you wrote that song? Unbelievable! I always knew you girls were talented, but like this? I never would have dreamed! And you," Mrs. Jacobovitz continued, wagging a finger at Elana, "you're an actress, a real star! For a minute, I really thought that Vashti and Haman had come back to life."

Nechama and Elana both blushed from Mrs. Jacobovitz's praise. They waited in embarrassment until she finished raving about their talents, and then they asked her how she was doing and what was new in her life.

"What's new? Nothing much," she answered honestly. "Here life continues on the same every day. Breakfast, activities, lunch, more activities, supper and then get ready for bed. It's nice and relaxing, of course, but there's nothing very exciting about it. The biggest excitement is when you girls come to visit each week. It means so much to all of us here."

"Well, we enjoy coming, too," Nechama and Elana replied sincerely.

After spending a few more minutes talking to Mrs. Jacobovitz, the girls said good-bye. Walking out of the JCE, Nechama turned to Elana and exclaimed, "You were absolutely amazing today! Mrs. Jacobovitz is right. You really are a born actress. How did you manage to keep it a secret for so long?"

Elana laughed. "Now, don't exaggerate, please. I'm far from a born actress, although I definitely do enjoy acting. I didn't mean to keep that a secret at all. In fact, in my old school, I performed in a few school plays. When I came here, though, whenever there was a class skit, the same few girls were always assigned the major roles. I didn't feel very comfortable speaking up and asking to be given a bigger part, so I guess that's why no one really knows that I like acting."

Nechama listened thoughtfully to Elana and said, "What a shame. Here you are, such a great actress, and no one even realizes it. I wonder how many other girls in the class have talents that no one knows about. You know, I wish there was an opportunity for each girl to get up and share a special talent or skill. It would be so nice for everyone."

"Nechama," Elana said, a spark of inspiration in her eyes, "I don't think that's such a far-fetched idea."

"What do you mean?"

"Well, I think you're right. It would be really nice to see all the talent that exists in our class, and I bet, between everyone, that there is a whole bunch of it. I'm sure that there are girls who can sing, dance, play musical instruments and do all sorts of things. That's why it only makes sense to organize a talent show."

"That's brilliant, Elana! Of course, a talent show would be the perfect thing. It would be fun for everyone to be in and to watch."

"That's exactly what I was thinking. And I even have an idea when we should put on this talent show."

"Really? When?"

"At the Purim *chagiga*."

Elana's words set the wheels in Nechama's brain spinning. "You know, Elana, you may really be on to something here! This idea of a Purim talent show really has potential. If we announce it in school tomorrow and have each eighth grader sign up for a slot, then we can have a whole show set up with hardly any hassle. As soon as I get home, I'll discuss it with the rest of the committee to see what they think, but, personally, I'm sold."

"Can you believe how excited everyone is about the talent show?" Nechama gushed to Leah as they were discussing this latest piece of eighth-grade news.

The girls were in the back seat of the Weisses' minivan, on the way to the hospital to visit Esther Bracha.

"It's amazing!" Leah enthused. "I didn't even realize all the different talents that girls had. For instance, even though Miriam has mentioned her guitar lessons once or twice, I never knew that she enjoys playing so much and that she's advanced enough to play a song with chords."

"Yeah, well, a lot of girls were surprised to find out that you can play the piano well," Nechama retorted. "You do keep pretty quiet about it, and the only reason I know is because I live with you. By the way, I noticed you signed up to sing and play a song. Did you already decide which song you're going to perform?"

"Actually, I do have something in mind, but I need your help," Leah confessed.

"My help? Please don't tell me you're counting on me to harmonize or anything like that!"

"No, that's not it," Leah laughed. "What I do need is your

help with writing the song. You see, Esther Bracha has made me see things in a new way. I used to just take it for granted that when a mother was expecting, after nine months she would give birth to a healthy baby. After everything that's happened in the past few months, though, I've learned that there are so many different complications that can come up and that we have to be so grateful when things go smoothly. So I was thinking that for the talent show, I would really like to sing a song to thank Hashem for my healthy baby sister. That's where you come in. Even though I have all these ideas that I want to sing about, I need your help to put them into a song."

"Wow! It sounds like a tall order, but I will definitely do the best I can," Nechama promised her friend.

"Thank you! I knew you wouldn't let me down," Leah said. "What about you? What are you planning to do for the talent show?"

"I would like to do a dance," Nechama answered.

"A dance! I'm sure it's going to be beautiful. Everyone at our Israeli dance class knows how graceful you are."

"Well, talk about discovering talents … I didn't even know how much I enjoyed dancing till I came here and you brought me along to the dance class."

Nechama and Leah discussed ideas for the theme of Nechama's dance until they arrived at the hospital. Entering the building, they grew quiet. Without talking, Levi and the girls followed Dr. and Mrs. Weiss to the ICU where Esther Bracha was kept in an incubator. The nurses there all greeted the family kindly. While the nurse who was in charge of Esther

Bracha gave Dr. and Mrs. Weiss an update on the baby's weight and schedule, Leah found her sister and pointed her out to Nechama.

"She's tiny!" Nechama whispered in awe.

"She certainly is!" Leah agreed.

The two girls stood staring in wonder at the miniature person before them until the nurse approached and took Esther Bracha out so that the Weisses could hold her. Mrs. Weiss kissed her baby gently and sat down to feed her. When she was finished, the nurse came back and took Esther Bracha, placing her gently down in her bassinet.

During the rest of the family's visit with Esther Bracha, Nechama didn't say much. Watching the baby, Nechama kept thinking about Leah's words in the car. Although Nechama had understood then what Leah was saying about appreciating the miracle of birth, seeing Esther Bracha made the whole idea seem so much more real for her.

On the drive back home, Nechama remained preoccupied with her musings.

"What are you thinking about?" Leah questioned.

"A lot," Nechama answered, adding softly, "I'm so glad I came along with you today. After meeting Esther Bracha, I really feel ready to help you write your song."

"Is it just me, or do you feel like you need a break, too?" Nechama asked Leah as the two of them studied for a history quiz.

"A break? From what?"

"I don't know – from everything, I guess. This past week has been so busy. Between schoolwork, preparations for the talent show and everything else, I haven't had a minute to relax."

Leah listened sympathetically. "I think I have a solution," she proposed. "Let's go to the Knit and Bead store tomorrow after school. Going there is always relaxing."

"Yeah, I remember when we went at the beginning of the year and made earrings. It was a lot of fun. Good idea, Leah. Do you think we should ask anyone else if they want to join us?"

"Why don't we invite Elana along?" Leah suggested. "It will be a great opportunity for me to spend time with her."

"Okay, so do you want to call her and see if she can come?"

"Sure." Leah made the phone call to Elana. After a brief conversation, Leah hung up and turned to Nechama with a wide smile. "So there. It's all arranged. Tomorrow afternoon, Elana, you and I have a date at Knit and Bead."

The next day after school, the three girls walked together to the crafts store. Naturally, the topic of the talent show came up.

"What kind of show will you be putting on?" Nechama asked Elana curiously.

"Well, I'm actually working together with Raizy, and we're creating a short comedy skit of the confusion that takes place when two friends dress up as each other one Purim." Elana started to elaborate, and her friends listened in interest, until Nechama gave a sudden gasp.

"What's the matter?" Elana asked in bewilderment. "Did I say something wrong?"

"No, it's not you at all," Nechama replied. "It's just that I thought I spotted a man from Woodhaven walking into the flower shop across the street."

"Which man?" Leah asked.

"I was almost sure it was Avraham, but I guess it couldn't have been him. I mean, what in the world would Avraham be doing in Lakeview City? Oh, well, maybe I'm just letting my imagination run a little wild."

Nechama had just finished saying these words when a man walked out of the flower shop holding a bouquet of blooms. "There he is!" she almost shouted.

Leah turned in the direction that Nechama was pointing and watched the man get into a car and drive off. "He does look exactly like Avraham," Leah remarked.

"That's because it is Avraham," Nechama declared firmly. "It has to be him because he's driving Avraham's car!"

"Then I guess that solves our little mystery," Leah said.

"Not really," Nechama disagreed as the trio entered the Knit and Bead shop. "It just makes the mystery bigger. What brings Avraham to Lakeview City? And what's more, why didn't anyone tell me that he was coming?"

The auditorium was packed. In addition to a large crowd of students and faculty, the audience was filled with many mothers who had come to see the talents of their daughters highlighted.

Backstage, the eighth graders hugged each other and wished

each other good luck. They all felt a mixture of nervousness and excitement.

Mrs. Solomon walked up to the podium and began to introduce the program. "Good evening, everyone, and *Purim sameach*," she began. "I want to welcome all of you here tonight and thank you so much for joining us.

"For those of you who don't know the history of tonight's program, originally, a very popular singer was scheduled to perform at this Purim *chagiga*. Because of a simcha, the singer had to cancel less than a month ago. At first, the girls on the Purim committee were crestfallen. Which entertainer would they get with such late notice? Sure enough, their attempts to find a last-minute entertainer were not successful, and they put their heads together to figure out how the girls themselves could prepare a program that would captivate each and every one of you.

"In an instance of amazing *hashgacha pratis*, one eighth grader got the brilliant idea for tonight's program. Who needs to search elsewhere for entertainment when so much talent exists amongst our very own students? And, indeed, over the last week and a half, I really got to see how our girls are bentched with so many unique talents. On that note, I am proud and delighted to present to you a talent showcase of our eighth graders. So please sit back and relax because you are about to witness the best show in our history of Purim *chagigos*."

The next hour proved Mrs. Solomon's words to be true. The audience watched spellbound as eighth graders danced, sang, acted, played musical instruments, recited poems and performed gymnastics and some other feats. The show reached its climax with the finale, as the whole class sang a song about the special gifts that Hashem has given each person to share with others and to use in serving Hashem.

When the girls were done, everyone burst into thunderous applause. There was no doubt about it. The talent show had been a big hit. With flying spirits, the eighth graders invited everyone to join them in dancing as Leah played music on the school's keyboard. The lively, unified dancing went on for a while, until some girls and their mothers gradually drifted out because of the late hour.

It was almost ten o'clock when the auditorium had cleared of everyone besides the eighth graders and their mothers. With a special sense of unity, the girls continued dancing in a circle until Mrs. Solomon reluctantly told them, "Girls, I hate to break this up, but it's really time for everyone to go home. Before you leave, though, I want to let you know that I am so, so proud of every one of you. I also want to say that although part of tonight's *hatzlacha* was no doubt due to all of your amazing talents, a bigger factor in your success was the incredible *achdus* with which you worked. In the past week and a half, I watched as you really came together as a class, discovering the special qualities in each girl and using all of these talents to create one beautiful show."

Mrs. Solomon looked at the radiant faces that surrounded her, and, spontaneously, she declared, "And now, if we dance to just one last song, I think that will be the perfect end to this wonderfully magical evening!"

Even before the dismissal bell finished ringing, Leah was standing at Nechama's desk with her coat and backpack. "Come on, let's go," she urged.

"Okay, okay," Nechama laughed. "Just give me one second."

Nechama understood Leah's impatience to get home already. After three weeks in the hospital, Esther Bracha had finally gained enough weight to be released. Her parents had made plans to go early that afternoon to pick their baby up and bring her home.

Nechama practically had to run to keep up with Leah's brisk pace. Panting, she begged, "Leah, slow down a little, please."

Compliantly, Leah slowed down – for exactly one minute. Then she quickened her steps once more. Nechama didn't bother protesting again. Instead, she jogged beside Nechama and breathed a huge sigh of relief when they finally reached their house.

Mrs. Weiss opened the door for the girls with a big, welcoming smile. "Hi, Nechama. Hi, Leah."

"Hi, Mommy," Leah said. Noticing her mother's empty hands, she asked, "Where's Esther Bracha?"

"She's sleeping in her bassinet."

Leah's face dropped.

Realizing how disappointed her daughter was, her mother offered, "If you're very quiet, you can go upstairs and peek in on her."

Leah didn't need a second invitation. Grabbing Nechama's

hand, she said, "Come on, let's go see Esther Bracha!"

Esther Bracha looked angelic as she rested in her bassinet, wrapped in a pink fleece blanket. Nechama and Leah silently watched her sleep until Leah reluctantly whispered, "Okay, let's go back downstairs."

When cries were heard a while later, Leah jumped up from her seat on the sofa and exclaimed, "Esther Bracha's up! Let me go get her."

"Just one minute," her mother said as she headed toward the steps. "First, I'm going to feed Esther Bracha because she's probably very hungry, but as soon as she finishes eating, I'll call you so that you can burp her and hold her."

Mrs. Weiss called for Leah just as Dr. Weiss entered the house. He greeted Nechama and Levi, who were sitting in the living room, and then went upstairs to check on Esther Bracha. A few minutes later, Leah and her parents joined Nechama and Levi in the living room. Leah cradled Esther Bracha in her arms, and her parents kept their eyes on the baby to make sure that she was okay.

There's no doubt about it, Nechama thought. *Esther Bracha has definitely become the center of attention around here, and for good reason, too. The Weiss family has waited for this little addition for so long!*

From her place on one of the armchairs, Nechama observed Leah and her parents as they cooed over Esther Bracha. She also observed Levi, who sat with his toy cars on the floor, a dark expression on his face.

Suspecting Levi's feelings of abandonment and resentment,

Nechama came up with a plan. As soon as Mrs. Weiss rose from the couch to set the dinner table, Nechama followed her into the kitchen.

"Mrs. Weiss?" she asked.

"Yes?"

"Would it be alright if I took Levi out for ice cream after dinner?" Uncertainly, she added, "I thought he might appreciate the treat and the extra attention."

Mrs. Weiss regarded Nechama with gratitude. "How sweet of you to think of Levi! You're right. He must feel a little neglected now, with everyone focusing on Esther Bracha. I'm sure he'll be so happy to go out with you after dinner, and that will give me a chance to straighten up and bathe Esther Bracha. Then I can give Levi all of my attention when he gets back."

Sure enough, Levi brightened considerably when Nechama mentioned the idea of taking a walk to the ice cream shop. After supper, the two of them bundled up in their winter jackets and headed outdoors. On the way to the store, Levi was quiet and didn't seem very interested in answering Nechama's questions. Walking home, though, after he'd thoroughly enjoyed his sprinkled, double-scooped ice cream cone, Levi seemed more up to talking.

"So how is it having Esther Bracha at home?" Nechama asked carefully.

"It's okay, I guess." Levi paused a moment before continuing, "I don't know why everyone's so interested in her, anyway. She's just a little baby. All she does is eat, sleep and cry, so I can't understand why everyone makes such a fuss over her."

"Levi, I think it's just because everyone's so happy that Esther Bracha is finally home. In a few days, when your family gets used to having her around, things will get back to normal. They'll still fuss over Esther Bracha, of course, because that's how people are with babies, but she won't take up all of their time and attention anymore."

Encouraged by Levi's interest in what she was saying, Nechama went on, "And I want you to know, Levi, that even though Esther Bracha doesn't do very much now, in a few months you'll be amazed! She'll be smiling, laughing, crawling and playing. One day you're going to have a lot of fun with her, and you'll be so glad to have her as your little sister. And what's more, she's going to be so glad to have you as her big brother. You'll show her all sorts of tricks and protect her with your strength. After all, you're still the only boy in the family, and that's very special."

Levi listened seriously to Nechama's words. Though he didn't respond, a glow of pride shined from his face when he and Nechama returned home.

"All aboard!" called the conductor. Bells chimed, and then the train was off, speeding down the tracks.

Nechama grinned at Leah. "I'm so glad you're coming home with me!"

"I'm so glad to be coming. I was surprised by how quickly my mother agreed to the plan. I thought she would really want me to spend Shabbos with the family, now that Esther Bracha's home, but she told me she still owed me one for missing out during winter vacation. Plus, she said that she's happy for me to take advantage of this last chance to sleep over at your house before Pesach, so here I am, on the way to Woodhaven with you."

"I can't believe that Pesach's almost here already!" Nechama declared. "It seems like the year is flying! It feels like such a short time ago that I was making my first trip to your house to check out the school and see if I wanted to stay."

"I know what you mean," Leah remarked, "but so much has happened since you came to Lakeview City that, in a way, it seems like you've been living with us for much more than half a year."

"A lot has definitely happened in these past few months," Nechama nodded. "Besides having to settle into a new school and making so many new friends, I also met Natalie and got to know her. And remember that whole episode when Raizy broke her leg?"

"I sure do," Leah answered wryly. "That was going on at the same time that I was so nervous about my mother. Seeing her so sick made me really suspect the worst."

"I was pretty nervous, too," Nechama admitted, "but look how happily everything turned out in the end."

"*Baruch Hashem*!" Leah exclaimed, and then continued reminiscing, "Remember when we first started going to visit the people at the JCE? It's funny to think back at how reluctant you were to make that your *chessed* project."

"Yeah, and now from a temporary *chessed* project, it's become a weekly commitment. Do you remember when we met Chevi Chein in Bella's room?"

"That was such a shock! At first I thought I was seeing things," Leah declared.

"We couldn't believe our luck when she agreed to sing at our Purim *chagiga*. It sure was a disappointment when she called to cancel."

"You're telling me! All of us were so upset, especially since we had no idea what kind of entertainment we were going to have instead. You and Elana really saved the day, though. The talent show was amazing."

"It was a lot of fun," Nechama agreed. "The night of the Purim *chagiga* was one of my best nights ever. As we all danced together, I felt so connected to every girl in the class, and it made me realize what a long way I've come since September, when I was the new kid in school."

"Well, the year's not over yet," Leah said. "After Pesach, we still have two of the most exciting months ahead. Besides for the mother-daughter tea, there's our graduation trip and then our graduation itself. We really have so much to look forward to!"

"When did you say your mother-daughter tea is?" Mrs. Greenberg asked the girls that night.

"It's the Sunday after Shavuos," Nechama answered. With a hopeful expression, she questioned her mother, "Do you think you'll be able to make it?"

"I don't see why not!" her mother replied.

Nechama looked elated by her mother's response. "Are you serious, Ima? It will be so special to have you there!"

"It will be my pleasure to come. It will be nice for me to meet all the teachers and classmates whom you've been spending the year with, and it sounds like there will be a very nice program there, as well."

"Can I come with you, Ima?" Rachelli wanted to know. "I would love to hear Chevi Chein sing live."

"Of course, you're welcome to join me," her mother smiled. "I'll be more than happy to have company during the long ride. Natalie, you're welcome to join, too."

"Actually," Natalie said, "you'll never believe this, but I'm pretty sure that's the same Sunday that my mother is planning to spend the afternoon with my aunt in Lakeview City for her birthday. If it is, I can just get a ride to Leah and Nechama's school with my mother. After the tea, my mother can pick me up, and then I'll baby-sit for my cousins while she and my aunt go out."

"I have a better idea," Mrs. Greenberg suggested. "Why don't you see if your mother wants to attend the tea, as well? I think it would be a great opportunity to expose her to the beauty of Jewish education. The program will only last for about an hour and a half in the morning, so that will give her the rest of the day to be with your aunt."

"That sounds like a wonderful plan," Natalie said, adding wistfully, "if only my mother would agree to it!"

"Bring up the idea to her, and see what she says," advised

Mrs. Greenberg. "Tell her that Nechama will be very touched if she comes. If that doesn't work, let her know that a very talented singer will be performing."

"Well, my mother actually enjoys music, so maybe that will draw her. Do you think it's all right if we come, though? After all, my mother and I are not involved with the school at all."

"Of course, it's alright if you come!" Nechama burst in. "You'll be my guests. I'll check with Mrs. Solomon just to confirm, but I'm sure she'll say that it's fine."

"In that case, I'm going to try very hard to coax my mother into coming with me," Natalie decided. "If this is a way to give her a positive impression of a religious school, then I really want to make it happen."

chapter Nineteen

The following week, Leah was talking to her mother excitedly. "What an exciting weekend we have coming up!" she exclaimed. "First, we have the kiddush for Esther Bracha on Shabbos afternoon. On Sunday morning, there's the mother-daughter tea, and then Mrs. Greenberg and Rachelli are staying to join us for a barbecue lunch."

"And that's not even all," Mrs. Weiss remarked, a mysterious smile on her lips.

"What do you mean?" Leah asked curiously.

Nechama, too, wondered what Mrs. Weiss was referring to.

"I mean that it looks like the celebrations will continue on Sunday evening."

"Mommy, please tell us what you're talking about!" Leah begged.

"Well, the good news is not yet public, so I don't feel comfortable being too specific. However, since Nechama did have a hand in this, I will give you a hint. Sunday night's simcha has something to do with Tanta Bracha."

"Tanta Bracha?" Leah asked, still puzzled.

Meanwhile, though, Nechama's mind was racing. Searching

her memory, she recalled a conversation she and Natalie had once had with Mrs. Weiss in the kitchen, as well as the image of Avraham leaving the flower shop with a wrapped bouquet.

In a flash, she gasped, "Oh, my goodness! This is just too much!"

"What?" Leah demanded. "What's going on?"

Nechama's eyes twinkled merrily. "If my suspicions are correct, Tanta Bracha is going to be getting engaged – and the *chassan* is none other than Avraham."

Mrs. Weiss's broad smile confirmed Nechama's conclusion.

"Tanta Bracha and Avraham? Getting engaged? I don't believe it!"

"I know!" Nechama nodded vigorously. "Now that I think about it, though, it makes so much sense!"

When the eighth-grade girls' mothers and other guests entered the school auditorium on Sunday morning, they were awed by the room's décor. Beautiful lavender and gold tablecloths draped each round table, which was set with matching napkins and cups. Near every setting there was an elegant place card and a copy of the program, and at the center of each table stood a vase filled with summery pink and purple blossoms.

"Everything looks magnificent," Mrs. Greenberg declared. "You girls did a wonderful job setting up."

"All we did was follow Mrs. Solomon's instructions," Nechama admitted candidly.

"Which of the women is Mrs. Solomon?" her mother wanted to know.

Nechama pointed out her teacher, who was engrossed in conversation with the principal.

"She's busy now, but I'll introduce you to her later," Nechama said. "Where are Natalie and Mrs. Golovyan, by the way? Aren't they supposed to be coming?"

"They are," Rachelli answered. "I just hope that Mrs. Golovyan didn't back out at the last minute."

"No, it doesn't look like she did," Mrs. Greenberg remarked, looking toward the door.

Standing there at the entranceway were Natalie and her mother. Mrs. Golovyan seemed uncertain, as if she didn't quite know what to do with herself, so Mrs. Greenberg hurried over to escort her to their table. Nechama went to greet Natalie.

"Hi, Natalie, I'm glad you made it."

"Me, too. I was scared my mother would change her mind in the end, and she almost did. Last night, she was getting cold feet, but my father insisted that she come. He finally convinced her, saying, 'It's not a religious ceremony, only a mother-daughter tea, for heaven's sake!' And he told her that she should appreciate the fact that I was requesting her company because so many girls my age want to have nothing to do with their mothers. Boy, was I relieved when I saw my mother give in to my father's arguments."

By then the girls had reached their table. "Where's Chevi Chein?" Rachelli wanted to know. "Is she here yet?"

"She should be coming any minute with Mrs. Jacobovitz,

her great-aunt who lives at the old age home that we visit. I'm sure you'll be very happy to hear that the two of them will actually be sitting at our table."

"At our table?" Natalie asked, her eyes wide. "Wow! So not only do we get to hear Chevi Chein sing, we also get to sit right next to her!"

"I don't know why you're getting so excited," Rachelli teased her friend. "You haven't even heard any of her CDs."

"What does that matter?" Natalie retorted good-naturedly.

"Shhh," Nechama whispered. "Here she is now."

The girls turned around to see the famous singer, who looked beautiful in a turquoise outfit that complemented her auburn *sheitel* perfectly. Noticing that Chevi Chein had arrived, Mrs. Solomon walked onstage to start the program.

"Welcome, everybody," Mrs. Solomon began. "We are all gathered here to pay tribute to a very special group of women – our mothers. This year, I had the privilege of teaching a wonderful class of eighth graders, girls who are bright and talented, caring and enthusiastic. The more I got to know them, the more I was filled with awe for you mothers who raised them and helped them become the beautiful young ladies they are now. Even greater than my admiration, though, is the appreciation of your daughters, who have worked hard to make this morning a memorable one, one that will convey their feelings of gratitude to you for all that you do. On that note, I would like to call the eighth-grade choir girls up to sing a song in your honor."

Leah, and several other girls wearing matching lavender

flower pins on their white shirts, rose from their seats and got into position on stage. On cue, they began singing about a mother's prayer as she lights the Shabbos candles, and many women in the audience had tears in their eyes as they listened.

Following the choir's presentation, Mrs. Solomon returned to the podium. "Thank you, girls. That was really beautiful. And now I would like to call upon one of our eighth graders to speak. Although it's true that every girl in this class has many words of appreciation to express to her mother, there is one girl who is in a particularly unique situation. This girl, at the age of thirteen, has lived away from her home this past year for the sake of her *chinuch*. Although it couldn't have always been easy for her to be so far from her family, it must have been even harder for her mother to be separated from her young daughter. And, without further ado, let me introduce to you Nechama Greenberg from Woodhaven, Pennsylvania."

"Nechama!" Mrs. Greenberg exclaimed. "You didn't tell me you were talking."

"I wanted to keep it a surprise," Nechama explained with a smile, and then she walked up to the front of the room. Taking a deep breath to calm herself, she began to speak. Eloquently, she talked about how supportive her mother had been from the start, encouraging Nechama in her decision to switch schools even though it meant living away from home.

"Not a day went by that I didn't speak to my mother," Nechama said. "Although I didn't see her for weeks at a time, I relied more than ever on her listening ear and sound advice. It may sound funny, but the truth is, over this year that I spent so far away from my mother, we've actually grown even closer.

"Ima, thank you so much for everything – for your unconditional love, your constant support and your guiding example. Mrs. Weiss, thank you so much, as well, for being my mother away from home. You've opened your house and your heart to me and made my stay in Lakeview City so much easier and more comfortable. And to the mothers of all my classmates, I'd like to say thank you for raising such wonderful girls. Your daughters have welcomed me into their circle so warmly, and I feel grateful to have them as my friends."

Nechama's moving speech was met with a round of applause. As she sat back down in her seat, her mother leaned over to kiss her, her eyes wet with tears.

Mrs. Solomon returned to the podium and said, "Thank you, Nechama, and thank you, Mrs. Greenberg, for sharing your daughter with us this year. Now, for the next part of our program, we are so lucky this morning to have with us the famous Chevi Chein, who has so graciously agreed to sing a few songs for us on the theme of mothers and their daughters. Chevi Chein, the stage is yours!"

Guitar in hand, Chevi Chein took her place on stage. It didn't take long for her to have the room full of women and girls clapping and moving to her music. In the next half an hour, she went through a mix of songs. Some were slow and serious, and others were more lively and humorous. Her audience thoroughly enjoyed all of them, especially Mrs. Jacobovitz, who proudly announced to everyone around her that the woman on stage was her very own niece.

"Well, my time is almost up," Chevi Chein announced into the microphone, "but I'd like to conclude on a personal note with a song that my mother always used to sing to me when I was little, a song that always brings me back to my childhood when there was no safer place than my mother's embrace. My mother was actually Russian, and this sweet, Jewish lullaby that she used to sing to me is in her mother tongue."

In her lovely, lilting voice, Chevi Chein began to sing. Although most of the ladies and girls didn't understand the words, they enjoyed the soothing melody and started to sway along.

In the midst of the serene atmosphere, the sound of sniffling could be heard at Nechama's table. She and several others were taken aback to see Mrs. Golovyan listening to Chevi Chein with tears streaming down her face. Natalie turned to her mother and spoke softly to her. Mrs. Golovyan mumbled something in reply.

Although everyone at the table did their best to avoid looking at Mrs. Golovyan, they all wondered why she was crying so intensely. Nechama remembered the way that Mrs. Golovyan had gotten so emotional at their Chanukah party, and her heart sank.

I can't imagine what is upsetting Mrs. Golovyan, but I really hope that whatever it is doesn't turn her away from Yiddishkeit even more, Nechama thought.

Watching Mrs. Golovyan from the corner of her eye, Mrs. Greenberg grew apprehensive, too. Was it a mistake to convince Mrs. Golovyan to come here today? Maybe she just isn't ready for this and needs to be left alone to come around at her own time.

As Mrs. Golovyan's sobs grew louder, Nechama and Mrs. Greenberg's doubts grew stronger. Mrs. Weiss, who was sitting across from Mrs. Golovyan, passed down some tissues from her purse, which Mrs. Golovyan gratefully accepted. Natalie, embarrassed by the scene that her mother was creating, asked her mother if she wanted to leave, but Mrs. Golovyan shook her head, doing her best to regain her composure.

Chevi Chein finished singing soon after, and as the crowd erupted into enthusiastic applause, she made her way back to her seat. She stopped by Mrs. Golovyan and put her arms around the weeping woman's shoulders.

"I noticed that my last song made you cry," she said in a voice of sincere concern, "and I am sorry if I've done something to hurt or offend you."

"No, no," Mrs. Golovyan assured her, finally managing to pull herself together again. "That's not the case at all."

Wiping her eyes and breathing deeply, Mrs. Golovyan explained, "It's just that the lullaby you sang brought to mind some images that have been long buried for me. Listening to you, I was carried back to my early childhood. Every night, my mother would take me to kiss the mezuzah before tucking me under my blankets. Together we would say the Shema, and then she would sing that very same lullaby as I drifted off to sleep.

"When I was five, though, she became ill and passed away when she didn't receive proper care from the Jew-hating hospital staff. Her death left me an orphan, since my father had been killed in an anti-Semitic attack when I was an infant. Parentless, I was raised by an aunt and uncle who brought me up to believe that a religious lifestyle is synonymous with persecution and pain. Influenced by their strong views, I firmly resolved to always keep a safe distance from observant Judaism.

"The lullaby you sang, though, unlocked a door of long-forgotten memories, memories of my mother lighting the Shabbos candles and preparing delicious treats for the holidays, memories of the two of us singing, praying and playing together. These memories are all warm and happy, very different from the dark, dreary picture that my aunt and uncle painted to me of religious life, and I realize that many of the prejudices that I've been harboring are unfair and unfounded.

"It seems like it may be time for me to question a lot of things, including my decision to guard my family carefully from the influences of Orthodoxy. Perhaps it would not be so bad to accept my daughter's interest in Judaism and to give in to her fervent desire to attend a religious school.

"I don't know where exactly all my soul-searching will take me, but one thing is for sure. Hearing this long-forgotten lullaby that you sang today has given me a lot to think about."

Following Mrs. Golovyan's emotional words, everyone at the table was speechless, overwhelmed by the incredible impact of Chevi Chein's final song. The singer herself impulsively embraced Mrs. Golovyan tightly before sitting down to watch the group of mothers and daughters dancing together on stage.

Although the dance was beautiful, it was difficult for Nechama to pay much attention to it. She was too busy trying to register the amazing transformation that had just taken place in Mrs. Golovyan.

Is it really possible that one song can have the power to affect someone so strongly? Nechama wondered in amazement. *Although we all hoped that Mrs. Golovyan would leave the mother-daughter tea today with more positive feelings about a Jewish education, who would have dared to dream that she would change her mind completely about her attitude toward Yiddishkeit and be open to seriously consider sending Natalie to a Jewish school?*

Caught up in thought, Nechama's eyes wandered around the table as one of her classmates concluded the mother-daughter tea with the recitation of a poem. There, in a circle all around her, were the faces of the women and girls who had played such a big role in the past year of her life.

Looking at them all, Nechama marveled at the way each of these women and girls had helped her grow, deepening her appreciation of so many things she had taken for granted – her family, her Jewish upbringing, the miracle of birth, the joy of living and the way Hashem orchestrates His world so that everything has a purpose and a reason.

Leah, sensing Nechama's eyes on her, met her friend's gaze and smiled. As if reading Nechama's thoughts, she whispered reflectively, "It's amazing how all the different pieces of our lives came together so perfectly this year."

Nechama nodded in response. She couldn't have agreed more.

Glossary

Achdus – unity

Baruch Hashem – thank G-d

Bentch – bless; to say the Grace After Meals or to recite a blessing

Bentch licht – to make the blessing over Shabbos and Yom Tov candles

B'ezras Hashem – with G-d's help

Bikur Cholim – attending to the needs of the sick

B'li ayin hara – lit., "without an evil eye"

Bnos – activity groups for girls on Shabbos

Bracha, brachos – blessing(s)

Bris – circumcision

Bubby – grandmother

Chagiga – party

Challah – braided bread used on Shabbos and Yom Tov

Chassan – groom

Cheshvan – second month of the Jewish year

Chessed – kindness

Chinuch – education

Chol Hamoed – the intermediate days of a Yom Tov

Chumash – the Five Books of Moses

Daven – pray

Divrei Torah – words of Torah

Dreidel – four-sided top used for a special Chanukah game

Eineklach – grandchildren

Erev Shabbos – Friday

Fleishig – meat, or food cooked with meat

Frum – religiously observant

Frumkeit – religious observance

Gut voch – good week; a traditional greeting on Motzei Shabbos

Halacha – Jewish law

Hashem – G-d

Hashgacha pratis – Divine Providence

Hatzlacha rabba – much success

Kabbalas Shabbos – prayers recited on Friday night to welcome Shabbos

Kaddish – prayer for G-d's name to be glorified, often recited by a mourner

Kiddush – blessing made on Friday night over a cup of wine, to sanctify Shabbos

Kollel – a yeshiva for dedicated Torah learning, usually full-time by married men

Lashon hara – gossip

Maariv – evening prayers

Mabul – the Flood

Maidelach – young girls

Mazel tov – good luck

Mechaneches – teacher

Meforshim – Torah commentaries

Megillah – the book of Esther

Melava malka – meal eaten on Saturday night

Mezuzah – encased parchment with certain Torah portions, attached to the doorposts in Jewish homes

Middos – character traits

Milchig – dairy

Mincha – afternoon prayers

Mishebeirach – prayer said for the sick during the public Torah reading

Mishloach manos – gifts of food sent to fellow Jews on Purim

Mitzvah, mitzvos – Torah-mandated commandment(s)

Modeh ani – prayer said when waking up in the morning, thanking G-d for giving one another day of life

Motzei Shabbos – Saturday night

Negel vasser – washing the hands upon arising in the morning

Neshama, neshamala – soul

Parsha – weekly Torah portion

Pasuk – verse

Perek, perakim – chapter(s)

Pidyon haben – redeeming a firstborn son

Purim sameach – happy Purim

Refuah shelaima – a complete recovery

Rosh Chodesh – beginning of a new month in the Jewish calendar

Sefarim – Torah books

Shabbos – the Sabbath

Shacharis – morning prayers

Shavuos – festival that celebrates the Jews receiving the Torah at Sinai

Sheitel – wig

Shema – prayer affirming the unity of G-d

Shpiel – play, skit

Shul – synagogue

Siddur – prayer book

Simcha – happy occasion

Simchas Torah – festival on which Jews express their joy in having the Torah; immediately follows the festival of Sukkos

Sukkah – temporary dwelling in which Jews eat and sleep on the holiday of Sukkos

Sukkos – festival that commemorates how G-d protected the Jews during their forty-year sojourn in the desert

Tefillah, tefillos – prayer(s)

Tehillim – Psalms

Tzedaka – charity

Tznius – modesty

Upsherinish – a boy's first haircut at the age of three, for those who have the custom to wait until that age

Yiddishkeit – Judaism

Yud Zayin – seventeen

Zaidy – grandfather

Zeeskeit – sweetie